Wake the Dead

Victoria Buck

I0690258

Wake the Dead

Contact Information: titleadmin@pelicanbookgroup.com

All scripture quotations, unless otherwise indicated, are taken from the Holy Bible, New International Version(R), NIV(R), Copyright 1973, 1978, 1984, 2011 by Biblica, Inc.™ Used by permission of Zondervan. All rights reserved worldwide. www.zondervan.com

Cover Art by *Nicola Martinez*

Harbourlight Books, a division of Pelican Ventures, LLC
www.pelicanbookgroup.com PO Box 1738 *Aztec, NM * 87410

Harbourlight Books sail and mast logo is a trademark of Pelican Ventures, LLC
Publishing History

First Harbourlight Edition, 2014
Paperback Edition ISBN 978-1-61116-336-0
Electronic Edition ISBN 978-1-61116-335-3
Published in the United States of America

Dedication

To my husband, Randy; my number one proofreader, Jackie Thomas; and my fellow writers at Word Weavers.

1

In the near future…

Chase Sterling, with great pride and sentiment, announced the unmatched prizes awarded by his primetime unreality program, *Change Your Life.* "A hundred million in a world exchange account and a ninety-foot yacht to take you to the Caribbean island mansion built for you and your family, Judy Bamber."

The five thousand fans lucky enough to hold tickets to the show that night applauded in wild astonishment.

Chase lifted his hand, and the cheers fell to a low roar. "That's not all, Judy. You'll have the best surgeons we can find to turn you into a goddess, and you're the new owner of a WR Selfdrive dealership sure to gross millions every year."

The cries of the throng rose louder. But without the glint of a tear or a single word of gratitude, Judy Bamber dropped to her knees and her portly middle-aged mug slapped the golden stage.

Chase pored over his shocked and simmering congregation. He had to sustain the momentum. The fans had just witnessed the biggest win in the show's history. And the most dramatic reaction—Judy's face hit hard. Not that a broken nose mattered now. She'd soon have a new one.

Electric blue beams coursed through the

auditorium and the music reached its peak, but the crowd hushed. Along with them, millions, maybe a billion, likely held a collective gasp in front of their GrapheVisions.

Chase had to deliver, to pull yet another miserable soul from the ranks of the poor, the sick, and the unattractive. His mission, his destiny, was to make winners out of losers. That's what he planned to do for the rest of his life. No one could stop him.

The glorious anthem that accompanied every win ebbed to the melodic equivalent of bated breath. Nice touch. The director played the situation well. But he'd better not flood the stage with medics. Chase could get this dumpling off the floor.

He knelt on one knee next to the show's newest chosen one and turned to the crowd. "People, help me out. Judy is missing the moment." He hoped it worked. "Scream loud enough to wake the dead!"

The hum escalated to a roar and the walls seemed to shake. Within seconds, Judy rose to her feet as though a hand had come through the stage to thrust her upright. Or else, from somewhere among the brilliant lights overhead, a puppeteer had tugged a string and lifted her.

Chase stood and clasped her hand. She smiled, having survived the greatest moment of her life with no visible damage. No broken teeth. No swollen nose.

A reverberation of awe, decibels lower than the dead-awakening shriek, swept through the assembly. Chase kept his eyes on the risen Judy Bamber, but he knew from where he stood that some in the audience dropped to their seats or to the floor of the narrow aisles. No one seemed concerned about this contagion of fainting. Those still on their feet held their stare on the newest victor.

Chase swallowed hard. It felt like the first time he'd announced a big win. What a privilege to bestow such a blessing. The network supplied the goods—by means of the advertisers, of course—but Chase bestowed the bounty on this floating, glowing gazillionaire. He was Judy Bamber's savior. She was the star, at least for the moment. He was the endless sky.

"Judy, are you all right? You gave us a scare hitting the floor like that."

She scarcely giggled as she nodded. "Forgive me."

"You are our biggest winner *ever*. How does it feel?"

She lifted her hands to the lights. "It feels like air, Chase. Like I couldn't breathe before, but now I can."

"Do you hear that, people? Resuscitation. This woman will never have to worry again. She has entered the world of the wealthy, the universe of the unrestricted. Thanks to SynVue, our generous global network, Judy Bamber is now one of the richest women in the Western Republic. Her prize is beyond anything our wondrous program has awarded to date."

Chase spread his arms wide. "And as you all know, the bigger the *winner's* prize…"

The crowd let loose with a frenzied shout.

"Judy, you know what to say." He faced her to wait with the fans.

"Yes, Chase, my prize is big. My fortune is *their* fortune." She turned her avid expression to him. "What will they receive?"

"Here's what I'm going to give them, Judy. Every one of them." He turned again to the crowd. "You're all going home with a brand new…" He paused until he thought a few eyeballs would pop out and roll down the aisles. "Autonomous fuel cell car, complete with front and rear reality shield."

The thunderous reaction brought a buzz to Chase's eardrums. Judy clapped her plump hands and smiled as she turned her gaze upward to the rear of the massive auditorium. A foretelling quiet descended on the fans, and then the soft voice called from above.

"Judy Bamber, come claim your prize and begin your new life." This invitation from the show's mystifying producer brought another ovation from the spectators. They knew the voice and turned as one to the blackened portal high against the far wall. From there, the illustrious Kerstin Bennett called forth the new winner. "I'm waiting for you Judy, with all that you will receive."

Judy blasted off the stage and took the center aisle like a nimble twenty-year-old. The fans reached for her as she passed by. They cheered as she climbed the golden stairs, and sighed as she vanished into the passageway between the lower level and the tiered balcony.

Chase took his usual spot—the center platform edged with shafts of white light. But this remarkable episode called for something different. He stepped onto the illuminated ramp and went down into the crowd. A spotlight followed him. The people cried out in delight as the nearest ones reached for him.

"And so we've sent another lucky soul to begin her new life. Remember, our aim is to change *your* life. Good night." He touched a few outstretched hands before racing up the incline. The musical finale resonated through the auditorium as he reached the backstage egress.

Chase retreated, knowing thousands stampeded the exits to form lines to the prize arena. Dozens of SynVue employees would spend the rest of the night handing out vouchers for the cars. Kerstin's team would devote the next several hours to Judy Bamber. They'd go over the regulations, sign documents, and schedule appearances.

But Chase's part, at least for tonight, was done.

"Nice job out there, boss." His right-hand girl thrust a bottle of cold water into his outstretched hand.

"Thanks, Mel. Can you handle the press?"

"Me? I don't think the queen would like that."

"Watch what you say, Mel."

"Sorry, *Ms. Bennett* wouldn't like it. Besides, you love the post-show interview, especially after a big win. And this—"

"Is the biggest win ever, I know," Chase said. "I'll be tempted to say too much."

Mel stepped close, her brown eyes growing wide. "About what?"

"Never mind. Don't worry about Kerstin. I'll take care of her." He put his hands on Mel's shoulders and turned her toward the approaching crowd. "Just handle it."

"You got it." She stepped toward the gathering of media reps. "This way to the press room. You know the routine."

"Chase, how's our favorite game show host? You've got to be running out of ideas. And money," one of the herd called.

Chase couldn't let this go without a response. "*Change Your Life* is no game. Unreality programming remakes the real world of helpless individuals. As for your other insinuations, ideas and money are limitless, my friend. SynVue knows no boundaries. And soon…" He forced his warmest smile before giving them just enough to rouse their curiosity. "Greater things are coming. Thank you all for being here. My assistant will answer any questions about our winner and her wonderful new life."

Chase left them and took the rear hallway. With his pulse racing and his ears still buzzing, he considered his show's future.

After this, they'd bring in a couple of contestants destined for smaller victories. Then, something big. Bigger than the massive fortune just awarded to Judy Bamber. Lucky lady. But her luck would soon be forgotten.

On to other projects. New contestants. Bigger prizes.

Something unforgettable.

2

"Did you see the look on her face when I told her everything she'd won?" Chase smiled. "She turned white as a ghost. I knew she was going to pass out."

"We couldn't have planned it any better." Kerstin kicked off her red pumps and put her feet on the coffee table. "But it would have been ruined if we'd had to carry her out on a stretcher. We're lucky she got up."

"She didn't just get up. It was miraculous. Somebody up there is on our side. We're jumping to the next level."

"We're going back to business as usual." Kerstin took the clip from her dark hair, and the long tresses fell against her shoulders.

"But Kerstin, sweetheart, business as usual means we have to make the next big win bigger than tonight's win. We've been on a progression for two years. We've got to keep the—"

"Chase, really, you're going to bankrupt SynVue." She sipped from a stemmed goblet.

"Not possible."

"We just gave away more money than the combined annual salaries of two thirds of SynVue's employees."

Chase dropped to the sofa and put both arms around her. "Two thirds of SynVue's employees don't make much." He kissed her ear. "But the rest of them—"

"Includes you and me. So stop giving away our money."

"I just do what I'm told. Besides, it's the advertisers' money, and they're not hurting."

The feel of her flawless skin energized him. Everything about her was perfect, from her unembellished beauty—the SynVue surgeons were not needed here—to her management of the show. She brought in the advertisers and their money, chose the contestants, arranged every detail of the winners' new lives, and then kept those fortunate souls from recklessness. They had to be maintained.

The show truly did change lives. But its success depended on the lasting triumph of the winners. No one wanted to see someone monumentally prized, outrageously wealthy, and virtually reborn come to failure. Kerstin made sure the winners stayed winners. If Chase was the adored one, and he was, then Kerstin was the revered one. She made it all happen.

But Chase was not left out of the running of the show. Ideas were easy—funding was the hard part. Kerstin would love this idea, and it wouldn't cost SynVue anything. He sat straight and looked her in the eye. "I've come across something new. Something better than plastic surgery and outrageous wealth."

"Life is money, Chase, and money is life." Kerstin's VirtuPad chirped. She reached for it and read the message. "We've got trouble." She slammed the VPad on the coffee table. "My gutless assistant says *you* will tell me about it."

"I don't know any—"

"Checked your messages lately, Chase? You can't be out of touch. I've told you that."

So much for timing. He stood, reached for his

jacket, and plucked his VPad from the pocket. It came to life at the touch of his hand.

Kerstin's creamy skin turned a mean shade of red. "I knew something like this would happen."

"We don't know what happened, Kerstin." He paced across the living room then out the open glass door and onto the moonlit patio. Kerstin's breath hissed on the back of his neck. "There's a message from Mel."

He punched the text-only option, and then grabbed hold of the iron railing that encircled the patio as he read the news. The very bad news. Why did he have to be the one to tell Kerstin? He turned to face her.

"Well, what is it?" Kerstin folded her arms.

He stuffed the VPad into his pants pocket. "One of our re-creations is having some issues. We'll need Dr. Jacobson. And a suite at SynVue Estate. And a good psychiatrist. Latmore, maybe. Or—"

"Chase. What happened?"

"Elaine Jenz. Remember? New face, new body, job anchoring for SynVue."

"Of course I remember. We made a star reporter out of a sow's ear. What did she do?"

Chase wiped his hand through his hair and then put both his hands on his hips. "She took a laser knife and cut up her own face. On the air, during a broadcast."

Kerstin covered her mouth with her hand.

"She said something about *Change Your Life*."

"What about it?"

"That it was our fault."

Kerstin turned to go back in the house and grabbed her VPad. "OK, damage control. I'll get the publicity team on this. We'll issue a sympathetic refute. Nobody can blame us for this. She cracked. That's all."

"Poor woman," Chase said. "What would make her do something so awful?"

"I'm not as concerned about that as what this will do to *us*—to the show."

"Kerstin, she's obviously sick. Shouldn't we stand by her?"

"Listen to me, Chase." Kerstin came beside him and put her hand on his shoulder. "We can't take blame for this. Our reputation is rock-solid. We make people's lives better. Wonderful. Perfect." She brushed her fingers against his temple. "We'll stand by her, yes. But only as long as it takes to distance ourselves as gracefully as possible."

3

Chase escaped to his dressing room while the directors planned the next shoot. He fell to the sofa and closed his eyes, but recent events flashed a show of their own.

In the last two weeks, he'd taken heat in countless interviews, rejecting conclusions of why a former winner turned to despair and self-mutilation. "Elaine Jenz had a drug problem," Chase told the reporters. She didn't adhere to the coaching she'd received, and she slipped back into old habits. The explanation sufficed. None of it was true, but he had to protect the show. Now that a little time had passed, the incident was hardly remembered, at least by the press.

As for Elaine, Chase tried visiting her at SynVue Estate, but after a few minutes, she pounded on the shatterproof windows of her private suite, screaming to be saved from the devil.

Kerstin was right. He had to distance himself. He didn't go back.

The episodes following Judy Bamber's big win spotlighted a middle-aged man in need of a kidney transplant. And major debt reduction, of course. How did these people get themselves into grave-deep debt? Chase came alongside Larin Andrews, as with all the poor souls chosen as contestants by SynVue, and acted the part of sympathetic confidante.

Larin played the game, though it wasn't really a

game. And he would win—there wasn't any chance he'd lose. After three episodes filled with emotional tugs and careful management, viewers would pick the winner's prizes, casting their votes on VPads and graphene systems across the world. Of course, SynVue execs picked the prizes ahead of time. The votes meant nothing. Chase shifted on the leather sofa and put both hands behind his head.

"A week and a day 'til I tell Larin he'll get a new kidney. But I don't know if I'll have the prize ready."

"Boss, are you talking to yourself again?"

Chase opened his eyes to find his assistant standing in the doorway. "Mel, how many times have I told you to stop calling me boss?"

"Stop calling me Mel and maybe I will."

He smiled, and Melody smiled in return. She came into the small room and began straightening items on the desktop. "You got a call from some doctor," she said.

"Dr. Fiender?" Chase leaned forward and put his elbows on his knees as Mel shuffled some papers. "Don't throw those out."

"Yeah, that was his name." She sat on the edge of the desk. "You know I'm not going to throw out anything important. What are you doing with all this? If we get caught using so much paper, we'll get fined."

"They're printouts from Kerstin. I have to look into some things for her."

"Why didn't she just send it to your VPad?" Mel folded the pages together, held them over the wastebasket next to the desk, and dropped them in.

"Mel...*Melody*, I told you—"

"They're filed right here, boss, where you can find them." She dropped to the desk chair and folded her hands on her lap. "What sort of doctor is he? You sick?"

"No, he's a scientist I met a few weeks ago."

"Why's he calling you?"

"He wants to talk to me about the show." Chase rubbed his hands together. "I think he can help with Larin."

"I don't like that look in your eyes." Mel crossed her arms. "What are you planning?"

He smiled at the way she studied him. Black curls framed her face. She looked like a kid, but she was one smart woman. And she was always on his side.

"I'm just looking into some possibilities," he said. "I was going to tell Kerstin about it. Then we got into the whole mess with Elaine Jenz, and I decided I'd better wait. Now we have a contestant who needs a transplant. It's like it was meant to be."

"I'm not sure what you're talking about, but you know you're not going to do anything without the queen's approval."

"If Kerstin heard you say that, she'd have your backside on the street. Then what would I do?"

"You'd get your own coffee and file your own papers." She motioned to the wastebasket. "Seriously, what's this science man got up his sleeve? You do something behind Kerstin's back, she'll put *you* out on the street."

"Says he can make body parts out of nothing. Parts that won't wear out. We could get Larin a kidney. Remember the last time we tried a transplant? We got a genetically altered liver grown in a pig. It was a disaster. Took three months for the ratings to recover."

"Boss, that poor man died. And nobody makes something out of nothing. Nobody but God."

"If God can do it, then it can be done."

"Don't go comparing some witchdoctor to God." She turned in the chair and gently touched the ceramic bobble-head figure on Chase's desk. "You don't want to mess with the man upstairs any more than you have already."

"Mel, are you still worried about that thing? I told you, there's nothing wrong with a bobble-head Jesus. It's just a souvenir."

"It's a joke," she said. "Something the devil would keep on his desk. A little harmless, do-nothin' Jesus."

She was a religious girl. Chase wasn't sure if anyone else at SynVue knew this. People didn't talk about such things. What Mel did in her private life didn't bother him, and he didn't want to offend her.

Nor did he care to hear another insinuation that he was some horned beast from the underworld.

"If it bothers you, throw it out. It's just something I picked up in the EU. I thought it would be funny, you know, since I change people's lives."

Mel shook her head. Silver earrings dangled against her brown skin. "Not funny." She picked up the bobble-head, but her confident expression was gone.

Chase laughed. "You can't do it, can you? You can't throw it out."

"Well…" She looked at the little figure's quivering head and then at Chase. "He does look kinda like Jesus, I guess. How can I put him in the trash?"

"You need to let go of the old ways, Mel. You're so intelligent. Wise beyond your years. Why do you believe that stuff? It's not like you're in the Underground Church or anything. Are you?"

"I wouldn't be here working for you if I was. Wise

beyond my years, huh?" She set down the bobble-head, stood, and headed for the door. "Well, you're just a wise guy." She flashed him a sly grin, and she was gone.

Chase remembered why she'd come—the call from Dr. Fiender. He fished his VPad from the pile of clothes on top of a wooden trunk. Dr. Fiender's message popped up. Chase ran his finger across the numbers highlighted within the text and touched the real-view option on the small screen. He put the VPad in a stand on his desk. The doctor's image appeared in the room, and Chase leaned forward and smiled.

"Good day, Mr. Sterling. You're a hard man to reach."

"My apologies, Dr. Fiender. The life of a celebrity…"

The doctor grunted and wiped a finger across his gray mustache. "I understand you've had some problems with a past winner. I thought you might have come to the conclusion that I could be of service in the matter of Elaine Jenz."

"No, that didn't occur to me. We talked about body parts. I have a new contestant who needs a kidney, but I don't know how you could help Elaine. She had a breakdown."

"Meet with me, Mr. Sterling. Come to my facility."

"Where?"

"South of Phoenix, near the town of Florence. I could send my jet. You'd be here in thirty minutes."

"You have a Globejet?" Chase lifted his hand to his forehead and then wiped the sudden emergence of perspiration from his top lip.

"How else could you get from Chicago to the Southwest Territory so quickly?"

"Why me? Why not one of the execs from SynVue?"

"Because, Mr. Sterling, people call you the most influential man in the Western Republic. And I need an influential man."

Chase drew a breath and straightened his shoulders. "I'd have to be back tonight."

"Be at BHO International in one hour. My associate will meet you at the information counter at Terminal 44."

"Can you help with the kidney?"

"I'll send one back with you."

"Should I bring a cooler?"

The doctor lifted his brow and grinned. "No cooler needed."

4

Chase held to the armrests of the padded seat. The other seven seats in the Globejet were empty. A curvaceous blonde flight attendant stood near the door to the cockpit. No sign of a pilot.

Chase wasn't a good flyer. He wasn't afraid of heights. Falling, however, was a different fear altogether. And speed. Going 140 on the city tram was bad enough. This was unbelievable. He dug his nails into the plump upholstery.

"Sir, we'll be landing in four minutes." The blonde moved toward him. She took the glass of melting ice and folded the tray upright. Chase kept his eyes on her elegant stride until she disappeared behind a partition.

It was a long four minutes.

The jet landed smoothly, and the blonde reappeared and bid a pleasant good-bye as Chase exited. Still no pilot.

Florence Jetport was small, with one long runway next to several shorter ones. An unmanned motorized cart carried Chase to the terminal building where Dr. Robert Fiender's driver waited.

The ride in the black limo gave Chase time to recuperate. His muscles, his mind, everything in him still soared. But the soft black leather warmed and massaged his thighs and back. The big electric vehicle made little sound, but when he closed his eyes, he heard the roar of the audience. Giving up on rest, he looked out the window at the wide, empty desert.

Could Fiender really change the way the show operated? Technology had given Chase the opportunity to bless so many. Barren couples and same-sex couples were given children genetically related to both parents. In one case, the baby was created from *four* parents. Paraplegics walked. The blind regained their sight. Widespread organ failure due to environmental toxins was dealt with regularly at *Change Your Life.* But donors were getting harder and harder to find. Poor people died with poisoned parts. Rich people outlived those awaiting transplants. And xenotransplantation was just plain unreliable. Lab-grown organs had been failing for twenty years.

That's why this scientist's claims intrigued Chase.

An iron gate swung open at the entrance to Dr. Fiender's facility. A fence, maybe ten feet high, surrounded the small compound. Four buildings, none too impressive, stood in the fenced area.

Dr. Fiender met Chase at the door of the two-story brick structure to the left of the paved driveway. A small man, he appeared to be in his late sixties. The doctor's wild gray hair and prominent nose were classic Einstein.

But Einstein never made a kidney.

"Dr. Fiender. Good to see you again." Chase shook the doctor's hand firmly.

"Yes, yes. Welcome. Come in and see what we've done here at the Helgen Institute."

"Named after Naomi Helgen? Did she work here? I thought her laboratory was somewhere in the EU." Chase took in the small lobby as he spoke. Southwest décor seemed at odds with framed posters of what appeared to be body parts covered with binary code.

"You know of her?" Dr. Fiender's bushy eyebrows went up. "Well, of course you do. She was the greatest scientist of our time." He walked toward a glass door. "She did her work overseas. She was a Brit, you know. Never came to the Americas."

"So, you named this place after her because of her renown? Understandable—she did cure cancer."

"Her research in synthetic antigens gave us our vaccine, yes. But her subsequent work is what I hope to complete. She swore me to the cause."

"You knew her well?" Chase said.

"I was her pupil. And her lover."

Chase stopped walking.

The doctor turned and smiled. "Don't be surprised. Everyone needs love."

"Oh. Yeah, I'm…" Chase moved forward, and the doctor waved his hand in front of a small screen. The glass door slid open. "How did she die? Some sort of accident, wasn't it?"

"No accident. She was silenced. I moved her laboratory to this location, away from the probing leadership of the EU."

"Somebody killed her? Who?" Chase stumbled over an upholstered chair then fell into it as the doctor took his seat behind a massive oak desk.

"Not important. Not anymore."

"Someone killed Naomi Helgen. Now they're not important?"

"Relax, young man. Certain people helped us move our operations to the WR. And now they protect us."

"Us?"

"Myself and a few other scientists. Certainly you don't think I could do all this alone."

Chase leaned forward. "All what?"

Dr. Fiender let out a laugh. "Come and I'll show you."

"Why me?"

"I told you, because of your influence. Because I want to change the world, and you want to change lives. We are of one mind."

"I doubt that." Chase stood and walked to a window. The desert spread out beyond the iron fence. "I'm starting to realize I don't have any idea what you have in mind."

"I can help you with your little show. I'll pay SynVue to supply me with hopeless, helpless individuals. And you will present to the world a new kind of winner."

"I didn't know you were a student of Dr. Helgen." Chase turned to look at the doctor. "My contestants are not guinea pigs."

"Why the sudden resistance?"

"Murder? Government involvement?" Chase returned to his chair. "I know a little about what Dr. Helgen did. She was a proponent of the transhumanist movement."

Dr. Fiender leaned back in his leather chair. "I have a kidney for you."

"I'm guessing you didn't get it from a cadaver."

"I made it, covered it with manufactured, universally accepted tissue, vacuum sealed it, and…" He put his hands on the desk. "Where did I put it?" He looked to the shelves and cabinets to his left, then down to his big white coat. "Oh, yes." He reached into his pocket, pulled out a small fleshy blob tightly wrapped in plastic, and tossed it on the desk.

Chase got up and backed away. "Won't it…rot?

You carry it around in your pocket then put in someone's body?"

"It's not going to rot. And it won't be rejected by your contestant's body. Carry it back with you, and give it to your surgeons."

"Would my contestant be the first to receive one of your homemade parts?"

"I have a few homemade parts myself. As do some of my colleagues. If it makes you feel any better, we tested the product on ourselves."

"What else have you got in your pocket?"

The doctor stood and walked toward the glass door, waved his hand, and stepped into the hallway of the Helgen Institute. "Come with me and I'll show you."

5

The next morning Chase eased to the sofa in his dressing room and lowered his travel bag onto the floor. He stared at the bag that held a kidney he'd brought back from the desert. Now what was he supposed to do with it? Fiender told him to give it to the surgeons. Chase pulled out his VPad.

"Mel, I need you."

"Be right there, boss."

He left a message for the medical coordinator. As he stood, he inadvertently kicked the travel bag across the floor.

"Geez." He reached for the bag. "Idiot." He tugged the zipper and spread the bag open to peer inside. The kidney remained nestled between a spare shirt and a green folder. It looked fine, he guessed. He pulled out the folder, zipped the bag shut, and set it on the coffee table.

Chase opened the folder and flipped through the handwritten pages. A few computer generated sheets were attached, some containing visual aids. A do-it-yourself guide to kidney transplants. How odd to manufacture a human organ and then send it off with a thrown-together manual. The doctor could watch the surgery live on a GrapheVision, if he wanted to, and instruct the surgeons himself.

Mel came into the room and handed Chase a cup of coffee. "What'd you find out? You get a kidney for

Larin?"

Chase reached into his bag and pulled out the shrink-wrapped organ. He held it up, looked at Mel, and raised his eyebrows.

She put her hand over her mouth and backed away. "Oh, Great Lord Almighty, please don't let that be what I think it is."

"Great doctor is more like it. He made this, Mel. He made a kidney. And that's not all he can make."

She sat at the desk and crossed her arms. "Sport to a fool."

"Huh?"

"To do evil is like sport to a fool."

"Mel, what on earth are you talking about?"

"He's playing a game, boss. That doctor's competing with the Creator." She stood and walked closer, bent down, and poked the blob in Chase's hand. "Fool." She sat on the sofa, and Chase sat next to her.

"You want to hold it?" Chase smiled.

Mel slipped her hands under her thighs. "Maybe you should put it in the fridge."

"No need. I could put it in a drawer if I wanted to and keep it there 'til we need it."

"I'm not going near your desk if that thing is in it."

"Don't worry. I already sent a message to the med team. I said you'd deliver it to the estate this morning."

"I just told you I'm not going near it."

He lifted the leather bag and dropped the kidney in. "Relax, Mel. It doesn't bite." He thrust the bag into her hands.

"OK, but I am not happy about this." She stood and walked toward the door. "Does somebody have to sign for it?"

"Give it to Mike. He'll get it to the surgical team."

He waved her off, and she disappeared, mumbling something about God.

Maybe he should have held on to the kidney a little longer to show it to Kerstin, but he'd better wait to tell her. He'd make it seem like her idea. She didn't need to know the manufactured organ she was about to order had already been picked up. She couldn't accuse him of going behind her back if she was the one to direct him to Dr. Fiender.

He picked up his VPad and spoke another message: "Mike, don't tell Kerstin about this. You know how she is. We'll let her take the credit." Then he sent it as type.

He wasn't worried about Mel letting out the secret. She avoided Kerstin as much as possible. He slipped on his blue blazer and straightened his tie. Larin would be here soon to go over plans for the day's episode. Then the makeup guys would make sure Larin looked sick enough. It'd be hard not to tell him about the kidney.

One more week 'til prize day. Chase had better start working on Kerstin. He left his dressing room and headed for her office suite.

Interruptions persisted as he thought over what he would tell Kerstin. First an intern giving a tour of the studio spotted him. It wasn't unusual for Chase to encounter audience members who'd won a tour. Fifteen fans were in this group.

"Oh, Chase, I can't believe I'm shaking your hand." A lovely young woman gushed over him. She didn't look sick or poor, and she certainly wasn't in need of a makeover.

"Welcome. I hope you enjoy today's show." Chase moved to the next outstretched hand, forced a smile, and rushed away.

Then a director stopped him for a brief go-over of the show to air live that night. The muscles in Chase's legs bounced like springs. At last, the director stopped his rambling, and Chase launched into the east hallway.

He dashed to the private elevator that would take him up to Kerstin's domain and waved his hand before the glowing green panel next to the door. Staring at the lighted panel, his mind raced. Something was wrong. His heart suddenly tried to climb out of his ribcage.

The green folder—he didn't put it back in the travel bag with the kidney.

On his way back to his dressing room, he prompted his VPad, but Mel didn't respond. She must be really mad. Chase wouldn't have time to deliver the folder before the shoot. It could wait, he guessed. He slowed his stride, took a breath, and then prompted the med coordinator.

"Mike, I'm an idiot. The matter we discussed, the thing Mel is delivering—I forgot to send the instruction manual."

"Yeah, Melody handed me the bag, and I reached in and got the little thing. But she said she didn't know anything about what to do with it. Except that I could stick it in a drawer if I wanted to."

"Is she still there?"

"No. Hightailed it outta here."

"I'll get her to bring you the notes from Dr. Fiender later today. In the meantime, like she said, stick it in a drawer if you want, but keep quiet about it."

"How about I put it in the safe instead? Weirdest thing I've ever seen, Chase. I don't want to misplace it."

"Right. Later, Mike. Thanks."

Chase stuffed the VPad in his pocket and opened the door to his dressing room. There sat Kerstin, the green folder open in her lap.

"Chase, darling, I haven't seen you since noon yesterday. Where have you been?" She didn't look up from the page. "And what is this gibberish?" Then she reached for another stack of pages and looked at Chase. "And why did you throw out my notes on the new Moonbeams Tour Company?"

He stood in the doorway. "I didn't throw them out."

"Someone did. I found them in the wastebasket."

"You went through my trash?"

She had a way of smiling through a scowl. "I wanted to know where you went yesterday. I thought I might find a discarded clue."

He smiled and came into the room. "Don't you trust me?" Bending to kiss her, he glanced at Dr. Fiender's notes.

"Chase, I don't think you went to meet another woman."

"What then? Do you think I would betray you in any way?"

She closed the folder and held up one hand. With the other, she held up the pages she'd retrieved from the wastebasket. "Explain."

"Well, the notes about the space vacation probably got knocked into the trash."

"That assistant of yours did it."

"No, of course not. Besides, it doesn't matter. The notes are saved, and I will look into the possibility of sending a winner to the moon."

"What about this?" She waved the folder in the air. He grabbed it and drew his arm behind his back. "Chase, give it to me."

"Listen to me. I want to tell you about something wonderful. If you like the idea, and only if you like it, we'll start doing business with the man who wrote these notes."

"And who would that be?"

"Dr. Robert Fiender." Chase sat on the sofa and leaned forward. "He's a genius, Kerstin. You can't even imagine what he can do."

"What I can't imagine is why you would meet with some quack without my permission. I know you went to BHO—I can track your car easily enough. But then your VPad put up a block. You didn't take a commercial flight, so I can assume you took a private jet. One belonging to the doctor?"

If she'd been a cat, her back would've been arched, her black hair standing on end. Chase stepped away. How did he think he could hide anything from her? But maybe he could stop this tirade.

He slinked to the sofa and motioned Kerstin to sit beside him. As she moved from the desk chair, he opened the folder. "You know more about medical advancement than I could ever hope to know. Now that you've read through this, what do you think?"

"I think your friend is telling you how to install a kidney. A kidney he created. Correct?"

"A manmade, universally accepted, fully functioning kidney. It's a miracle, Kerstin. We can heal all kinds of ailments now." He closed the folder. "Don't you think we should take advantage of this technology?"

"How much?"

"It wouldn't cost SynVue anything. The doctor is just trying to—"

"Trying to test his product. What about liability?"

"It wouldn't be the first time we've asked a contestant to sign a waiver."

She sat motionless, her green eyes steady. "In the future, remind your contacts that *I* run this show. In fact, you need reminding of that as well. You may be the one who gives good things to the poor and the pitiful, but I determine what is good."

He lifted her pale hand, kissed it, then rose and walked across the room. "My mistake. I thought we were a team."

"Your mistake was to go off on your own. It makes me think you want to take credit."

"I just want to help a man who needs a transplant." He turned to open the door. "Now if you will excuse me, it's almost show time, and I haven't even been to makeup."

He looked back at her. "May I order the kidney?"

"Don't be hurt. Of course you may order the kidney. In fact, I'll do it myself. But before we take this relationship with Dr. Fiender any further, I will meet with him."

Chase nodded and left the room. Mel was right.

Kerstin *was* the queen.

6

Chase closed his eyes while his personal presentation assistant combed and plucked his brows. A one-eyed glance at the countdown screen told him it was twenty-two minutes to show time. Today Larin Andrews' doctors would deliver monologues alternating with a digital diary of Larin's existence. Between shots, Chase would conduct a live interview, asking questions about the contestant's past, and meager hope for a future now that his kidneys were kaput.

In a week, Larin would be awarded a kidney, and nobody had to give up one of their own. The slimy thing was in a safe on the other side of the hundred acre SynVue complex. Chase quivered.

"Mr. Sterling, please be still," the assistant said. "One wrong move and you'll lose those curly lashes."

"Sorry." Chase relaxed into the chair.

After a moment, the girl removed the cover from Chase's neck and pushed the chair upright. "There now. All done and handsome as always. Blue eyes shining under a perfect brow. A touch of gold added to your chestnut hair." She sighed. "You're a vision."

"Thank you…uh."

"Nanette." She smiled, but her eyes showed the hurt.

"Nanette. Of course. What happened to the other lady?"

"I don't know, Mr. Sterling. Alma's been gone awhile. I've been here two months."

"Really? Well, thanks." Chase left the small room and the makeup girl he didn't know. He wondered briefly how many people worked for him that he couldn't name.

The stage welcomed him as always—the one true constant in this job. That and Mel. And Kerstin. The golden tiles were among his closest friends. They helped make him who he was—the giver of gifts. The changer of lives. He stood in the middle of the splendor and prepared himself for the show. The crowd on the other side of the retractable lighted partition rumbled with impatience.

Larin waited in the low lights on the left side of the stage. Chase caught the dying man's eyes. The poor guy looked sicker than ever. His wrinkled shirt and trousers hung on him. Drab, graying hair fell across his forehead. He should be on a hover cart—it would have been better than letting him walk onto the stage. The directors should have thought of that.

The lights at the bottom of the partition swelled in shades of blue and green, and the audience roared as the partition lowered into the underbelly of the auditorium. Chase lifted his hands.

"Welcome to *Change Your Life*, my fellow comrades in hope. Today we take Larin Andrews a step closer to the wondrous generosity of SynVue. This time next week, we'll find out what you, the viewers, have chosen as his prize. Will he live his final days in peace and security? Or will he have a long and healthy life blessed with endless bounty? You decide. Now let's bring out our contestant and hear his story."

Larin walked with effort to the center of the stage,

and Chase took his arm and turned him to the right. A spotlight illuminated the set-up of a comfortable living room. Larin lowered himself gently onto a plush sofa. Chase sat across from him in a wing chair. Glasses of water waited on a small table.

"Larin, how are you feeling? You look well." Chase leaned forward and clasped his fingers together.

"I look like death, Chase." Larin's hands dropped to the sofa. His breath dragged. He did have a look about him like someone about to pass on. Chase wondered if the makeup team or the Grim Reaper had painted that picture.

"It won't be long now, my friend. In a week we'll find out just how much your life will change. We'll know if we've found a match, and if the world has decided you deserve the prize." Chase lifted a water glass and offered it to Larin.

The fragile man took a sip. "I can tell you this. No one deserves such torture. My health is gone. The medical bills have put my family on the streets. We sleep in a van, the kind that used to run on gasoline. Now it's our home." He looked above the audience. "Home sweet home."

The revelation surprised Chase. He didn't like surprises. Someone should've told him about this. But now he was curious. "You're nearby, I assume."

"Whole village of old vans ten miles from here, just outside the city. Where good citizens don't go, I guess. People like you, like these people here." He looked at the crowd. "Those who have what they need don't go out of the city anymore. Nobody does but the poor souls who've got nothing."

"But you spend a good deal of time in Med World, don't you?" Chase asked. "Surely they take better care of the sick."

"Med World is for paying customers. My WR med fund ran out a year ago. Without that I can't pay for a kidney. Without a kidney, I can't keep up my strength for the WR workforce, which means I can't replenish my med fund. Which means my family lives in a van outside the city."

"What was your job in the workforce before you got sick?" Chase knew the answer, but the viewers didn't.

"I was a sweeper. My assigned lot in life—to run a refuse sweeper. Did you know I went to Yale?"

Chase knew this. An educated man, a Yale graduate, became a common sweeper. The ineffectual methods of the government that gave this man his job also gave Chase his. How could an intellect end up at the bottom, and a man who couldn't pass trigonometry end up on top?

As if Larin knew what Chase was thinking, he asked, "Where were *you* educated, Chase?"

"Today is about you, Larin. We *are* going to change your life. I *am* going to get you a new kidney."

"Do you ever think about dying, Chase? It's not such a scary thing."

Where was he going with this? "Like I said, Larin..." Chase gave him a firm stare. "It's your day." Then under his breath he said, "Use it wisely."

Larin put on a weak, pitiful smile. "Not that I plan on dying anytime soon. I know my life is about to change for the better."

Chase looked to the crowd. "Let's give Larin a round of applause." The crowd cheered and clapped. "Now, lift your eyes to the GVs. Larin's doctor will tell us about the technology that's kept him alive. But techno-meds, for Larin, are at the end of their usefulness."

Larin looked at his own shoes as a beautiful redhead named Dr. Tara Brown spoke.

"My patient, Larin Andrews, needs something I can't supply. Our advances in kidney reconstitution have kept him alive for years, but what he needs now is a good old-fashioned transplant."

Chase nearly chuckled—an old-fashioned transplant.

The doctor continued. "Of course, with regulations and waiting lists, the cost of a good kidney is nearly two million. Mr. Andrews would never be able to afford that."

Chase looked at his latest contestant while the doctor continued her woeful explanation of the disease. Larin looked up from the floor, and his gray eyes glared back.

ॐॐ

"What's with Larin? He should be trying to win over the audience, not scare them." Chase spoke louder than he should as he stormed past the media reps backstage. Mel followed on his heels.

"Don't know, boss, but now's not the time to go there, you know?"

Chase slowed his pace and softened his furrowed brow. "Right."

"I'm sure nobody noticed but you," Mel said. "It wasn't like he was outright rude or anything." They came to the hall leading to Chase's dressing room.

He turned to Mel. "Did *you* notice?"

"Maybe he's just feeling bad. Maybe it's the

meds."

"And why didn't I know the guy lives in a van?" Chase raised his voice. "In a field of vans."

"I don't know, boss. Ask the queen."

Chase started to lecture her for this, another *queen* reference. But he stopped. Kerstin had to know. Why was she holding back information? "I will," he said. "Believe me, I will."

7

Chase went straight to Kerstin's office. "Why didn't you tell me Larin lives in a van?"

"It's not for you to know everything, Chase. You're just the host. You don't run the network."

He didn't respond to her belittling. "Kerstin, look at me. I want an explanation, and I want it now."

She met his eyes but without emotion. She didn't appear frightened by his tone. And she didn't seem to feel the need to apologize. "Don't worry. We've got it worked out. He'll get a nice home—at least 8,000 square feet."

"I don't care about that. I want to know why you're keeping me in the dark. We could have played the angle all along. The fans love this kind of thing." He banged his fist on the desk. "And I'm the one the fans rely on. A contestant shouldn't surprise me in the middle of a show."

Still no apology. She just looked at him. "Larin lives in a van, Chase. Satisfied? Our consultants said it would be too much for the show. We can make over a life but not a village. And our audience would want to know why, if *Change Your Life* couldn't fix the problem, the government doesn't do something about it. It's best to leave widespread poverty alone."

"So that's why I've never seen or heard of the place until now," Chase said. "The government doesn't want to admit people have to live that way."

"Exactly. You and I, and our winners, give the world hope. But there's only so much we can do, Chase. We can't fix everybody. Better to bless a few extravagantly than to give a worthless boost to the masses." She tapped her fingers on the desk. "Now forget about it. What you ought to be worried about is why Larin isn't drooling over you like he should be at this point. What did you do?"

"What did I do? I got on a globe jet—something I hate—and flew to the desert to get him a kidney that will live longer than *he* does."

"*I* got the kidney, Chase. I sent word to your assistant, Melanie, this morning. She ordered it for me."

"Her name is Melody."

"Whatever. Now go on and let me work. I'll see you at dinner."

"This isn't over." He turned to leave the office but stopped at the door. "I might not make it to dinner. I think I'll take a drive—I could use some fresh air. I'll see you tomorrow." He walked away before Kerstin could deny consent.

Chase realized on his way out of the studio that he hadn't driven his steel blue Selfdrive in a while. He didn't even know where it was. He rode in a limo most of the time—SynVue property—chauffeured by a man named Hiram, or something like that. He flipped out his VPad and prompted Mel.

"Yeah, boss?"

"Where's my car?"

"Your car? In your slot. Plugged in. Where else would it be?"

"It's been a while. Where's my slot?"

"Boss, are you OK? Want me to call Liam and tell

him you need to go somewhere?"

"Fine. I mean no. Don't call Liam. I'm going to take a drive."

"Where are you going?"

"Where is my slot?"

"Did you ask your VPad?"

"I'm asking *you*, Mel."

"You want me to come? I'm about through for the day."

"The slot, Mel. I don't want company."

"Level six. Turn right when you get off the elevator. Slot 327."

"Got it." He thought Mel started to say something, but he ended the call. The elevator took him to the underground garage and he exited on level six, turned right, and walked a few hundred yards before he found his slot. He was sure he'd never been here. Someone else must have put the car away for him when he drove it last. The steel blue looked more like dusty blue. The push of a button inside the small slot started the air-washer, which swooshed away the filmy grime.

He stood beside the driver's door, and a tiny camera on the end of a black rod rose from the dark window's frame. The camera flashed in Chase's eyes and the door opened. Once inside, Chase commanded the vehicle.

"Power up."

The car unplugged itself from the panel in the rear of the slot and gave a soft hum.

"Disable autonomous mode."

Chase took hold of the steering bar and pushed his foot onto the motion petal. He'd take control of the driving today.

Another small car and a limo pulled into the sunlight. The car went left, the limo straight, and Chase turned right. He wanted to get away from anyone else leaving the SynVue complex.

Driving through downtown gave Chase time to think. Larin's eyes would not leave him alone. But the voice he heard was that of Elaine Jenz, inferring he was the devil. All he wanted to do was help these poor people. Why were they turning on him? Maybe Elaine really did lose her mind. But Larin? He was so friendly, so eager, at first. Maybe it was the meds, like Mel said.

Ten miles outside Chicago, Larin had said, was a village of old vans. Chase got on the north city exit line. South would take him to what was left of the suburbs, east to tech row. And west was nothing but maintained nature preserves where school children went on field trips. The government wouldn't allow a neighborhood of junk vehicles to spring up there. It had to be to the north.

Traffic moved along and Chase was out of the city in minutes. A few commuters whizzed overhead with flight packs.

"Lunatics—flying around like birds," he said to no one.

A few hotels and a shopping arena dotted the landscape. Trees rose from the rolling hills to touch the gray sky. Chase pulled into a coffee drive-up and turned on his outside speaker when he came to the order window. His own window he left up—the coffee girl could hear him through the speaker. He didn't dare show his face.

"Can you tell me if there is a place nearby where old vans are parked? Sort of like a junk yard, I guess."

"The village," the girl said with a nod. "About two

miles." She pointed right. "Go past the dairy plant and turn left. You can't miss it. Can I get you some coffee or something?"

Chase really could use some coffee. But the girl would recognize him, and she'd tell everybody where he was going. And then the press would show up. "No, but thank you for the directions." He took off and turned right onto the highway.

The place was easy to find. Surely it wasn't as big a secret as Kerstin let on. Chase parked at the ridge of a shallow valley and looked over rows and rows of vans. Thousands of them, all colors, all obsolete. The rows were neat with wide passageways between them.

Several cars drove between the rows. People walked alone and in groups. Children played. Small GVs lit the interior of some of the vans. Campfires smoldered in front of others. Lines of clothes hung here and there. A dog rambled between several vans and finally jumped into one. This really was a village, a neighborhood. These were people's homes.

Why were these poor people living like this? Why didn't the government do something? The changes brought by his show were outrageous—Chase knew that. Not everyone could be so blessed. But everybody deserved a place to raise their kids. Some place better than this.

He cracked his window just enough to let in the smell of barbeque and the sounds of community. Summer's warm air carried the squeals of children. A mother gave instructions, and three kids settled around a folding table in front of a green van. They bowed their heads. No father was present.

Somewhere else in the village a couple argued, but the fighting quickly turned to laughter.

A GV blared out the news from SynVue. "Fighting today in Damascus was quelled by North Republic forces. The rebels were forced back by cyber soldiers with little effort, and no deaths or injuries were reported. But informants insist a bigger battle may be in store for the United Arab Territory. In other news, the current contestant on *Change Your Life,* Larin Andrews, seemed at odds to most viewers, and to this anchor. What's going on over there? We'll follow up later with an interview with Chase Sterling."

"Interview?" Chase took out his VPad. This alleged interview must have been planned after he made his afternoon escape. He had a message from Mel, four from Kerstin. And he'd missed eleven calls—he'd turned off the sound.

He looked over the world of archaic vehicles turned into homes, the sight of families living their lives. A boy, maybe ten, jumped from the open side of a van and called out, "Switch, come on boy."

The same dog Chase had seen running moments earlier barreled from the van and followed alongside the boy. The child's blond hair came to his shoulders. His T-shirt was too big. He smiled as he scratched the top of the dog's brown head.

Chase smiled too. "I wonder why he calls him Switch." His VPad chirped, and he let go of the smile. "Playtime's over."

But before he could power up the car, sounds from the village caught his ear. There was a lot of mumbling—a low, unhappy roar. But one voice shouted.

"What's the matter with Larin? He's gonna bring the government down on all of us. Today he told the whole world about us, and for what—so Chase Sterling could get interviewed on the news? Let him pluck Larin out of the real world and set him up in a castle. Leave the rest of us alone."

Chase pushed the button to shut the window. "Loud mouth. I'm just trying to help. I just want to give a few people a new start. Is that such a bad thing?"

8

"Boss, you've got to get back here. The queen's about to blow. Correction, she's about to blow again. She already went off a couple of times."

With the VPad secured to the console, Chase could see Melody on the screen. Her look told him this was serious. "I heard about my interview. Are they waiting on me?"

"Dain Alexander is on the interview set. He's been here about an hour. He's not too happy."

"I hate that guy."

"Kerstin seems to like him." Mel lowered her voice. "She's here, too, waiting on the set for you to show up."

"Tell her I'm on my way. I'm almost to the parking entrance."

"She's been yelling about you not staying in touch."

"Tell her my VPad broke, and I had to take it to the shop down on Pulaski. I just got it working. I went out to my house on the lake, realized my VPad was out, and came all the way back to town for a repair."

"Is that what happened?"

"Just tell her, Mel."

He knew by the position of her shoulders that she'd folded her arms across her chest.

"That's a good sized lie, and I don't think I can keep it all straight. You better just feed her that bull yourself."

"Just let her know I'm coming. Can you do that?"

"I'll tell her. But you better get here fast."

He clicked off the VPad. "Smart-aleck girl. What happened to respect? What is happening to my life?" He pulled his car into the parking facility under the SynVue studio. "What was that slot number?" His VPad chirped—Mel again.

"Level six, boss. Slot 327."

"Thanks, Mel."

"I got you covered. Told the queen you're on your way up."

When Chase came down the hallway, he found Dain Alexander and Kerstin deep in conversation on the far side of the interview set. Kerstin looked up and her face went from charming to gray with no in between. She left the reporter's side and stopped Chase before he came into the room.

"How many times do I have to tell you not to be out of touch?" Her voice was as dark as her expression. "SynVue decided you needed to make a statement about today's show, to display some of that lovable charisma of yours." She threw her hands above her head. "And you're out for a drive. With your VPad turned off."

"It broke. I had to stop and get it worked on."

"No one cares, Chase. Now get over there and apologize for making Dain wait."

Chase walked to Dain. "Sorry to keep you waiting."

The reporter ignored Chase's outstretched hand. "Let's get on with this."

Dain cued his camera guy, took a breath, and struck his best reporter pose.

"We're coming to you from the *Change Your Life* studio with my dear friend, Chase Sterling." He gave Chase a look of deep concern and empathy.

Chase nearly laughed. "Hello, Dain. So good to see you again."

"Yes, it's been too long. It's not often we have something other than glorious news to report from these hallowed grounds. But today people are questioning if your latest subject is worthy of his rewards."

"Larin had a bad day, that's all. Medication issues. He's a wonderful man, a friend. He deserves only the best."

"And why were you surprised by his living conditions? You were surprised, weren't you? It seemed that way to me."

"About the vans outside of town—I didn't know Larin lived there. My only concern is getting Larin the help he needs. Of course, I do know where he'll be living when...if the fans vote as I believe they will." Chase smiled.

"What do you know about that town of old vans?" Dain asked.

Chase hesitated. He'd like to give the world a little honest reporting for a change, but throwing those poor people into a media circus would not help them. "I don't know anything about it." He shifted in his seat. "As you noted, Dain, I was surprised by Larin's admission that he lives there. I never heard of the place until today. It's irrelevant. As I just said, Larin won't be there long if the voters come through."

"Why do you think Larin was so discourteous, so removed from the process today?"

"I told you he's on some pretty strong medication.

I'm sure it's nothing."

"Have you spoken to him since the show?"

"No. Have you?" Chase really wanted to know.

The reporter gave an empty laugh. "Your producer told me that wasn't allowed."

"Whatever my producer says, goes." Chase glanced in Kerstin's direction but didn't make eye contact.

"Will Larin Andrews get a kidney? Will he live to enjoy his life outside that village of vans?"

Chase would not reveal the outcome of the show a week before prize day. He put on his best *Change Your Life* smile. "Like the rest of the world, Dain, you'll have to wait to find out."

The interview ended, and Chase left quickly, not slowing long enough to get Kerstin's opinion of his performance. She was probably too busy showering Dain with compliments to notice. Mel followed him. They both went into his dressing room, and Chase fell to the sofa and rubbed his face.

"Can I get you some dinner, boss?"

"Coffee, please."

She walked to the counter against the far wall and placed a mug under the auto-drip.

"Here." She handed him the cup. "Let me go down to the cafeteria and get you something to eat."

"Just sit with me, Mel." He looked at her.

She settled onto the sofa. "Did you go check out those vans?"

"Yes."

"I saw the expression on your face when Alexander asked about it."

"And you knew I went there?"

"I knew you didn't want to tell him about it."

"It wouldn't have done anybody any good."

"You wanted to protect the people there, is that it? You didn't want to subject them to the media?"

"Right. It's kind of a...I don't know, Mel. It's a world apart from this one. Kind of peaceful, you know?"

She nodded. "I know. It's a homeless camp, but it is home to those people."

"You've been there?"

"I go there with my...group. We take food and clothes once a month."

"Your group?"

"Charity stuff, boss. You know."

"Yeah. I didn't know you and your friends did that sort of thing." He leaned forward. "Did you know about Larin?" If she did, she better be ready with an explanation.

"No, boss. Thousands of people live there. I never saw Larin."

"I believe you." He patted her knee. "So your group goes out there and gives stuff away? Where do you get the stuff?"

"We buy it. And then we give it away." She smiled. "Not much different than what you do, except we don't have advertisers."

"What happened to those people, Mel? Why don't they have jobs? It's not like the old days—everybody has a job."

"Occupation assignment is a good thing, I guess. Some people make enough money to live a good life. But sometimes people just can't do the job they get put into. And sometimes the government doesn't reassign them, and they fall into poverty. They quit filing work reports, and they get kicked out of the system. And then they're just lost. Nobody can just go get a job—you have to be assigned. And if the system kicks you out, then you don't get assigned."

"So all those people out there living in old vans are government throwaways?"

"Most of them. But some were never in the system. They're dissenters."

"People brought up to resist the changes made by the Western Republic."

"Right," Mel said. "Their parents raised them up in the old ways. They believe they can restore the Constitution."

"Crazy radicals." Chase stopped short of calling them criminals. "I'm sorry, Mel. Does your group believe that way?"

"My group doesn't care about that, only about..."

Chase looked at his desk, at the bobble-head. "About saving souls?" He turned to Mel.

She didn't say a word.

9

Before the final episode of the current run of *Change Your Life*, Chase had a private meeting with Larin Andrews. The man apologized for his attitude during the previous episode, but he seemed rehearsed. The one-on-one talk left Chase feeling like a third person was in the room. But things were better, and Chase left the meeting confident they'd have a good finale.

Things were back to normal with Kerstin as well. Dinners at his place, or hers, or an upscale restaurant. He'd stay at her high-rise penthouse, or she'd stay at his courtyard townhouse on the edge of SynVue property. She'd been more agreeable, amiable, the past few days. But the notion that she'd had her own private chat with Larin Andrews gnawed at Chase. Three days before prize day he had his cook fix Kerstin's favorite pasta, a big salad, and a marbled cheesecake. Dinner was waiting for them when they arrived at the townhouse.

"Chase, darling, this is wonderful. You fixed my favorites."

"I *requested* your favorites."

"Same thing."

"Not at all," he said with a laugh. "I don't even know how to turn on the oven."

"That's why SynVue gives us cooks." She took her place at the table and pulled the clip from her hair.

He sat across from her and lifted a forkful of the creamy pasta. Kirsten, did you meet with Larin during the past week?"

"Yes. Why do you ask?"

"I don't know. It's just that when I met with him he seemed like he already knew what he would say. And what he said sounded like what you might say."

"What on earth do you mean?"

"You coached him, that's all. I'm not surprised or offended or anything. I know you coach the contestants. But you don't usually tell them what to say when they go to a private meeting with me."

"You're very astute. I just didn't want to risk another episode like last week. We couldn't take a chance that Larin would blow the finale by coming off unappreciative."

"Of course. He was back to being the eager contestant, and I was satisfied with the meeting. But he said something."

"What did he say?"

"He said, 'This will be the show the whole world remembers.' What did he mean by that?"

Kerstin nibbled on the salad. "Did you ask him what he meant?"

"I just assumed he was being positive. But later, I felt like he knew something I didn't."

"What could he possibly know?"

"I guess it's the whole thing with the vans. I feel like you're keeping things from me."

"Chase, it was nothing. I told you all about it when you asked."

"I'm asking now. Is there anything else I don't know about this contestant?"

"He's just a poor soul who needs us," she said.

"That's all. Like always."

Two days until prize day. Chase waited in the director's suite for some lackey to come in and go over the list of prizes with him. A few employees walked past the open double doors. Chase dropped into a desk chair and swiveled. Then a woman came through the doorway. Elaine Jenz. Chase jumped to his feet as she smiled.

"Mr. Sterling, so good to see you." She took his hand in both of hers. "Thank you for everything. My time at SynVue Estate was wonderful. I am completely better."

"I had no idea," Chase said. "I thought you were…"

"Beyond hope? So did I. But Dr. Fiender brought me back."

"Dr. Fiender? I don't understand. You know Fiender?"

"Of course I know him. He's my savior. He did some minor little operation, and I am back to myself. I'm going back to work today in the news studio. I heard you were in here, and I just wanted to come by and thank you." Her smile was warm and grateful.

"Well, you're welcome, Elaine. Good to have you back."

She left the room just as the guy with the list came in. Chase excused himself. "I have to make a call," he said. "I'll be back in a few minutes."

"But Mr. Sterling, we need to go over this. I've got to be back downstairs in five minutes."

Chase turned around. "Fine. Get on with it then."

The young man settled at the desk and pushed a few keys on his pad. "I'm sending the list to you now."

Chase pulled out his VPad and prompted his personal data. The list appeared.

Kidney transplant at Med World. A mansion in the Northwest Territory—Seattle area. An upsized Selfdrive. New occupation assignment after recovery: Professor of Government at Pacific University. "Nice," Chase said. "Anything else I need to know before I make the announcement?"

"There are more details if you click on the occupation assignment, but I don't think the audience would be interested. Just stuff Ms. Bennett will go over with Larin after the show."

"Thank you." Chase got up to leave. "What's your name?"

"My name?"

"Yes, your name. What is it?"

"Jesse."

"Thank you, Jesse." Chase turned back to the hallway and headed for Kerstin's suite. He found her yelling at some poor girl who'd brought lunch. He didn't wait before he started yelling, too. "I want to know why you didn't tell me I could expect to see Elaine Jenz at work today, completely healed."

The delivery girl disappeared into the hall, and Chase slammed the door.

"Chase, darling, calm down."

"And I want to know why Dr. Fiender is fixing contestants behind my back."

Kerstin folded her hands on top of her desk. Her shoe tapped the tile floor. "Have you spoken to Robert?"

"Robert? You're on a first-name basis?"

"He is our associate now. Our medical consultant and supplier of wonders. But you know that. He contacted you first. Really, I owe it all to you, Chase."

"Well, thank you very much, Kerstin." His anger slipped into a muddled simmer. He took a breath and sat in the chair on the other side of her desk. "I don't understand."

"What you mean is you don't understand how you could have lost control of this situation. The doctor called you. You met with him. *You* brought a kidney back from his laboratory. And you were supposed to be the one to receive the accolades for taking our show to the next level. For introducing the world to your amazing find."

"Well, no, not exactly."

"*Change Your Life* is *my* show. You're just the handsome face that tells the poor saps what they've won. You don't need to worry yourself with the production of my show, Chase. All you need to do is come to work, get in front of the camera, and smile."

"But people depend on me. I'm the one they trust. I'm the one they watch." Something else crept into his thoughts. "I'm the one who cares about them." He looked her in the eye. "Not you."

She let out a laugh. "You're right about that. I care about the ratings. When did you go all soft for the contestants? It's a job, Chase. An assignment. It's a paycheck, and a fat one at that. When did you start caring about them?"

"When did you *stop* caring?"

"Darling, nothing is any different. But soon, things may change." She reached across the desk and cupped his face in her cold hand. "New assignments are being discussed. That's what I hear."

He rose from the chair and backed away from her. "What are you talking about? This is my life. This is who I am."

"You are who the government says you are. Trust me, you won't be out of the spotlight." She put her palms flat on the desktop. "But that's really all I know. I'm sorry. I shouldn't have said anything."

"Where did you hear it?"

"Production meeting with some WR officials. They think it will be good for SynVue. And for you. Don't look so worried."

Chase backed against the wall. "Wouldn't you be worried if somebody said your life was about to change?"

She laughed. "Chase, changing lives is what we do."

"What about Elaine?"

"What about her?"

"What did he do to her? Dr. Fiender, I mean."

"Oh, I couldn't begin to explain it. Something about nano circuits."

"He turned her into a puppet," Chase said.

"I wouldn't say that. He made her manageable. That's all."

"I saw the implants when I went to his lab. I told him I wasn't ready for the show to go that direction."

"As I said, Chase, it's *my* show. And I'm ready." She smiled. "Anyway, it wasn't on the show, not really. Elaine Jenz is old news. Nobody cares about what goes on in her brain. Now go get some rest, and try not to think about what I said. I shouldn't have mentioned anything."

Chase headed out the door without looking at her. "I don't want anything to change. I won't allow it."

10

Chase retreated to his townhouse. He pushed the light filter key to darken the windows and then powered down his computer and turned off his VPad. He took a shower, put on sweatpants, and fell onto the bed. His hands rested on his bare chest.

The room had already been decorated when he'd moved in, and he never liked it. Now he looked at the teal walls and rust colored bedding, the lacquered ebony dresser, the plush chair in the corner that matched the duvet. A chandelier hung over his head, antique, or made to look that way. Dozens of prisms danced in the wake of the air system's stream.

"I can't do this. I won't change," he said to the ceiling. He really had no choice. SynVue was owned by the government. Or was it the other way around? Nobody could say for sure. The two entities were one. "I like my life. I'm happy."

He fell deep into tortured dreams.

ॐ◅

The next day didn't bring its usual excitement. The run's final show always put Chase in a good mood. He would check the votes, even if they were meaningless. He didn't know if anybody but him even looked at the outcome. Certainly Kerstin didn't. But the votes were real—SynVue kept a file. Today Chase didn't even open the vote program.

For the past week, SynVue had blasted the fans with updates and reviews of the Larin Andrews' story. Now the voting was over, and it was time to give the contestant his rewards. People were stupid enough to believe they were the ones determining how blessed this poor buffoon would be.

Chase walked into his dressing room and poured himself some coffee. "This is all such a joke." He gulped too fast and burned his tongue. "My life is a joke." He threw the cup across the room just as Mel entered.

"Boss, what's wrong?" She rushed to him, and it seemed to Chase that she would embrace him. But she wrapped her arms around herself instead.

"I don't know what to do." Chase paced the room and then settled on the sofa.

"You don't know what to do about what?"

He realized then that his assistant might get reassigned as well. If he got a new position, she might not be necessary. "I feel like I'm losing it."

She sat beside him and put her hand on his arm. "Losing what, boss? You're scaring me."

"I heard from Kerstin that things might be changing around here."

"And you're worried about it? Maybe it's nothing. We've made changes in the past. It's never been anything to get all upset about."

"I think this is a big one, Mel. I think they're getting rid of me."

"That can't be true. People love you. The fans wouldn't stand for it."

She was right. But maybe the fans, like their votes, didn't matter. "Things have changed," he said. "Larin's been all weird. And Elaine Jenz was certainly not showing me any love when she had her breakdown. Of course, she was very nice yesterday when I saw her. She's better. Well, I don't know if you can call it better. She's been…adjusted. And that man who was yelling out there at the village—I don't think *he's* a fan." Chase jumped off the sofa. "Maybe I don't have as many fans as I thought. Maybe people are—"

"Boss, calm down."

He dropped to the sofa, took her hand and held on tight. "Did you see her?"

"Elaine? No, but I heard she's back. Isn't that a good thing? What do you mean about her being adjusted?"

"Dr. Fiender put something in her brain. He told me how it works, and I told him I didn't like the idea."

"But he did it anyway? Who...?" The realization showed on her face. "Kerstin."

"Exactly."

"So, how does it work?"

Chase leaned back, still clinging to his assistant's hand. "I don't understand it all."

"Is it a drug or a chip?"

"More like a chip, I guess, but a new kind. Without the side effects. Or so they say. If nothing else, the side effect is that she's no longer herself. Now she's less, or more, of the person she was. Either way, she's been partly replaced with something made in a lab."

"At least she's better now." Mel squeezed Chase's hand, and he let her go. "Do you think this doctor wants to do that to everybody?"

"It'll be a new world if he does."

"What about *Change Your Life*? You think we'll do it to contestants?"

"I don't know, but things are happening. And I don't know where I fit in. Or if I even want to fit in." He looked into her caring eyes as he breathed in a faint, flowery scent. She always smelled of lilacs. Lifting his hand, he nearly touched her cheek.

She quickly stood and walked to the door. "It's time to get ready, boss."

"Yeah, OK." He rubbed his face. "I hope they don't split us up."

"You and Kerstin? I know."

"No," he said. "You and me."

⚜

Chase took center stage. The crowd was ready. Larin was ready. Chase breathed deep and shook his head. Then he put on his best *Change Your Life* smile. The partition dropped. The light came up. And the crowd roared.

"Welcome." Chase lifted his arms. "Welcome to this, our final chapter in the rebirth of Larin Andrews. Today we'll find out what you, the generous fans, have chosen for Larin's future. Will it be a transplant and good health? Will it be a new home? Or will he get both health and wealth?"

The audience cheered and a few voices called out, "Yes. Yes. Health and wealth." The crowd began a unified chant. Chase motioned to the left of the stage, and Larin Andrews came to him as the crowd applauded.

"Larin, my good man, today is the day. How do you feel?"

"I'm excited, a little nervous. I'm ready for this." He gave a weak smile. But he looked better than he did the previous week. It wasn't his appearance—he was still gray and sickly. Something in his eyes showed a new determination or hope. Or power. Maybe it was just the knowledge that his life was about to change for the better.

"Let's take a look back on your life, Larin." Chase lifted a hand to the giant GVs over the stage, and the audience quieted their rumble.

Larin's face appeared on the screens. "My name is Larin Andrews. I have no future. No hope. That is, without the help of *Change Your Life*." Chase heard Larin snicker. "What a pitiful sap I was," Larin said quietly. "I'm glad that's over." The screens played out Larin's life for all to see. His failing health and his poverty carried the story.

"What are you talking about, Larin? This is not over until it's over," Chase whispered. "You won't know what your prizes are for another thirty minutes."

"Right. You're right, Chase." Larin had that gleam in his eye again. "Are you OK?"

"Are *you*?" Chase looked away.

After a few minutes, the screens went dark and the stage lights came up. Chase faced the crowd and began his verbal climb to the announcement of the prizes.

"Larin, tell us what your life will be like if you receive a transplant?"

"My family won't have to dispose of my ashes in six weeks. I'll live."

"And what if you and your dear wife and kids are given a new home? A grand home." Chase looked to the crowd.

"Then I'll know that when I'm gone, my family won't be on the streets. So to speak." He didn't mention the village. "And I'll live out my final days in peace."

"And what if your health is restored? Will you go back to your job as a street sweeper?"

"I can only hope to be so blessed as to get my assignment back from the WR. I'm out of the system, you know. But I'd take the job if they'd let me have it."

"Tell me, Larin. If you could do anything, get reassigned, what would you like to do?"

"Oh, I don't know. Job like yours, maybe." Larin smiled big and lifted his hands to the crowd. A roaring laugh met his imitation of Chase. "Of course, I'm a little too old for the gig, and I don't look the part. But with a little surgery…"

Chase forced a laugh. "Listen to that, people. Don't worry. I'm not going anywhere. I bring the blessings, Larin, and you receive." He turned to the camera and smiled. "Stay with us. We'll be right back."

The partition rose from the floor as makeup assistants and directors hurried on stage. Chase could not look at Larin. He looked past the stage for Mel. He caught her eyes and motioned her to come to him.

"Doing all right, boss?"

He turned her around and walked her away from center stage. "Larin knows something. I think he's going to get my job."

"That's ridiculous. He's a little weird, boss. That's what's got you so worried. You've got this unpredictable contestant to deal with on top of the queen telling you stuff that might not amount to anything." She turned him back to his place on the stage and patted his back. "Let's just get this episode over with, and get Larin out of here. Then everything will look better."

"Yeah. OK." He brushed his hands down the front

of his suit. Mel hurried off the stage. Larin peered over the top of his water glass. The partition went down and Larin limped to the center of the stage.

"Larin Andrews, today your life will change forever," Chase said, more to the crowd than the contestant. "The fans have voted. And this is what they've decided."

Larin brought his hand to his mouth, dropped his head, and closed his eyes.

"He wants your job, Chase!" The shout came from somewhere in the audience.

"No." Larin looked up in surprise. "Of course not. Chase, I was just talking nonsense. You know that." He turned to the crowd. "I could never hope to be as wise and generous…" He paused a moment. "And loved as this wonderful man."

The fans applauded.

A muted thud came from among them. Then a light. Chase saw the angry burst of fire coming right at him. There was no time to run.

11

A dream or something…

He awoke in a quiet place. Definitely not on stage. Wherever he was, it was dark. Beyond dark. A bed held him at an elevation so that he was almost sitting upright. Shaking his head, he blinked. Nothing. He was blind. But in his mind, he could still see the light coming for him, and Larin standing beside him.

"Hello? Is anyone there?"

"Tell me your name?"

"Chase Sterling. Where am I?"

"I mean your real name. The name your parents gave you."

Why would he ask him that? Nobody knew Chase Sterling wasn't his real name. Well, his mother knew, of course. And Kerstin knew. "Charles Redding, but I don't go by that. Nobody even knows my name was changed when I got my assignment."

"Named after your father. He used to call you Charlie. It was your mother who first called you Chase, and the nickname stuck."

"How do you know that? Who are you?"

He didn't answer.

Chase rubbed his eyes. He still couldn't see a thing. His hands were wet, but it didn't feel like water. He touched his fingers to his nose. Blood.

"Excuse me, I think I'm bleeding. Could I get some help?"

"You'll be all right. Reach beside you—there's a bowl of water and a towel."

He felt in the darkness until his hand was submerged in cool water. He put his other hand in and rubbed away the bloody mess. He dried his hands on the towel and used it to wipe his face. There was no pain, but something seemed very wrong.

"What happened to me? There was some sort of flash. Was I shot? I was on stage when a light came at me. Am I dead?"

"Do you feel dead?"

"I'd really like to know who I'm talking to. I don't recognize your voice. Are you a director?"

"Something like that."

"You're with the WR." He was some government bigwig. This was it—Chase's career was over. And judging by the blindness and blood on his hands, he wasn't ready for any new assignment. "Can I talk to my assistant? Her name is Melody Reese."

"I know her."

"Can you get her for me?"

"We have some things to go over."

"Like what? New job? New life? I really don't want things to change."

"Let's review your life, Charles Redding. Let's take a look at where you came from."

He was mocking Chase—it sounded like a line from the show. Then a screen lit up. "Hey, I can see now. My vision is coming back."

"Good. Watch this."

Chase looked at the big screen, only it wasn't a GV. It was more like an old movie screen. Landscape, lush and green, filled his vision. It looked like the place where he'd grown up. A seagull whizzed past. The sound of rushing water told him he was near the river. And then, he was on the screen. Only there wasn't a screen anymore. Chase looked at his hands. They were small and sandy. He looked at his feet, at the blue sneakers he wore when he was ten.

"Hey, get me out of here," Chase whined.

No one answered.

He thought he might cry, but he didn't. He was a grown man. An influential man. This was some kind of new game. A new prize for contestants. And SynVue was trying it out on him. Well, OK, he could play along. As if he had any choice. He turned a circle. He knew the way home.

He came up past Braden River High School. Stupid teenagers. They were always messing with him. His house was just a couple of blocks away. He started to run.

"Hey, Chase." A little girl waved from across the road.

Chase waved back to her. "Hey, Kathleen." He ran a little faster.

He came to his house and went up the walkway to the front door. Chase could hear his mother singing. What was that? Something about the light of the moon. She had a lovely voice. Chase had forgotten she used to sing. He opened the door. "Mom?"

"In here, Chase. I'm baking your birthday cake."

"It's my birthday?"

She walked into the front room with a dish towel in her hands. "You silly boy." She smiled, and he ran to her and threw his arms around her.

"What's this? Did you miss me that much? You've only been gone for a couple of hours." She patted his back and kissed the top of his head. She smelled like chocolate and soap. That's when the dream, or the game—whatever was happening on the screen—became real.

He looked up. "I think it's been more than a couple of hours."

"Don't be so silly. If you were gone more than two hours, I'd have the whole Braden River City police force looking for you. All six of them. And if they couldn't find you I'd call the FBI."

"What time will Dad be home?"

"In time for dinner. You sure you don't want to invite a couple of friends over tonight? I hate it that we're not having a party like last year."

"Eleven is nothing special. Ten was a big deal. And twelve is a big deal, you know, 'cause then you're almost a teenager. I'll have a party next year."

"OK, then. Whatever you say." She turned back to the kitchen. "I'm making homemade pizza, just the way you like it."

"That sounds great, Mom." Chase sat on the floor and turned on the TV. The big old tube popped when it lit up, and he turned to the station that showed old reruns from when his parents were kids. Chase's dad was a real TV buff—he knew all about hit shows from the '70s. He knew when they aired, who starred in them. He even knew a lot of the episode titles. That afternoon Chase watched one of his father's favorites. Chase couldn't wait until supper so he could tell him about it.

Mom started singing again. Chase closed my eyes for a minute and wished he would never grow up. He wanted to stay eleven forever.

Dinner with his mom and dad made it the best birthday ever. By the time they got around to blowing out the candles and cutting the cake, Chase was telling his dad about that day's episode of *The Six Million Dollar Man*.

"Oh, I love that one." Dad shoveled in a forkful of the chocolate cake. "Guy puts a bomb in the Liberty Bell. It was when the country was getting ready for the bicentennial. Lots of celebrating."

"It all seems kind of hokey, you know? Compared to what's on TV now," Chase said.

"Sure it does. We've come a long way," Dad said.

And then Mom started singing something about coming a long way.

Chase raised his eyebrows.

"Old jingle from a commercial." She took a bite of cake.

Chase nodded.

Dad hummed the tune for a moment. "Steve Austin was something. So fast and he could see better than anybody alive. I used to think it would happen, you know, in the real world. But now I doubt it."

"Why?" Chase asked.

"Well, for one thing, it's too much money. Besides, who would allow themselves to have all that stuff put in their body?"

"But, Dad, Steve Austin didn't know it was happening until it was all over."

"Yeah," Mom said. "Same with Jaime Sommers on *The Bionic Woman*. Then they wiped out her memory or something."

"Well, it was more complicated than that," Dad said. "But I guess if some secret branch of the government wanted to turn people into cyborgs—"

"Yeah, and look how far we've come since *The Six Million Dollar Man*. Look what happened in *The Terminator*," Chase said.

"I love that movie. Best cyborg story ever. Still, it's just fiction," Dad said. "Nothing like that is ever going to happen."

"Not to my sweet boy," Mom said. "You're getting so big." She reached over and tousled his hair. "Happy birthday."

Chase opened his presents—a collector's edition of the Star Wars movies and a new pair of high tops. Then he watched TV while Dad helped Mom clear the dishes and clean up the kitchen. He could hear them talking, so he turned down the sound a little.

"He spends too much time watching TV, Kim. He needs to get out more."

"He gets out plenty. He was outside playing for two or three hours today—came inside all covered with sand," Mom said.

"Does he have any friends?"

"Sure he does. He doesn't see a lot of his friends during the summer. Some of them live on the other side of the county. But he plays with that Dawson kid. And he's always been buddy-buddy with Kenny Larson down the road. And have you noticed the way the girls coo over him? He's really getting to be very handsome."

"Now, don't push him into that, Kim."

"I'm not pushing, I'm just saying his social life is nothing for you to worry about, Chuck."

"You ought to take him down to the church on Main. They're having some kind of summer thing for kids."

"You know, you were the one who got him watching all those old shows. Let him enjoy his summer. They'd probably try to save his soul, or whatever they do, down at that church. You really want him to give up TV for God, Chuck?"

Dad came out of the kitchen and turned off the TV. "Come outside with me," he said.

Chase got up and followed him, and they looked at the stars. "What do you want to do with your life, son?"

"I don't know, Dad. What do you want me to do?"

"I want you to be someone who makes a difference in the world."

"How do I do that?"

He didn't tell Chase. He didn't say much else at all. Chase got the feeling he had something else to say, but he never said it. After a while, they went inside.

Chase turned off the TV in his room at eleven thirty. A yellow beam from the street light out front sneaked in through the split in the curtain and fell across his bedspread. He grabbed the edge of the curtain and pulled it closed. Then he slept the good summer sleep of an eleven-year-old boy. Until the voice woke him.

12

"Did you like it there?"

Chase opened his eyes but couldn't see anything. He was blind again. "Yes. It was a good game. I liked being a kid again. After I was there awhile, I forgot it was a game. I thought it was real. How did you do that?"

"Go back to sleep. You need your rest."

"Are you going to get somebody to come and check my vision? I think I was injured on the set last night."

"Do you want Dr. Fiender to take a look at you?"

Chase sat up. "Am I at SynVue Estate?"

The voice didn't answer.

"Don't let them do anything without my permission."

"The doctor could restore your vision. If fact, he could make your vision much, much better than it was before."

"Don't do this."

"Relax, Charles. Go back to sleep."

Chase laid his head on the pillow and blinked his useless eyes. Fear kept him awake for a while, but sleep finally took him. The next time he awoke, he could see. No super vision, just 20/20. He was in his room at the old house again. Only it was different. The walls were no longer blue, but beige. The furniture was the same, but the movie posters were gone. So was his

TV. An early model GV hung on the wall. Chase jumped out of the bed and looked in the mirror over the chest of drawers. He remembered the stupid haircut. He was twenty-one.

"Mom?" he yelled.

"In the kitchen, Chase. What's the matter?"

"Let the game continue."

"What?"

"Nothing, Mom. I'll be in the shower."

"Hurry up, dear. If we're going to do this on the way to the airport, we need to get going."

OK, he could figure this out. When did she say that? Where were they going?

"I can't believe it's been a year since your father died."

Chase closed his eyes. His father was gone. They were going to the beach to scatter his ashes. Mom had kept the urn in their bedroom for a year. Then she said she couldn't keep him trapped in there—she had to set him free.

Chase wondered if it were really herself she wanted to set free.

He had a new job waiting in Nashville. That's why they were going to the airport. The job was with a production company. He had full realization of all this, and he knew he was a thirty-four-year-old playing some kind of regression game. Maybe the game didn't work as well when you were re-living an adult experience. He took his shower, threw on the only clothes he hadn't packed, and walked to the kitchen to eat breakfast with the figment of his mother.

That's when the game became real life for him.

"Mom." Chase bent to kiss her cheek. "You look so pretty."

"Well, thank you, Chase. I wanted to look nice for this little ceremony. Your dad always liked this dress."

"Are you sure you're OK with me leaving today?"

"Absolutely. You spent a year with your widowed mother. That's enough. But are you sure about this job? You're really ready to leave grad school and go to work?"

"Mom, I told you, the virtual classes are all I need. I'll be done quicker than if I was still on campus. And yes, I'm sure about the job. It's what I want."

"Your dad was always worried about your spending too much time alone. You can't meet a girl in a virtual classroom."

"You'd be surprised what you can do in a virtual classroom." Chase smiled, and his mother raised her eyebrows. She had nothing else to say about *that*.

Chase drove Mom's new electric car that morning. They took the long way through town. He wanted one more look. He'd miss this place.

They went down Main. A sign stood in front of what used to be a church. Chase read it aloud. "Now they won't even miss us when we're gone."

"Do you remember your eleventh birthday?" Mom asked.

"Like it was yesterday."

"Your dad thought you spent too much time watching GV. Well, I mean, TV. He wanted you to go to some kind of summer program at that church."

"I wonder what the sign means."

"Maybe it means what it says. Nobody misses them."

"Yeah. I guess so." Chase turned onto the highway. "That was the night, on my eleventh birthday, that Dad told me he wanted me to make a difference in the world. I didn't know what he meant then, but I think I do now. That's why I took this job. Making a difference is all about communication. People need to know what's going on in the world. They need information, education. Working for this company, with the media, will allow me to give people what they need."

"Your dad would be so proud, Chase. I think you really will make a difference."

Chase drove over Clearwater Pass to Sand Key. His dad always loved it there. He stood on the shore and opened the urn. The wind was with them—with Dad—and the ashes floated like a gull over the gentle waves and out to sea.

Chase missed him. He was a good man.

They went on to the airport, and Chase handed Mom the keys to her car. "Don't forget to have it serviced in three months. I already made the appointment for you. It's programmed into your computer. You'll get a reminder prompt."

"Then why are you telling me not to forget? If the computer remembers, I don't have to."

"OK, Mom." He smiled.

"Call me when you get there," she said. She grabbed him around the neck and held him tight. Chase put his arms around her.

"Are you sure you'll be all right?" he asked.

"Of course. Now go on." She pulled away and smiled. "I love you, Chase."

"Love you, too, Mom. I'll call you."

Chase would miss her, but he was glad to be getting on with his life. For the first time, boarding that plane, he felt like a man. Like he was in control.

Once he got settled on the hydro jet, he buckled

himself in, turned on his reader, and ignored the instructions given by the robotic flight attendant whose digital nametag read *Haley*. The little mechanical "girl" dropped from an overhead compartment, then retreated when she was done.

"Look at that, they're naming the robots," the guy next to him said. "I like to see a real person when I get on a jet. You know? But they're a rare find. The cheaper airlines are still using them. And the private flights. But us middle-classers get the robots."

"You don't like robots?"

"Oh, sure, I like them just fine. They make great lamps."

The guy was probably sixty. Old farts like him kept things real. Real backward.

"Can't stop progress."

"I can try," he said. "Unless that idiot gets elected."

"You don't like Cosimo?"

"He'll throw out the Constitution for good."

"The Constitution's been on its way out for a while now."

The man turned in his seat to look Chase in the eye. "It'll be the end of us if Cosimo gets elected. We'll be living in a new country."

"You sound like my father."

"Then you've got a smart man for a father." He smiled, and there was a twinkle in his eye.

"I just scattered his ashes over the gulf at Sand Key."

"Oh, I'm sorry, son."

"He's been dead a year now. My mom wanted to set him free."

"Well, you're a good son to be there with her."

They didn't talk politics after that. After a while, Chase acted sleepy, and the man quit talking altogether. Chase really did start to doze.

But then the nosedive began.

His head jerked forward, and his shoulders followed. He dug his nails into the padded armrests. A body rolled down the aisle. He didn't know if it was a man or a woman. The political commentator at Chase's side wasn't wearing his seatbelt, and he fell away into the spiraling tunnel, screaming as he went spinning.

He forced his head back against the seat and gritted his teeth. Then he opened his mouth and screamed. He couldn't help himself. The sound from his throat met the discord of a terrified choir. After what seemed an eternity, though it was only half a minute, the front of the tunnel and the end of it came level. The bodies stopped rolling. His body stopped its strain to stay in the seat. And then the crying started. Chase cried along with them.

He vowed to never fly again.

After a look-over by med-techs in the airport triage center, Chase signed documents and stared at the free meal he'd been offered. He picked up his rental and escaped that compound of winged vessels bound for hell. He knew he would fly again—he'd have to. But it'd be a long, long time.

He took the Briley Parkway to the complex that housed the company that would be writing his paycheck.

"Good to have you here at last." His new boss met him in the reception area. "Pleasant flight?" He was middle-aged and pudgy.

"Not at all."

"Well, no matter. You're here now and we have a

lot to do."

He familiarized himself with the company's upcoming projects for about three hours until the boss came back. He'd heard about the flight. Chase was on the phone with Mom, trying to convince her he was fine, when the boss told him to take the rest of the day off. "I've got to go," Chase told his mother.

The boss chided Chase for not telling him he'd almost died that morning. Then he sent Chase home.

Home was a company apartment he'd been given to use during his probationary period. Chase didn't look at it—the colors or the furniture or the view. He found the bed and plunged headfirst into it.

ॐ∻

The voice woke Chase, who didn't understand what he asked at first. The voice obliged in repeating himself.

"Did you pray when you faced death?"

The room was black. "I don't know. I don't remember what was going on in my mind." Chase hoisted himself up on his elbows. "Look, I don't like this game. Just get me a doctor. And my assistant—I want to talk to Mel."

"What about Kerstin? Don't you want to talk to her?"

"Sure. Get her in here." Chase felt the nightstand for a VPad, or a lamp, or a glass of water. Nothing but a metal bowl. "Why can't I see anything?" His voice grew loud. "I want a doctor."

"In good time, Charles Redding. We're not finished."

"Well, it's a sick game. I won't allow it on my

show."

"This is *my* show."

"Get me out of here."

"Soon, Charles. Look up. Kerstin is waiting."

The screen came to life. The studio in Chicago filled his vision. Only it wasn't the way it looked the day before, or whenever he'd last seen it. Before him was the modest lobby of an organization not yet born. *Change Your Life* was only a dream at this point.

Kerstin came from the hallway at the far end of the lobby. Her silky ponytail bounced and swayed as she walked his way. She was young, beautiful, and almost sweet with her innocent smile.

Chase hadn't seen that hopeful expression on her face in years. He felt pity for her. And love, he thought. She held out her hand as she approached. He wanted to embrace her. This game just got much better. When she took his hand, the game became reality once again. This was his life.

"Kerstin Bennett," she said. "So glad to meet you, Mr. Sterling."

"That's sounds strange—'Mr. Sterling.'"

"No one else knows about the name change. Well, no one here at the studio, I mean. It suits you." She looked him over and then cupped her hand under his elbow and led him toward the hallway. "Chase Sterling. I like it."

She was right. It did suit him.

13

Somewhere in that hallway, a couple of years went by. The next thing he knew, he and Kerstin were standing in the newly built auditorium.

"You are going to do great things, Chase," Kerstin said.

Workers surrounded them. They were installing seats and unrolling carpets. Dust covered Chase's designer suit. Kerstin's VPad chirped interminably, but she ignored it. She wrapped both hands around his arm and stood on her toes to kiss him.

"*We* are going to do great things." Chase looked over the vast theater. "This is our show. I can't do it without you."

"True," she said, and she laughed.

In Chase's time with the studio, SynVue had become the only government-funded communications company in the world. They supplied all news, all information, and all entertainment. A few renegade broadcast signals remained, but involvement in that activity could lead to years in prison. This new show, *Change Your Life*, was not just about entertainment. It would literally change lives. The WR had chosen Chase as the face of the show, and he was ready to start handing out fortunes and health and hope. What a marvelous opportunity. He never dreamed this would happen to him.

"Chase, darling, pay attention."

"I'm sorry, what did you say?"

"Really, this is no time for daydreaming. We've got two days to get this auditorium ready. Now listen, when you hear my voice, you'll look up at the booth hidden there among the balconies." She lifted her pale hand and pointed to the area. "You'll look up as though an angel has called your name. Do you understand?"

"Yes, love. You are my angel."

"You will relay to the audience that I am the one who gives the prizes. Giving from a higher place, you see, will instill dedication in the viewers."

"Yes, dedication. We want these poor saps dedicated."

"Watch your language. We don't want anyone thinking we have anything but sincere affection and concern at the heart of this program."

"Of course, I understand."

She leaned close and whispered, "Poor saps they are, of course. But a few of them will get obscenely rich. As will you and I."

"We deserve it," he told her. "We deserve all of this."

She kissed him again and left him in the dust of the nearly finished complex. She walked up the golden staircase. He had an amazing assignment to host a program that would change the world. Soon he would have everything he ever wanted. And he had her. Life was perfect. If this was a dream, he never wanted to wake up.

14

"Wake up, Chase. It's time to wake up." The garbled sound surely came from the bottom of a water bucket. Chase strained to open his eyes, but he couldn't connect his thoughts with his actions. Another voice said something. The sounds were getting louder and clearer.

"He's conscious. Look at his readings. All systems are working at top performance. It's just that his brain is not used to all the new signals. Give him a few minutes. He'll come around."

Chase wondered what it meant—systems and signals. Neither of the voices sounded like the one he'd heard during the regression game. The new director must have taken the day off. And somebody finally got him a doctor. That was it—the voice was Dr. Fiender. And the other voice, the muddled one, was Kerstin.

"Chase, you're recovering from an injury and extensive surgery. Wake up." The voice from the bucket rose clear this time. Kerstin's hand cupped his face. He could smell her musky cologne.

He still couldn't open his eyes, but his lips spread and he said two words. "Great game."

"He spoke!" She rubbed her hand across his face and down his arm. "But what's he talking about? Chase?"

"No telling what sort of dreams he's been having these past few weeks. Or what visions of death he may have experienced." The doctor spoke quietly. "He may just be delirious."

"Death visions? We can't have him spouting nonsense, Robert. This is too important. He needs to be perfectly sane, perfectly augmented. He needs to be perfect."

Chase listened, but it may no sense. The voices drifted away, and he opened his eyes for only a moment.

Relief flooded his emotions as he realized he could see. Kerstin and Dr. Fiender huddled near the doorway. He looked around the room. He was definitely at SynVue Estate.

He needs to be perfect. They'd done something to him. Something wonderful.

Something horrible. He closed his eyes.

"He is as perfect as any human could be," the doctor said. "We made sure of that."

"Human. He is still human," Kerstin said. "And humans are unpredictable. Can't you program him or something?"

"Kerstin, my dear, relax. You will not be disappointed."

The door to the room slid open on command, and the doctor and Kerstin left him. Chase opened his eyes when he heard the door shut. "I can see. Thank God."

He tried to move, but his muscles didn't respond. Monitors and screens surrounded him, relaying codes he didn't understand. The big screen, the memory device he assumed he'd been hooked to, was not in sight. The game was over. The bugs would have to be worked out of it. Terrifying memories should be excluded. Only happy ones, like the birthday and the early days with Kerstin, would be allowed if contestants were going to play this game.

"I want to call my mother," he said. Soon the door slid open and nurses streamed in, followed by Kerstin and Dr. Fiender.

"See, I told you he was awake." The doctor hovered and then smacked his fingers against Chase's cheek. "You are playing games with us. The monitors indicate that you spoke again after we left the room. Why didn't you open your eyes and talk to us?"

"He has a habit of talking to himself," Kerstin said. "He doesn't care if anyone's listening. But soon, somebody will always be listening." She laughed.

Chase turned his eyes to her. Her smile seemed more pride than concern, more accomplishment than affection. He blinked, and he almost couldn't pull his lids open again. "Back when *Change Your Life* first started," he said. "I think you loved me."

"What about now? I saved you, Chase. Isn't that love?"

The doctor turned his attention to Kerstin. "Well, if it's saving we're talking about, I believe I'm the one who restored what was left of this man."

"Of course, Robert, you did all the work—you and a dozen other doctors. I just paid for it."

"*You* paid for it?" Dr. Fiender's bushy eyebrows rose above his befuddled expression, and Chase might have laughed if he hadn't been physically paralyzed and emotionally jolted beyond anything he'd ever known. He wanted to scream, but all that came out was a quiet request. "I want Mel."

Kerstin came to him and sat on the edge of the bed. "She's gone, Chase. But I'm right here. You don't need anyone else."

"What did you do to her?"

"I didn't do anything to her. The production team shut down."

"Was I shot? Who else was injured? What about Larin? He was on the stage beside me. Wasn't he?"

"Yes, that's right. He saw the M-snipe, and he tried to push you out of the way. But the rocket swerved, and I'm afraid you got the worst of it. Larin suffered some burns but the surgeons made him good as new." She smirked. "Well, better than new."

"M-snipe. A robot shot me? How did that happen? How did it get in? Who would do that?"

"We all have a lot of questions, Chase," she said. "Truth is we don't know the answers. We may never know."

"That's ridiculous. We know everything."

"The good thing is we put you back together," she said.

"We?" The doctor mumbled something as he moved toward the door. Some of the nurses followed him out, but two stayed, checking the monitors and poking Chase with all sorts of implements.

"Why can't I move?" Chase asked.

Kerstin looked to one of the nurses.

"Swelling around the spinal column," one of them said.

"That's it? It'll get better then, right?" Chase attempted to lift his head from the pillow.

"Once the swelling goes down," the nurse said, "the processors should work fine."

"Processors," Chase said. "There are twelve processors in my new spinal column, three in each leg, four in each arm. There are seven more in my upper body, for a total of thirty-three. I can give you the exact location of each of them. There is a small infection forming around the one beneath my left lung, which is made of a manufactured membrane similar to my own cell structure." Chase gasped and squeezed his eyes shut. "How do I know that? What have you done to me?" His eyes flew open, and he found Kerstin practically dancing with the nurses.

"It's a miracle!" Kerstin shouted.

"Answer me! What have you done?"

15

Chase stared at the monitor that thumped the coded rhythm of his replicated heart. The organ, like most of the others in his body, was made by Dr. Fiender, or someone on his team. The perfectly designed fleshy chambers of this pump, untouched by the sins of living, would never cease their thrusting of blood through flawless arteries.

He didn't need the monitor to tell him his heart rate. He knew it moment by moment. Even in his anger, the rate didn't alter. His blood pressure remained constant as well. He knew it without checking the machines surrounding him. He still wasn't clear on how he knew these things. Kerstin said it was wired into his brain. He could monitor his vital signs and maintain every new augmented system. The nurse had given him something for the infection under his lung. The old parts, not the new, were giving him a few problems. Swollen muscles kept his hard-wired brain from getting signals to his arms and legs. Some of his digestive system remained intact, and his stomach was not happy about all the new materials surrounding it. Kerstin said they may still have to replace the stomach and the small intestine. Then he'd never feel hungry again. He'd just eat when, and what, his brain told him to.

"Let my brain tell me what to eat? What fun would that be?"

"Excuse me, Mr. Sterling? What did you say?" A med-tech stood near the door, moving her finger across a VPad.

"Nothing. Get me my assistant, Melody Reese."

"I'm afraid your team was dismissed when the show got replaced. I'm really going to miss *Change Your Life*. Everyone will." The nurse, a full figured young woman with dark hair, walked to the bedside. "But I think the new show will be great."

"New show?"

"*Reach Your Destiny*. It's still in the planning stages. The studio is remodeling the auditorium, giving it a scientific feel. They won't actually do the medical procedures on the set, but the audience will think they do. That's what I hear."

"Who's the host?"

"Well…"

"Larin Andrews?"

"I'm not sure you're supposed to know that, Mr. Sterling. Don't tell anybody I told you. OK?"

"You didn't tell me, I guessed."

"He's a good man, Mr. Sterling, and he didn't want to take your job. They made him a whole new show. And you're going to get a great new assignment, I'm sure."

"What does the press say happened to me? Does everyone think I'm dead?"

"No, Mr. Sterling. Well, at first everyone assumed you were dead. Your injuries were beyond repair by traditional medicine. But the SynVue press release explained that you were rebuilt using methods perfected at the Helgen Institute. And now the world is waiting."

"Waiting for what?" Chase pushed his elbows into

the bed and lifted his head an inch off the pillow.

The nurse smiled. "Mr. Sterling, you just pushed yourself up a little." She pressed her VPad. Only seconds passed before a slew of uniforms filled the room.

"He's moving," the dark-haired nurse told the first of the arrivals. "Mr. Sterling, can you squeeze my hand?" She wrapped her soft hand around his.

He concentrated and then drew his fingers together until the woman smiled again. "What's your name?"

"Anna," she said.

"Anna, you have a cancer growing in you. I can feel it."

She jerked her hand away and stumbled backward, knocking a tray of needles and probes from the hands of the young doctor standing behind her.

"Mr. Sterling, you've been given some extraordinary abilities," the doctor said as he came close. "But you're going to have to learn to use them. You can't just go blurting it out to people that they have cancer. The employees here at SynVue Estate undergo regular scans. I'm sure we'd know if Anna was sick. These days, only the destitute get cancer. And maybe a few people who won't give up their inner-pods. Nothing like communicating device free, but it did do a number on the brain. Anyway, cancer is practically a thing of the past."

"Don't you think I know that?" Chase asked. "We haven't had a contestant with cancer since we started *Change Your Life*. Organ dysfunction, sure, but not cancer. I'm telling you, she's got it."

"Let's concentrate on you now," the doctor said. "Lift your arm."

Chase lifted his right arm above his chest and wiggled his fingers. Then he grabbed the doctor's arm and held on tight. "What's your name, doctor?"

The young man jerked free. "Dr. Gray. Harry Gray."

"Harry," Chase said. "You're as healthy as a horse."

Anna ran from the room in tears, and Chase sat up and poked Dr. Gray in the chest. "Go get somebody to take care of her. She needs some tests done."

"Oh, are you going to tell me what kind of tests? Doctor? I'm telling you, nobody gets cancer anymore." He flipped his finger across a VPad and yelled into it. "Get Dr. Fiender in here right now. I don't want to deal with his Frankenstein."

The doctor left the room, and the nurses trailed behind him. All except one—a young man.

"Did he just call me Frankenstein?"

"I think so," the nurse said. He shuffled to the bedside and held out his hand.

"I've always wanted to meet you, sir."

"Do you want me to take your hand and tell you what's wrong with you? Because if you do, get out of here. I'm nobody's Frankenstein."

The young man dropped his hand. "No, I just wanted to…I'm a fan. That's all. And I'm glad you're alive."

"Yeah, me, too. I think. But I'm afraid life as I knew it is over."

"It'll get better. Imagine all the people you can help now. Even more than before."

"But I have no show. *Change Your Life* was my identity. Now I don't know who I am."

"Who were you before the show?"

"What?"

"Well, you had a life, didn't you? You were Chase Sterling before you ever hosted *Change Your Life*."

"What's your name?"

"Jimmy Perris."

"Tell me, Jimmy, what do you know about the game, or program, or whatever it was they had going in here while I was unconscious? The regression thing."

"I don't know, Mr. Sterling. Nothing like that happened. They kept you in a coma. They didn't have any kind of mind game going on."

"Can you do something for me, Jimmy?"

"Sure, anything."

The door slid open, and Dr. Fiender rushed in with his hands on his head. "Chase, you've upset this whole place." Then he smiled. "But I don't care. You're a marvel."

The nurse slipped out of the room, but he gave Chase a nod before he left.

Dr. Fiender bounced onto the edge of the bed like he was an old friend coming for a visit. "Let me see you move your arms."

Chase lifted his brow and huffed. Then he waved both arms.

"Now," the doctor said, "stand."

"Don't think I can do that. Maybe tomorrow. If you get me any assistant."

"You no longer have an assistant, Chase. You have a team of medical experts, neuro-techs, personal hygiene maintainers, dieticians, and therapists, both physical and mental. And you have Kerstin. And you have me. When you are ready for your new assignment, we'll talk about an assistant. But it won't be your old one—that one has likely been reassigned already."

Chase sat straight in the bed with little effort. "Find her. Bring her here. And maybe I'll cooperate with you."

The doctor's brows drew together until they resembled a furry caterpillar resting above his nose. "Why is the girl so important? What was the nature of your relationship?"

"Friendship. I trust her."

"Don't you trust *me*, Chase? And Kerstin? We only want the best for you."

"Tell me what you've done to me."

Dr. Fiender climbed off the bed, grabbed the back of a metal chair, and pulled it to the bedside. He sat and crossed his arms. "Do you want to know about your injuries?"

"That would be a good place to start."

"The blast tore clean through your mid-section, ripping apart your heart and lungs, shattering your ribs, sternum, and spine. Your kidneys, liver, pancreas, and esophagus were destroyed."

"I had a hole all the way through me?"

"Yes, Chase."

"How could anybody survive that?"

"No one could."

Chase leaned back on the pillow. "What happened next?"

"You were rushed here to the estate. Your brain, and the other organs that remained intact, were kept alive while we replaced the parts that were destroyed."

"Replaced with parts you made."

"Yes, of course. No need remains for anyone to require an organic replacement."

"Was my brain injured?"

"No," the doctor said.

"But it was enhanced."

"In a manner of speaking."

"I just told a nurse she has cancer! In a manner of speaking, I couldn't do that before you brought me back from the dead."

"Calm down."

"I will not calm down," Chase yelled as he slammed his fist into the bedrail. "I've got some god gadget in my brain."

"Chase, are you familiar with the Wilberton?"

"Yes, of course, we use it here at the estate."

"It can tell what's wrong with a patient even before the doctors can."

"So you made a miniature Wilberton and stuck it in my head?"

"Something like that."

"And now I can tell what's wrong with people just by touching them."

"I have to say I didn't think it would be so efficient, or that you'd be able to utilize it without training. It was meant to be, Chase. We picked the right person for our beginning. You are the firstborn of the evolutionary leap."

"I was dead." Chase dropped his head onto the pillow.

"You were reborn."

16

Chase got little else from Fiender, except to learn that his new organs were real flesh, grown in the lab at the Helgen Institute. He was also stocked head to toe with machinery—silicon crystal and titanium covered with lab-grown tissue. It wasn't like the old movies where someone ripped off the cyborg's face and found a hideous robot. But the metal was there, wrapped in a new man's skin. The doctor promised more information would come as Chase healed. Now he found himself alone with Kerstin, and he had questions for her, too.

"Tell me about Larin," Chase said.

Kerstin circled the room, looking at the monitors. She didn't bother to answer.

"Why do I need these machines? I can tell you anything you want to know about my physical condition."

"True," she said. "But we don't know that you *will* tell us everything."

"An issue of trust?"

"After your outburst with Robert, I think we have good reason."

"Kerstin, how would you feel if somebody tried to turn you into some kind of wired-up super hero?"

"I look forward to the day."

Chase shook his head and looked out the window at the gray sky. "Tell me about the new show." He turned to face her.

Kerstin's eyes locked on his, and her lips curled downward. "I think it would be good for you to see Larin."

"No."

"Well you're going to. We have a prime time special scheduled in two weeks."

"You've got to be kidding. Larin is going to interview me?"

"No, silly, you're going to interview *him*. Why would you think otherwise?"

"Because he's the host of a brand new show, that's why. And I'm the one who just got turned into a robot."

Kerstin came to the bedside and rubbed her delicate hand across Chase's forehead and then kissed him. "You are more important than Larin will ever be." She took hold of his hand. "How did you find out about the new show? Don't tell me you can read minds."

"Not that I know of."

"Then someone told you. I've been careful to protect you from anything that might cause stress."

Chase didn't offer her anything.

"People need to know that you're in full support of Larin and his new show," she said. "And that there are no hard feelings."

"I am not in full support. I want my show back."

"*Our* show served us well. But those days are gone. Larin will move ahead with *Reach Your Destiny*. And you will have an amazing destiny of your own, leading the way into the future."

"Am I going to be a reporter?"

"No." She slipped her hand from his and walked

to the window.

"An anchor on the evening news?"

"No."

"The host of a new talk show? Are we reviving the old tabloid format?"

"No, Chase." She folded her arms across her shimmering black suit.

"Then why am I interviewing a new game show host?"

"I told you, people need to know—"

"That I support him. No hard feelings."

"Yes."

Chase pushed away the blanket, dropped his feet to the floor, and stood. "I'd like to go home now."

She looked like a little girl with a new doll. "You can stand. Is this the first time you've done it?"

"I said I'd like to go home."

"Chase, darling, for now this is your home."

He walked past her to the door and stood there, waiting to step into the hall after the door slid open. The door didn't move. He waved his hand in front of the green panel. Nothing. He turned around. "Why is it that this door opens for everyone who comes and goes from this room, but when I walk up to it, nothing happens?"

Kerstin pulled at the security tag hung around her neck. "Everyone here is coded for extra security—you know that. You're wearing a hospital gown, Chase, and little else."

He walked to the window. "Why are there no mirrors? Am I hideous? Burned?"

"No. There's a mirror in the bathroom—go in there and take a look." She came close behind him and put her hands on his shoulders. "There were some burns. The surgeons didn't even have to use any skin product—not on your face anyway. You healed well. Your eyes may look a little different."

"Why? And what do you mean by skin product?"

"Implants for night vision made your eyes a little darker. As for the skin, most of the mid-section of your body is covered by a manufactured product. It's bioorganic, matched perfectly to your own skin. But it doesn't change. It doesn't regenerate like real skin."

"It won't age."

"That's right," she said. "A crazy old woman made it."

Chase rubbed his hand across the hospital gown, over his chest. The feeling there was as normal as it had always been. "An old woman?"

"She's a genius, they say. One of Robert's scientists."

"Kerstin, why on earth do I need night vision? Why would they give me that?"

"Well, why not?"

"Why haven't you asked me to touch you?" He moved to put his arms around her waist.

She smiled. "Chase, really, this is not the place."

"You know what I mean." He grabbed both her arms. She gasped and her eyes went wide.

"Don't you want to know what's wrong with you?"

She fought loose and stepped back. "There is nothing wrong with me."

She was right, but he couldn't resist. "Your blood pressure is dangerously high. And your heart rate is off the chart."

"That's because you startled me."

"Oh, I don't think so, Kerstin. You better go get

your buddy, Robert, to check you over."

She practically hissed before she turned to the door.

"And I think you should cut down on the rodent."

She spun around. "What are talking about?"

"You do eat rat, don't you, my kitten? I'm sure you've served it to me a time or two."

She scowled as he laughed. The door that kept him prisoner gave way for her.

Chase walked to the bathroom and touched a panel. The small room came to light. The mirror was before him. He looked the same, and it was good to see his own face looking back at him. His eyes were indeed a bit darker. He dropped the hospital gown to the floor and looked at his chest. Only a slight mark encircled his midsection. He turned so that he could see the reflection of his back. The same kind of line circled from shoulder to shoulder and down to his waist.

"Hey, wait a minute." He touched the panel and lights went out. He couldn't see anything. "Good, they failed. Night vision—who needs it."

But then he knew—he just knew—the night vision was under his control. And he thought it into operation. Everything in the dark room came into view within an amber haze.

"Crap," he said. "This is pretty cool."

17

That night Chase looked around the amber room long after he should have been sleeping. Sometime after midnight, the door slid open and the young med-tech who'd confessed his admiration stepped in. "Jimmy," Chase said. "I'm glad you came back."

"How'd you know it was me?" The man said. His eyes did not focus on Chase but shifted about the room. "It's dark as night in here."

Chase touched a small lamp on the nightstand and a dim light filled the space between the two men. "Did you use the night vision thing? I didn't know they told you about it. They say everybody's gonna have it in a year or two."

"Like cats on the prowl, huh?"

"I guess."

"What other kind of gadgets have I got in me?"

"Better let the doctors fill you in. I don't know what works or what's still in the testing stages. Does Fiender know you can see in the dark?"

"No, and don't tell him," Chase said. "At least warn me if I'm going to start shooting lasers out of my fingertips. Can I run a one-minute mile? Or leap across the Chicago River?"

"Nothing like that. But I think you should be able to turn on a hearing modifier—some kind of cochlear implant. And you're probably a lot stronger than you used to be." Jimmy sat in the chair by the window.

"But the best part is the information they put in you. You're a walking computer."

"That's ridiculous. Why would they do that?"

"Because they can. They can program a human brain the same way you program a computer. The thought is that in the future nobody will have to go through the trouble and expense of learning. You'll just know what the government needs you to know."

"And what does the government need me to know?"

"Don't know. Could be just about anything."

"Give it a try. Ask me a question."

"OK," Jimmy said. "What is the distance between Mars and Mercury?"

Chase closed his eyes and then shrugged and looked at Jimmy. "I have no idea."

"Well, maybe you're not all hooked up yet."

"Yeah, maybe." Chase pushed himself up and swung his legs over the side of the bed. "Jimmy, did you come in here tonight to see what I wanted you to do?"

"Yes, sir."

"I appreciate that. I don't want to get you into trouble."

"Do you want me to do something illegal?"

"No, I just want you to see if you can find out where my assistant went when she got reassigned."

"Might be hard for me to find out. Too bad you're not all programmed yet. You'd probably know where she went without having to ask."

Chase smirked. "Surely they aren't going to fill my head with every detail of what goes on in the WR."

"I guess not. You'd be a security risk. I shouldn't have said anything. I really don't know what they plan to do with you."

"I'm glad you told me."

"What do you know about your assistant? I mean, besides her name and stuff. Do you know her family, her friends outside of work?"

"Not really. I know she did some work with a church house."

"Well, now, you're asking me to do something illegal. I'm not gonna go snooping around that kind. I'm mean, they're nice people, I guess. A little backward. And they *are* breaking the law, you know."

"I know. But the WR leaves them alone for the most part."

"You know anybody else in that movement?" Jimmy asked.

"Not to my knowledge. You?"

"No, I'm not into it."

"I mean do you know anybody?"

"Oh. Well, I think there are a couple of nurses here who might be. So they might know your assistant."

Chase rubbed his eyes. "I want to meet them."

"Chances are they won't tell you anything. They spook easy—those church people."

"I'll deal with that. You find a way to get them in here."

"Mr. Sterling, I don't have any pull in this place."

"Just ask one of them to do something for you, take your place for a few minutes."

"It may not amount to you getting the information you want."

"I know, Jimmy. But you'll try, right?"

"Yeah. There's one more thing you ought to know."

Chase looked into the young man's brown eyes.

"What is it?"

"If they want to see what you see, hear what you hear, they can. They don't have it hooked up or anything. No reason for it with you stuck in this room. But anytime they decide they want to get in your head, they can."

"Thank you for telling me. I'll keep that in mind if they ever let me out of here."

Jimmy left the room, and Chase stood and walked to the window. No moonlight fell on the dark garden outside his room, but the amber hue revealed every detail just the same. He watched a small cat in the rose bed. "I wonder..." He activated the hearing modifier. He could hear the cat scratching. He tapped on the glass and the cat, its eyes glowing in the amber, looked directly at him and meowed. Chase smiled.

But then a noise came from the hall outside his room. Somebody dropped a tray or something, and the sound reverberated through his head. He bent down and put his hands over his ears.

"Turn off. Turn off," But it did no good. The sound of clanging metal pierced the silent midnight as scattered items were thrown onto the tray. "God, help me! This is too much. Turn it off." He reached for the bed, crawled in, and pulled the pillow over his head. "Help me."

18

Sometime around three in the morning, Chase turned off his super hearing. He wasn't sure how he did it. He just thought hard about stopping it, and then it stopped. Before that he caught enough conversation between late-shift estate personnel to know that Dr. Fiender was well liked, though his motives were questioned. And he found that, although Kerstin was generally adored by the masses, those closest to her found her not only untrustworthy, but scary. "Treacherous," one nurse called her. "A shifty, two-faced feline," a cohort added.

Hearing through walls caused hours of pain and left Chase with a headache, but discovering he might find some allies out there in the hall was worth it.

The sun was not quite up when a nurse stirred him. "Come on, Mr. Sterling. You're gonna have a long day. Let's get some food in you before the team gets here."

He opened his eyes. His head throbbed. A black woman, tall and slender, stood over him, a breakfast tray in her hands. Her green scrubs indicated she was a mid-level nurse.

"Come on now. Sit up. I've got eggs, a soy patty, some oatmeal,"—she smiled—"and a fruit cup."

"How about pain meds. Got any of that on your tray?"

"Where is the pain, Mr. Sterling?"

"My head."

"I'll have to get authorization. You want me to call the doctor?"

"No. Just lower your voice. And get me an instruction manual for all this stuff they put in me."

"Oh dear, what have you been doing? You shouldn't be turning on your—"

"Super powers?"

"Well, yeah. You need some training."

"No kidding."

She placed the tray on the bed table and leaned over Chase. "I'll send for Dr. Fiender."

"Please don't," he said. "What's your name? I haven't seen you in here before."

"Patty. It's my first time in here with you. Some kid named Jimmy asked if I could take over for him. Said he got a double shift, and he was wiped out this morning. Said I was the only one he could reach." She walked to the door and folded her arms. "I hardly know the boy, and I'm sure there were others available. It's not like we need a full staff on duty—we only have three patients in the whole place right now."

"Me and who else?"

"Elaine Jenz is back for some adjustments, and Judy Bamber just had her final plastic surgery."

"Is Dr. Jacobson taking care of them?"

"Yes, and Dr. Fiender was called in for Elaine."

"To make the adjustments."

She sucked in her breath until her nostrils flared.

"Patty, come and sit with me. I could use some company."

She shrugged and then sat on the chair at his bedside. "Eat your breakfast, and I'll stay for just a few minutes."

Chase forked a bite of scrambled egg and shoved it into his mouth. "Do you know Melody Reese?"

Her eyes grew wide as she stopped a smile.

"You do, don't you? Where is she?"

"Why would you think that I know her?"

"I learned you might share the same beliefs. I don't care about that. I'm not giving you grief about your activities."

"Sir, my activities are—"

"Not my concern. Mel is a good friend of mine. I just want to see her."

"I know she was your assistant. She thought of you as a friend, too."

Chase gobbled the fruit, hoping his compliance would loosen the nurse's tongue. "Please tell me where she is," he said. "I need to see her."

"Did Jimmy tell you I was—"

"A Christian?"

She came to her feet.

"He said you might know Mel, that's all. So—"

"So I've got to be more careful."

Chase scooped a spoonful of oatmeal. And waited.

"She was reassigned to the Northeast Territory. New York City. I don't know if I can get in touch with her."

Chase dropped his spoon onto the tray. "I thought she would stay until she knew how I was doing. I thought she'd be here for me."

"Mr. Sterling, do you know what *reassigned* means? She had no choice."

"I know." He looked into the woman's black eyes. "Call her for me."

"And tell her what?"

"Tell her it would be easier to get through this if

she were here to help me. Tell her to at least give me a call sometime."

"If I'm able to find her, I'll get that message to her, but I don't know if she's even allowed to speak with you at this point. You're sort of off limits. As far as the outside world knows, you're being kept in a vegetative state. There's talk that the experiments done on you might not have worked as planned."

"Funny. Another nurse told me the world was waiting to see the new me."

"That's what the staff was told to say to you, if you asked. Nobody on the outside knows you're awake."

"But I am recovering, right?"

"Yes, of course you are." She moved toward the door. "I'll see what I can do about getting in touch with Melody."

"Thanks, Patty. And don't worry, I won't tell anybody you follow Jesus or anything."

"Follow Jesus? I'm tired of following Jesus." She put her hands on her hips and shook her head. "I think I'll just let Him carry me the rest of the way."

Chase laughed though he didn't really know what she meant. "OK. Either way, unless the room is bugged, or my head is bugged, nobody will hear it from me."

"I believe you. Melody says you're a good man. But you're right to be careful what you say—somebody might be monitoring."

"I'll be careful."

A smile crept up one cheek as she turned to leave the room. The door slid open, then shut, and she was gone.

19

Before noon, the doctor and his parade of nano-geeks invaded Chase's prison and began the indoctrination. They came to teach him how to turn on his night vision, which he already knew, and how to utilize his hearing enhancers, which he never planned to invoke again. The agony Chase had experienced was never brought up when Jaime Sommers got *her* super hearing in *The Bionic Woman* series.

After an hour of lying about what he'd already figured out and pretending to understand what he didn't, he made a game of the team's pride in the greatest mega technology accomplishment to date. That's what Fiender called Chase. "You are a bionomic number one," the doctor said. "The firstborn of many to come."

Chase moved ahead with the game. "A-Life versus B-Life."

"No, son, there is no versus. Artificial life and biological life are one, at least in your case."

"The rosebush outside my window—who made it?"

"It came to be from the processes of biology. Maybe there was a little engineering by a botanist to make the blooms so brilliantly red."

"But it's one for B-Life, wouldn't you say?"

The doctor furrowed his bushy brow. "Chase, we are not here to compare the wonders of nature to—"

"And this monitor, the one hooked to my head, who made it?"

"I don't know, Chase. I suppose some engineer designed it, and then a team of technicians manufactured it."

"So, is that a point for A-Life?"

"No. It can do nothing but monitor brainwaves."

"So, Dr. Fiender, it's another point for B-Life." Chase smiled. "It's only use is to monitor a biological function."

The five team members read screens and punched buttons on their VPads, seemingly ignoring the adolescent science drill. "Chase, please, no need for formalities. Call me Robert. After all, I made you. That reading on the monitor, the one you believe to be your brainwaves, is more my doing than yours. More A-Life than you know. Your brain, son, is keeping track of—"

"Of processors and nanodevices and technocytes that you put in me," Chase yelled. "You turned me into a freak." He pulled the wires from his head and arms, and stood to walk from the doctor and his skillful disciples with their up-to-the-minute contraptions. They were nothing but clowns with can openers.

He came to the door, but it didn't open. He turned around.

The doctor stood there, arms folded. "Young man, you must cooperate. It's your only option."

Chase stood still, his eyes fixed on the man who'd taken control of his life. "Tell me about Elaine Jenz."

"What about her?"

"When did you meet her?"

"You know when I met her. I came to repair her abnormalities after she became unmanageable."

"Not before."

"No. Why do you ask?"

"What happened to her during her initial surgeries? What kind of device was put in her?" Chase moved to the window and dropped into a chair. "What made her crack?"

The doctor turned to his team. "Everyone out." The men left without question. Fiender kept his back to Chase. "What makes you think any sort of augmentation was done to Elaine prior to the time I met her?"

"She lost her mind. You tweaked her. And then she was fine. Somebody messed up in the beginning, isn't that right?"

"Chase, tell me. How do you know this?"

"Do you think it showed up in some information reservoir you hooked up in me?"

The doctor turned around. "How do you know I hooked up any such thing?"

"Maybe because it's working, Robert. Maybe I turned it on."

"Information about Elaine Jenz would not come from your enhancements. Did Kerstin tell you?"

"She knew about this?" Chase wiped his hands across face. "Of course she knew. She got some half-wit scientist to work on Elaine, right? And it made Elaine go nuts. And you fixed her."

"Something like that, yes. But the woman is fine now. I just updated a few of her sensors, that's all. Her changes were strictly limited to personality. We made her outgoing and confident. That was the intent of the initial surgery, and that's what the adjustments have achieved. She's here at the estate right now. Would you like to see her?"

"What else has Kerstin done behind my back?"

"I'm sure I don't know." Fiender came to sit in the chair opposite Chase. "Did you really tap into your data bank?"

"No. It made sense, that's all. Somebody messed with Elaine Jenz's brain before you showed up."

"But you knew about the capability. I know Kerstin told you about the night vision. What else do you know?"

"I have super hearing. I've used it, and the night vision, without your help."

"Amazing."

Chase leaned back and stretched his legs. "More like useless. Why would you do this to me?"

"To show the world what we are able to accomplish. People trust you, young man. If you show them the benefits of selective augmentation, they will not be frightened of the future. They will embrace it. The night vision and the hearing are gimmicky, yes. But people will love it. They'll want it."

"*I'm* frightened of the future, Robert."

"Only because you have not been taught all that you are capable of. Let's begin right now."

"I can monitor my own body, and everyone else's, without any instruction. Why is that? And why have I not been able to utilize the data…whatever?"

Fiender leaned forward, his eyes bright with excitement. "I wish I could tell you." He nearly giggled. "The exoself seems to have its own ideas regarding the timing of its emergence."

"The exoself being what was added to my…*self*?"

"Yes, that's right. Systems linked to the self, extending mind and body beyond their normal capabilities. In your case, the systems monitor all your functions, both organic and augmented. But some systems are operative outside the exoself, including the Wilberton module and the sensors that allow you to control your vision and hearing. When you unlock the exoself you'll find systems that allow you to tap into a wealth of information."

"Those systems are more complex than the upgrades on my eyes and ears?"

"Yes, yes. I told you those are gimmicks to draw in the multitude that trust and respect you."

"But there's a knowledge thing, a part of the exoself that hasn't kicked in. Something to make me wise." Chase looked out the window at the red roses and the gray sky.

"Your ability to reason was not enhanced. The ability to store data is what is different. Wisdom is something else entirely. I'm sure I can make a simpleton smart. I'm not sure I can make a foolish man wise." Fiender giggled again. "Give me a couple of months to work on it."

"What kind of information?"

"Excuse me?"

Chase turned to face his creator. "What kind of information is in the exoself?"

"Useful factors that will help your followers. Assignment issues, pay scales, housing availability. That sort of thing. Facts and figures."

Chase closed his eyes and concentrated. Hard. But nothing happened. Not a single fact or figure popped up from the exoself. "I got nothing, Robert. I don't think like a computer. I'm not spouting off useless information."

"It may be that the imp needs adjusting, but it's not useless. I do not support info glut."

"If the imp was working, would I know what an

imp is?"

"Electronic implant."

"Oh. Info glut, I get it. Information overload, right?"

"You will not be crammed with things you don't need to know."

"The whole thing sounds like a complete waste— filling my head with stuff accessible on any WR computer. What on earth are you people trying to do?"

"Don't you find it fascinating that you could think like a computer?"

"No. No one will find it fascinating. It's a stupid idea."

"The time is coming when you will relish the capability."

"I'd like to rest now."

"I know you're not tired, Chase."

"Did you program fatigue right out of me?"

"No, I'm looking at your monitor. It indicates your responses to both physical and mental stimuli are prime."

"I yanked the monitor off ten minutes ago."

"Doesn't matter. You're still registering." The doctor pointed to the monitors on the wall and then pulled a VPad from his pocket. "In fact, I can leave you and still monitor your readings." He held the device in front of Chase.

The coded readout meant nothing to Chase. But he wasn't tired, he was wide awake and eager to understand how all this worked. And Fiender knew it—the doctor could read him. No attachments needed.

"Can you read my mind?"

"No, Chase."

"Can you hear what I hear and see what I see?"

"Yes, if I so choose. That's what my team did here today. The program was activated that will allow me that privilege."

"It's a good thing you can't read my mind, Robert."

"You must not despise me, Chase. You won't survive without me." The doctor turned toward the door. "Tomorrow we will see what can be done about the imp that hasn't kicked in, as you say. In the meantime, try ripping some towels or bending the IV pole. Your upper body strength is greater than before. Not like Superman, but great nonetheless. Another gimmick to make the people *ooh* and *ahh*."

The door slid wide, and the doctor lurched through before it sealed shut.

"Tomorrow," Chase said—he didn't care who heard him on the other side of the door. "I will learn how to unplug this monster."

20

Chase spent the evening wondering if he really had a huge bank of WR resources inside his head. What would happen when he figured out how to turn it on? Would he know everything about everyone? Would he be the one to decide who moved up and who got booted out of the system? Would he find Mel?

Somewhere between revulsion and curiosity, he found the switch. He knew the number of people assigned to the job force—86,676,331. Wait—332. Somebody must have just gotten their assignment. He found no access to the names or locations of workers. No record of Mel's reassignment. Maybe with a little training he'd be able to get more information.

He knew how many people were scheduled for reassignment. A figure of how many workers were in need of a housing upgrade came to mind. He thought about the village and wondered where Larin Andrews lived now. Chase didn't have trouble with too much data popping into his head all at once. It came orderly, slowly. Once there, it was available for instant recall. But what was the point?

As he processed what came from the exoself, he played a game with the staff. He found he could go without blinking, so he stared at the faint outline of the window for hours on end, his night vision turned off. He controlled his breathing to make it inaudible. The only sound was the occasional bump or whisper that came from the hall. He waited, wondering how long it would be before someone came to check on him.

Of course, they knew he was alive. They probably knew exactly what he was doing. No one came.

Somewhere between a list of houses available in the outer regions of the Pacific Island Territory and a tedious catalog of reassignment opportunities, a record of seemingly little consequence came to mind. Chase knew the number of the main branches of the Underground Church in each territory, along with the names of major cities where a branch existed. Some main branches listed one or two sub-branches. He wondered if Mel and her friends were aware the WR knew so much, and he questioned what the government planned to do with the information. And why on earth would they put it in his head? Were they going to use him to eliminate the organization?

After a while he stopped running the current of the system, and his mind wandered. He figured he was getting tired, and the exoself was giving him a break. He thought about Elaine Jenz, about her personality alterations—surely something she'd wanted. But if they could do it to Elaine they could do it to anybody. They could alter the core of anyone they chose.

He broke his stare at the dark window, turned on his night vision, and pulled a VPad from his nightstand drawer. His old VPad was gone—too many outside contacts stored there. This new one was clean, and he couldn't communicate outside SynVue Estate. But he could make notes and record data, and prompt the nurse's station. Or Kerstin or Dr. Fiender. He typed a message on the small screen. He didn't send the memo to anyone, but simply held it in front of his eyes.

I'M RUNNING DATA NOW. EVERYTHING IS WORKING.

In only a minute a nurse—a big woman with a gruff voice—came through the door.

"I see your data bank kicked in. I'll call Dr. Fiender in the morning."

"So you're the one invading..." He checked his attitude. "You're the one watching my monitors tonight."

"Yep. Don't see why. You spent three hours staring at nothing. Didn't even blink." She snorted. "Kind of creepy."

"Did you know the data was streaming before I told you?"

"Nah, I don't know what's going on in your head. I only know what the monitors tell me."

"Which is..."

The woman huffed. "Vital signs, activity, sight, and sound, that sort of thing." She turned for the door. "And I can tell you're wearing down. Get some sleep, Mr. Sterling. You can't go forever without blinking. Let the lids fall."

Before she was gone, Chase's eyes were begging shut. He drifted into dreams of numbers and meaningless data.

❧

"Chase, come look at this."

"What is it, Mom?"

"Some sort of sea creature. It looks like a jellyfish. Ever seen anything like it?"

"Nope. But I don't think it's a jellyfish."

"I suppose it isn't. I mean, it has the face of a man. A mad scientist, I'd say."

"You're right, Mom. It must be a—"

Chase's eyes flew open. Sunlight glimmered through the filtered glass. Sweat beaded on his forehead.

"Does anyone out there know I just had a nightmare? Fiender? You look good as a jellyfish." Chase threw back the covers, put his feet on the floor, and went to the bathroom. Splashing cold water on his face, he replayed the comforting sound of his mother's voice. Even a bad dream wasn't so bad with her in it. He looked in the mirror.

"I want to talk to my mother," he said. "Do you hear me?"

Back in his room, he did a few morning stretches. He looked at the IV pole next to his bed. He didn't know why it was there—he'd not been hooked to it for days.

"OK, Fiender. Here goes nothing." Grabbing the pole, he turned it sideways over one knee and readied himself to bend it in two. Nothing happened, except that he hurt his knee, and he thought something snapped in his back. "Crap. That hurt." He dropped the pole and turned to look at the door. "Are you listening?"

Lifting the pole again, he sparked a couple of processors to life—he wasn't sure how. This time the pole bent easily. Well, as the doctor said, he was no Superman, but the metal stick bent nearly in two before his strength gave out. "Somebody come get this piece of junk out of my room." He threw the pole at the door. "And get my mother on my VPad!"

He knew losing his temper was a bad idea as soon as he'd done it. "Sorry about that. I'm just feeling a little cooped up in here." He walked to the window and sat in the chair. "Besides, the doctor told me to see if I could bend the IV pole. Well, yes, I can."

Sunlight came in brighter now. "Wait a minute," he said. He searched his mind. No, his exoself. "Twenty-seven minutes past eight." He had a built-in clock. He deliberated on the strength sensors again until he was certain they were disabled. He purposefully unhooked himself from the newly found time piece. His night vision and hearing enhancers rested in the off mode. With little effort, he disengaged the WR data bank. "I'm turning off my powers. Can you hear me now?" He slumped into the chair and grinned. "If you can hear me, get somebody to bring me breakfast. I still have to eat, you know. Soy bacon and a poached egg. And some apple juice. And a bagel with strawberry jam." Twenty minutes passed before curvy scrubs came through the door. The young blonde carried a tray. It held everything he'd requested.

"I see you heard me."

"Actually, I had the audio turned off or I would have been here sooner," the girl said. "I saw the text on the monitor when I walked by my desk." She put the tray on the small table beside him. "Enjoy your breakfast, Mr. Sterling."

"What about my other request?"

"To call your mother?"

"Yes, get her for me. You can't possibly have a reason to keep me from talking to my own mother." Chase picked at the bagel and then licked the jam from his finger. "Does she know about the new and improved me?"

"I really have no idea, sir. I'll make sure Dr. Fiender knows you want to speak to her."

"I'd like to see Elaine Jenz."

"She left the estate this morning."

"Didn't even tell me good-bye. Or did she even know I was here?"

"Again, sir, I have no idea."

"How about Patty? Is she around?"

The tech straightened the blanket on Chase's bed as she spoke. "Patty got reassigned."

Chase sat straight in the chair. "When did that happen? I just talked to her a couple of days ago."

"I have—"

"No idea." He nodded. "Thanks for breakfast. What's your name?"

"Shane."

"Know any of Patty's friends, Shane?"

"No, sir. Why do you ask?"

"No reason."

She gave a shy smile before exiting. Chase leaned back and moved the plate to his lap. Patty was his only hope of getting in touch with Mel. Why was it that everybody who could help him disappeared? He grabbed a strip of the fake bacon and bit off a chunk.

21

"What did you mean when you said I look good as a jellyfish?"

"Don't you know?"

"No, Chase. If I knew I wouldn't be asking."

"Then you can't see my dreams."

Fiender laughed. "You dreamed I was a jellyfish? Tell me about it."

Chase wondered what the multiple screens surrounding him with codes and flashes meant. He'd finally left his room, under what seemed an unnecessary presence of a security force. They took him to Dr. Fiender's new laboratory at the estate. The armed men entered by waving their security tags in front of the door and left the same way. This was just a new cell in the same old prison. It'd only been a week since he woke up a new man. Seemed like forever. "I'd rather not tell you about my dreams, Robert. They are all I have left of my privacy."

"Fine, fine. No matter." He laughed again. "I love the sea, you know. When I was a boy, my father took me sailing clear around the globe."

Chase continued to study the implements in the room. He stood and walked to the far side of the lab. Probes and wires, some quite outdated, littered a metal table. He picked up an implement. "I'd like to talk to my mother."

"Put that down. You might hurt yourself."

Chase dropped the thing and returned to his seat. "What are we going to do?"

Dr. Fiender swiveled in his chair in an almost childlike manner. "We're going to talk about your future."

"My reassignment?"

"Yes, exactly—your role in SynVue's new venture."

"I'm a little confused about how all this happened, Bob. Can I call you Bob?"

"No one calls me that." The doctor tapped his finger on the desktop. "But if it makes you happy, I suppose it wouldn't hurt."

"Do you want me to be happy?"

"Chase, please, stay on course."

"OK, back to my confusion. You see, I don't understand how we went from you helping me with *my* show to me being turned into some kind of showpiece for *your* benefit."

"I saved your life. You sound unappreciative."

Chase checked his tone. "I am grateful to be alive, Robert. I just want to know how we got here. You had to have been in touch with Kerstin, or someone at SynVue, before I was attacked. It's like you were on notice to come and save me. How else could it have all happened so fast?"

"Chase, are you suggesting someone inside SynVue planned for you to be shot that night? Do you think I had something to do with it?"

"It's all a little too convenient."

"I can see how you would jump to conclusions, not knowing about my dealings with the network. Believe me, it's not what happened. No one knows how the M-snipe got into the auditorium or who would have wanted to kill you. That's why you're under guard. If the person, or organization, wanting you dead could get a weapon in there, they might get one in here. We won't allow that to happen."

"Protecting your investment?"

The doctor tapped again and sighed. "I brought you here to discuss the future."

"If you don't know the truth about your past, you have no future."

"Now you're a philosopher. I didn't program *that* into your exoself."

"I'm a realist, that's all. I was really, *really* happy with my life. And now everything is gone. My show, my purpose, my relationship with Kerstin. I can't even talk to my best friend or to my own mother. You can see how I would be discouraged, can't you, Bob?"

"Why would you think your relationship with Kerstin is over?"

"She's moved on." Chase slumped into the chair. "She has a new show with a new host. She treats me like a lab rat." He picked at the frayed blue fabric on the armrest. "Besides, I said some things to her. I made her mad."

The doctor didn't ask any questions, only waited.

"I told her she should stop eating rats."

"Like yourself? A lab rat?"

"Her feelings have changed."

"She hasn't mentioned that you insulted her. In fact, she speaks of you fondly. No doubt she's quite busy with the new show, but her focus these past days has been your upcoming special with Larin. She wants it to be perfect. For your sake."

"Everything Kerstin does is for her own sake."

The doctor shrugged. "Then why don't you move

on, too? Why would you want to be involved with her on a personal level?"

"I guess it's hard to let go."

"Who is this best friend with whom you're not allowed to speak?"

"Melody Reese, my assistant. Right now she is the only person I trust. If she told me to go into this thing wholeheartedly, I'd do it. I'd take what you've given me and use it to the best of my ability. But I have a feeling she'd tell me to…"

"To what? To run? There is no way out of this, Chase." The doctor stood and studied one of the screens. "Turn on your data bank."

"I have to be in the mood."

Fiender gave him an impatient stare.

"Fine" Chase said. "What do you want to know?"

"Think of Melody. Do you know her assignment code?"

He thought for a moment, and there it was. "21076-44."

"Put a tracker on that number."

"I don't know how."

"Figure it out. You just pulled up a number you didn't know. Now track the number."

Chase's thoughts merged into the exoself, and he took hold of a numerical program sorted by quadrants in the WR. He zipped through the northeast files, pulling up Melody's number in seconds. "She's working for a SynVue subsidiary," Chase said. "Office is in Brooklyn. She's got a desk job, no contact with the public. She's a fact checker." He folded his arms. "She's better than that."

"Does it matter?" Fiender asked. "You know where she is. You have her office number right there in your head. Call her if you want."

"You're really going to let me do that?"

"I don't see what it could hurt."

"I thought when you got rid of that nurse, Patty…"

"I don't know anything about getting rid of a nurse. Was this person going to contact Melody for you?"

Chase hesitated. "I don't know. We talked. Then she was gone—reassigned."

The doctor shook his head and raised his brow. "Maybe she was needed elsewhere. I wouldn't give it much thought."

"What about my mother?"

"Pull up her number."

Chase found the number assigned to Kim Redding. But it took him nowhere. "It's not coming up in the southeast." He checked the other quadrants. "I don't understand."

"How long has it been since you spoke with your mother?"

"Three months, maybe four."

"We ran her number already, Chase. She's out of the system."

Chase stood and walked to the edge of Fiender's desk. "What do you mean she's out? She's got a good job with the parks department. She's not old enough to be put out, unless she's sick or something."

The doctor lifted his hands, his palms up. "We can't find her."

"So put some data thing in me that locates the ousted. There's got to be a way to tell where people go, even if they're not working for the WR."

"Of course, those receiving assistance, people

waiting for new assignments—they're accounted for."

"So let's find her." Chase walked aimlessly in front of the lighted screens. "Program me or something."

"Your mother is not on those lists."

"Which means?"

"She's gone rogue—probably joined a militant group. Or else she just got tired of the system and removed herself. Either way, she'll not be able to support herself or receive benefits from WR programs."

"Militant group…Like the Constitution Rebels? My mother never objected to the rewriting."

"There are other groups. Dissenters of the Republic. Or perhaps she found religion."

"Not my mother. My father maybe, but he's dead."

"Could be that you don't know her as well as you think, Chase. People change."

"She must have heard about me being shot." Chase ran his fingers through his hair. "I know she cares what happens to me."

"I'll leave you for a moment, and you can call your friend Melody. But you mustn't tell her too much. Don't reveal your identity to anyone else who may answer that number. And don't even think about trying the hologram mode—it's disabled."

Chase nodded. "I get it." He sat across from the doctor. "Not everyone involved in religious activities gets ousted. Not that I think my mother is involved in anything like that."

"You know anyone who is?"

"I just don't believe the WR can oust everybody who says a prayer or helps the underprivileged."

"It's the responsibility of the government to take

care of the needy."

Chase thought about the poor souls gathered for family dinners in the field of vans. "People fall through the cracks."

"I'll go and get us both some lunch," the doctor said. "When I come back, we'll talk about your re-entry into society as the first man of the new form."

"A living, breathing computer man. New wonder of the world."

The doctor laughed. "That's my boy."

As soon as he was alone, Chase roamed the place looking for a way out. No back door, no windows. Plenty of cameras and motion sensors. He dropped into the blue chair. Scanning Mel's data again, he came across a contact number under the heading WR/Brooklyn. He pulled his new VPad from his pocket and spoke the number into the small screen.

"WR Special Assignments, Brooklyn office. How can I direct your call?"

"Melody Reese, please."

"Ms. Reese has gone home for the day."

He closed his eyes. He had nothing to lose by telling the truth. He might even learn something. "This is Chase Sterling."

"That's not funny. Poor man is so bad off he'll probably never wake up."

Chase had to think fast. "It was worth a try. My sister was his assistant. Poor man. I thought maybe you'd give *him* Melody's private number. But you wouldn't give it to just any old guy saying he was her brother."

"You're right, I wouldn't. If you're her brother, why don't you know her number?"

"She just got reassigned. She got a new number

when she left Chicago and moved to New York. I didn't get her new number programmed, and I forgot it."

"Uh-huh."

"I'm serious. What's your name?"

"Hillary, but don't think you're going to sweet talk me."

"I wouldn't try that, Hillary. The thing is I need to talk to my sister. It's about Mr. Sterling. I'm working here on the old *Change Your Life* set, and I know she'll want to hear the news."

"News?"

"Top secret stuff, Hillary. Please, just give me her number."

"Well, OK, if it's about Mr. Sterling. Poor girl tears up every time his name is mentioned."

Chase swallowed hard. He was taking a chance getting hold of her number this way, knowing the powers in charge of his life were probably listening. "She's been crying?" He swallowed again.

"Yeah. She's all torn up over what happened. I think that's why they sent her here." The girl gave him the number, and he thanked her. Then he wiped the screen and spoke the new number.

"Hello, this is Melody's number. Can I take a message?"

Chase couldn't believe what he heard. He stood to his feet. "Mom?"

The call went dead.

22

Chase tried the number two more times but got no answer. When the doctor came back to the lab with sandwiches and colas and asked how the call went, Chase simply told him he wasn't able to speak to Mel. But he wondered if Fiender knew more about the call than he let on.

"Too bad," Fiender said. "But you've got her number. Try her again later."

"Why? Why did you allow this?"

"You wanted to talk to a friend, and I gave you permission. You think I have ulterior motives?"

"Of course," Chase said. "Did you listen in when you left me?"

"On the contrary, I turned off the program. I gave you your privacy."

"Again I ask, why?"

The doctor cupped his chin with the palm of his hand. "I don't understand you, Chase. I'm trying to be nice. I know this is hard for you."

Chase wanted to believe him. "Thank you. I'll try the call again later."

"Now eat your lunch."

The men shared some conversation, along with tuna on rye. But Chase didn't forget the old rule about keeping your friends close and your enemies closer. Fiender talked more of his sailing adventures, and Chase told him about the beach where his father's ashes floated across the waves.

"It's a shame the man succumbed to cancer when the vaccine was in reach," the doctor said.

"He died a month after the diagnosis. He thought he had more time. We all did." Chase looked out the window on the far side of the room. "Speaking of cancer, what happened to the nurse I diagnosed?"

"She has a tumor in the intestine. Highly treatable. She'll be fine, but she wouldn't have known about the disease if you hadn't told her."

"How did she end up with cancer?"

"Just a random occurrence. Sometimes things happen that medical science can't explain. There are about a hundred cases like hers discovered every year. You just don't hear about it."

"So cancer is still a problem. The public just doesn't know it."

"A hundred cases a year is not a problem. It's a fluke. That's all."

"Unless you're numbered in the hundred." Chase bit off a chunk of the sandwich.

"I suppose."

When the food and drinks were gone, Fiender took the conversation into the future. Chase tried to keep up, but his mind was on what he believed was the sound of his mother's voice. Now that an hour had passed, he was less sure about what he'd heard. If it were her, why did she disconnect without saying a word?

"Kerstin has some ideas about a new show," the doctor said. "Personally, I don't think you need a show, but she says no one ingests information that isn't presented as entertainment."

"She's the producer. But she's busy with her new

show. Hers and Larin's."

"You'll be the one to start them off with the special prime-time program."

"But the world thinks I'm all but dead. And soon I'll be conducting a prime-time interview?"

"How do you know what the world thinks?" The doctor stopped. "You talked to someone in Brooklyn. Maybe it was a mistake letting you make a call. You'd better tell me what happened."

"Nothing. That nurse, Patty—the one they reassigned—filled me in on what the public was told. As for the call, I got some receptionist who said Mel was upset about what happened. The girl referred to me as 'the poor man who would probably never wake up.' That's all. I didn't tell her anything and she didn't know it was me she was talking to."

"If Kerstin finds out about this…"

"I won't tell if you don't." Chase smiled. "Are you afraid of her?"

"No, no. Of course not." He drew a breath. "Mildly intimidated, perhaps."

"She has that effect."

"Next time you make that call, you may be monitored."

"I know. Why is it that I can control the vision and hearing enhancers, and even the data bank, but I can't turn off the—what do you call it—the thing that lets you or anybody else know what I see and hear?"

"Crypt offloading program, or COP."

"Yeah, exactly what I would have called it." Chase smirked. "What does that mean? Why can't I turn it off? I can tell you about sensors and processors. I can read my own vital signs. I can tell you what time it is. I can use the night vision and super hearing at will. But I can't stop you from monitoring my senses. Why is that, Robert?"

"Chase, I can't explain to you how to turn off something that was designed to be left on."

"You just don't want me to do it."

"I told you I turned it off earlier. *I* turned it off. It's external."

"But it's also internal. It's in me. So I can turn it off, too."

"If that were true—"

"It is true."

"*If* that were true, don't you think you would have been able to do it by now?"

Chase leaned back. "It took me two minutes to turn on the hearing thing and several hours to turn it off. But I figured it out."

"Chase, accept the fact that you are not your own. Not anymore."

"But I am. Nobody can own a person. Not even when that person is less than, or more than, human."

"Which do you consider you are?"

Chase studied the doctor's curious expression. "Both."

"You must be tired. Let's call it a day."

"In two hours, will you check to see if the staff on duty has the crypt thing turned on? And if it's on, will you turn it off for a while?"

"Tell me, Chase. Do you consider that I am your friend or your enemy?"

There was only one way to answer the question. "Both."

The doctor smiled, and his bushy brows lifted. "Let down your guard, young man. In two hours, I will turn off the monitors."

"Thank you."

"We will come to an understanding, Chase. And then, the world."

"I'd like to say I'm onboard, Robert, but you've got a lot of convincing to do before we take on the world."

"You know what you need? A trip to my compound."

"What's there that you didn't show me before?"

"The desert, son. And the spirit of the Helgen Institute. Very inspiring. Very peaceful."

"Just because you can finagle a forbidden call to Brooklyn, doesn't mean you'll be able to take me out of here. Kerstin will show you who's in control."

"We'll take her with us," the doctor said. "The three of us have a lot of planning to do."

Chase would not fight the idea. He'd take whatever chance he got to see the outside world, even if it meant another trip on the death jet. Even if the world was nothing but an eerie laboratory and a bunch of sand. No escape would come here. But maybe things would be different there.

"I'd like that, Robert. I'd like that very much."

23

Back in his room, Chase fiddled with his VPad, waiting for the two hours to pass before the doctor turned him off. He knew the nurse on duty was monitoring because when he sneezed, she came in to see if he needed an antihistamine. In twenty minutes, he would try to call Mel again. Her private number waited in the memory of the VPad. He paced the floor for ten minutes and then sat by the window. The sun was nearly gone. He thought of his mother's voice. Was it really her? Mom didn't know Mel. Chase was sure he'd never even mentioned her. He must be mistaken in thinking it was his mom on the VPad. Five minutes and he'd find out.

The door came open. Chase stuffed the VPad in his pocket.

"Chase, darling, I understand you had a very productive day." Kerstin circled the room, looking over the monitors. She stopped in front of him, put her arms around his shoulders, and kissed him deeply. "I'm very proud of you."

"I didn't expect to see you again. Not like this anyway. You're not mad about the other night?"

"You mean about your cat reference?"

"You were pretty upset when you left."

"I'm not mad anymore. And I really am proud."

"What for? I sat around with Fiender and talked about some ridiculous idea for a new show. I'm not taking that route, Kerstin. Why can't we continue with *Change Your Life*? Think of the incredible things we could do for people."

"Things won't be so different. You've always loved helping others, and you will do that. Just in a different format, and with much, much greater admiration. The people will worship you. You'll like that, won't you?"

"You're wrong. The fans will get no joy out of watching me pull a new job assignment out of my hat or informing a mid-level worker he's getting a housing upgrade. They get that sort of information through their VPads every day. And I don't care to be worshipped. Is that what you think of me?"

She dropped her hands down his back. "I think you are a man who has always wanted to impact the world in a great way. Am I right?"

"Maybe I'm different now." He had to be careful with what he said, and he had to play along. "Of course, I *am* able to show the world exactly how great the future can be."

She smiled. "That's my Chase." Her hands came up his back, and she ran her fingers through his hair. "I've missed you."

The old feelings, the touch of her, nearly drew him in. "Me, too." But it wasn't right. "Only I'm kind of worn out from the day. I think I'd like to get some dinner and then turn in." He knew the time had passed for the monitors to be shut down, and he didn't know how long they'd stay off. He had to make that call.

"Oh." She let him go. "Just as well, I have plans with Robert." She turned and picked up the bag she'd dropped on the bed when she came in. "I have something for you." Out of the bag came a VPad. "I know they gave you one, but I thought you should have your old one. It's got all your music in it, and some recorded shows you might like to see." She held the VPad in front of him. Her green eyes held his stare.

"The new one is fine."

"I think you should have the old one, Chase. Give me the new one, and I'll leave this one with you."

"I've got some notes in the new one that I'd like to keep."

"I'd like to see those notes."

Chase reached into his pocket, powered the VPad, and wiped it clean with one stroke of his finger. He pulled it out and slapped it into Kerstin's waiting palm.

She handed him his old VPad and powered the new one. "There's nothing on it. What happened to your notes?"

"You know, I just remembered I sent the notes to SynVue memory. If you want them, I'll retrieve them with my old VPad and forward them to you."

"You do that, darling. I'll see you tomorrow."

"What do you and Robert have planned?"

"Just a dinner meeting." She came near and kissed him. "Good night, Chase." She turned and left the room. The door slid shut.

Chase dropped to the chair by the window. Mel's number was lost. But he had other contacts in his old VPad. He could reach any number of people on the outside, and his mother was on speed mode. Powering up the device, he had a surge of hope.

But the thing was wiped clean. Nothing except his music, like Kerstin said, and a few recorded shows. No access to news, no numbers except Kerstin's and Fiender's.

But he could get the number for the Brooklyn office just by running Mel's WR assignment code. He thought the data bank into operation and ran the number. The name and main office number of the Brooklyn office came up. He typed it on the VPad. No answer. He'd try again tomorrow during business hours.

But tomorrow they'd be listening.

If his replicated heart could have skipped a beat, it would have.

❧

Fiender came to Chase's room at noon the next day. The doctor had a warning—Chase was sure of that. But he gave it as a matter of conversation. "Kerstin had the COP added on her VPad, and she told the staff to make sure it remained activated," he said. "Isn't that nice, Chase? She cares a great deal for you."

Chase wanted to ask what she knew, but he didn't dare. There would be no more calls to Brooklyn. "Yes, of course she does. Is she watching all the time?"

"As much as she wants," Fiender said. "But she has to sleep sometime. If you want to do anything in secret you'd better know when she takes her nap." He laughed. "Just kidding, Kerstin, if you're listening. Don't want to get the young man in trouble."

"If I'm in trouble, *you're* in trouble," Chase said.

The doctor got a look of panic, but he shook it off quickly and laughed again. "Funny, my boy. No one is in trouble."

"Yeah, just kidding."

"Now, let's get to work on your recall program," the doctor said.

"I didn't know I needed a program for that. I have an excellent memory." Chase moved from the bed to the window. He placed his hand flat against the glass.

"Really? What did you have for lunch today?"

Chase glanced at the tray holding an empty plate and wadded napkin. "That's easy, I just ate. Grilled chicken, a baked potato, salad, chocolate cake."

"You got cake? I didn't see any cake in the cafeteria."

"Sorry about that, Bob."

"Think about your lunch. Picture it in your mind. Do you see it?"

"What's the point of this?"

"Do you?"

"Yes, I can see it in my mind."

"Take a picture."

"Huh?" Chase plopped down on the chair beside the window, and the doctor grabbed the desk chair and sat in front of him.

"Snap a picture of the memory using your exoself."

The memory of the lunch held his concentration. He pictured the tech carrying it in and placing it on the table by his bed. The tech left the room, and Chase looked at the tray. In his mind, he held that image. And he knew, somehow, he'd recorded it.

"OK, did I do it? Did the exoself save a picture of my lunch?"

The doctor held his VPad for Chase to see. The picture from Chase's mind appeared on the screen.

Chase jumped from the chair. "How on earth did you do that?"

"I didn't do it. You did. Do I really need to explain the science, Chase? The fact is, you can store and send images. Not only still images, but moving ones. Show me your lunch as you ate it."

"I can't do that."

"Give it a try."

He closed his eyes and pictured his lunch as he consumed it. His hands held a knife and cut the chicken. He lifted a bite on the fork. He pictured the whole experience. After a moment he opened his eyes and looked at Fiender.

The doctor lifted the VPad. "I have a record of you eating your lunch."

"Why would you want that, Robert? Why would you want to see what I did twenty minutes ago instead of what I'm doing right now?"

"That is the question."

Chase stared at the man's confidant and calm expression. "I don't understand."

"Don't you see, Chase? You ate lunch already, but I can watch you eat lunch now. Isn't that interesting?"

"Yes, it's interesting. And weird, and creepy. And pointless."

"No, son, it's very useful." Chase realized the man was trying to tell him something without actually saying it. He wiped his hands over his face. "Yes, it would be very useful, I'm sure, for something."

"In time you'll understand more about the exoself." Fiender turned to leave. He stopped at the door and placed his hand on the nightstand. "Pay attention to what I tell you, son." His finger tapped once. "You have everything you need to accomplish seemingly impossible tasks." Then he tapped four times. "Do you understand?" He tapped two more times and his hand rested there for a moment before he powered the door open and left.

"Not at all, Robert," Chase said to the door. With his privacy completely gone, Chase wasn't sure he could maintain the attitude expected of him. But he had to if he wanted to avoid losing his will. He wouldn't let them steal that.

He turned off the exoself, to the best of his ability. With his own meager intelligence, he replayed the doctor's words. He considered the tapping on the nightstand. Once, then four times, then twice: 142. Maybe. But so what? A code? A password? Chase settled by the window for a long afternoon. He pulled out his old VPad and prompted his collection of classical music. A soft rain fell against the window, and the rose bush turned its blooms upward.

He hoped Kerstin shared the sight and sound — she hated classical music. The cat that lived outside the estate appeared on the other side of the window. Its black fur and green eyes melded with thoughts of Kerstin.

But the cat was more welcome in his mind than the woman.

24

Days passed with little to do but search the new highways in his mind. Chase found everything from the gross profits of every corporation in the WR to a list of the best restaurants in China. He even found a trail of information that told where to get a meal if you're out of the system. That baffled him. How did the system know what was going on outside itself?

By the end of the week everything moved into rapid mode. Preparations were made for the interview with Larin. Chase got a haircut and manicure. Kerstin, much to Chase's surprise, agreed to take the trip to Fiender's lab. Five days before the scheduled SynVue news special, Chase was moved, again under heavy guard, to the underbelly of the estate and loaded into a dark limo. Kerstin and Fiender were already in the center seats. Chase took his place behind them. A security agent with a readied laser rifle sat beside the driver.

Even the air felt different outside his prison. He wanted to pull open the door of the limo and run. He didn't for fear the laser would catch him. They could just shoot a hole in him and patch it again. The limo pulled right up to the doctor's globejet, and in the dark of night, Chase climbed the familiar steps.

Kerstin came behind him, the doctor after her, and the armed guard entered the jet last. Just like last time, Chase didn't see a pilot. The attendant was a young man this time. He seemed shocked to see Chase. Kerstin pulled the man aside and whispered something.

"Robert, who flies this thing?" Chase asked.

"An EP345."

Chase stood from the seat he'd just taken. "That sounds like the name of something not human. Am I right?"

"A robot is less likely to crash a plane than a human. Relax, son. And buckle your seatbelt."

During the flight, Kerstin and the doctor laughed and drank. Chase held tight to the armrests. The doctor glanced at him occasionally. Kerstin seemed intent on avoiding eye contact. Soon, she demanded the flight attendant play a movie on the retractable GrapheVision. She insisted Chase watch the film from 2005—an alien flick—and she went to the rear of the jet, turned her back to the screen, and pulled out her VPad.

Chase endured the movie while Kerstin giggled at her ability to watch it through his eyes.

"It's amazing, Robert. How did you come up with this?"

The doctor sat near her, but faced the GV, watching through his own eyes. "I designed the program for military use, Kerstin, not for your entertainment. It would be very useful in certain situations to know what a spy sees and hears. No risk of monitoring systems being discovered."

"But it's also useful in allowing us to monitor the spy," she said. "Or in this case, the product of our creation."

Chase turned in his seat.

"Darling, I can't see the movie if you look at me."

She turned to face him, tilted her head, and adjusted her barrette as she saw herself in the VPad. "Watch the movie, Chase."

He stood and walked to her. "I am not your plaything. I'm still a person with rights. And I shouldn't have to stare at some boring old space movie if I don't want."

"He's right, Kerstin," Fiender said. "He's not a techno-gadget. Let him be."

The plane wavered a bit, and Chase grabbed the nearest seatback. He dropped into the seat and shut his eyes.

"Fine," Kerstin said. "Chase, what's wrong with you? It's just a little turbulence."

He opened his eyes to find her sitting across the aisle. "I don't like flying—you know that. But it's not as bad as being treated like a toy, Kerstin. Please, just show me some respect, would you?"

"I'm watching the movie without you, aren't I? I'll leave you alone. For now."

"Thank you."

"I know you could break me in two, darling. You wouldn't, would you? I don't want to make you mad."

"I know you're not afraid of me. You're not afraid of anyone."

She smiled in her catlike way. "You're right, I'm not. But the strength sensors are as unnerving to me as the crypt offloading program is to you."

"I don't intend to ever hurt anyone with the enhancements that have been forced on me."

"You're such a good boy. Going to keep the world safe, are you? Like some kind of superman?"

"I don't intend to do that, either," Chase said. "I only want to—"

"What, Chase? What do you intend to do with your powers?"

"You tell *me*. You and Fiender made me. What do you plan to do with me? Besides entertain yourselves."

"Robert's plans are his own. My plan, as always, is to make money for SynVue."

"Of course. What about your personal plans? Darling."

She didn't answer.

"Why do you want to watch my every move?" he asked. "It's awful, you know. I can't go the bathroom without you, or someone, watching."

"There is one thing I fear, Chase. I fear you'll run. But if you do, I will find you."

He *would* run if he got the chance. But he knew that wherever he went his own eyes would give him away.

∂∾∾

The ride to the Helgen Institute was uncomfortably quiet. Fiender occasionally mumbled and shook his head. Kerstin stared out the window at the black desert. Chase wondered if having them both near might give him the opportunity to know when he wasn't being monitored. If they were both busy, he might have the chance for another call to Mel's office. Not that the doctor cared. At least, he wouldn't have cared a few days ago.

The limo pulled through the gate, and the doctor sighed. "It's good to be home."

"Do you really live here, Robert?" Kerstin asked. "It's an awful place. So glum."

"Wait until you see the inside before making such

a judgment, my dear." Fiender had his hand on the door release before the luxury vehicle stopped. "It's a place of miracles."

"I have the miracle I need," she said, and she turned her gaze to Chase. But her eyes were cold.

The limo came to a stop and the doctor leapt from the warm leather seats and met a waiting associate in front of the first brick building. The men hugged and whispered, and the man Chase had never seen walked to him, a look of amazement on his face. "You look much better than the last time I saw you," he said.

"I'm sorry. Have we met?" Chase extended his hand.

"I was on the team that restored you. I have to say, I thought there was no hope. You were a dead man. But now you are a living, breathing wonder." The guy's blue eyes sparkled in the light of the solar shafts surrounding the dark compound. "I'm Dr. Frederick Davis. My friends call me Dave."

"Dave," Chase said. But he wasn't sure he could call one of Fiender's cronies a friend. Inside the building, Fiender introduced Chase to a number of other scientists. Chase remembered only a few of them from his first visit. Kerstin seemed acquainted with almost all of them, though a couple of men came alongside her to state their names and specialties.

Fiender reveled in his accomplishment as his peers circled Chase. An older woman with a shrunken posture and wrinkles on top of wrinkles grabbed hold of the collar of Chase's striped shirt. Before he could stop her, she unbuttoned the shirt and looked over the repair.

"I did this," she said. "I made the skin and welded you together."

Chase took a step back. "Oh, well...thanks. You seem pleased with the outcome."

"It looks like it was grafted from your own organic skin, doesn't it?"

"It's, um...You did a fine job." Chase buttoned his shirt.

"How does it feel?"

"Like skin. I didn't know it wasn't my own until someone told me."

The lady came closer and lifted on her toes to bring her face close to his. "Guess how old I am."

"I'm not very good at guessing people's age."

"Guess," she insisted.

Fiender laughed. "Go ahead, Chase. And be honest."

Chase looked at the doctor and then back at the old woman. "OK. You must be about eighty-five."

The woman grinned. "I'm a hundred and ten."

Chase raised his brow and turned to face Fiender.

"Still working in her field, Chase. She's a genius."

"How does she—"

"How do I keep going?" the woman asked.

Chase looked into her eyes. "Yes."

"Had most of my organs replaced. They won't wear out. Funny thing about scientists—we're like dentists who don't get their teeth fixed or plumbers who let the faucet drip."

A few of the other geniuses nodded and snickered, but Chase didn't follow.

"You see," she said. "I make skin. Miracle skin—never wears out. But I didn't bother with it for myself. Didn't trust the rest of these imbeciles to do it right, so I just let it go." She smiled big. "But the rest of me will be young for a long, long"—she came even closer—

"long time."

"That's enough," Kerstin said. "Dr. Gaha, you are something. Now leave him alone. We all need some rest. We'll wait until morning for the examination."

"Examination?" Chase crossed his arms.

"Never mind, darling," Kerstin said. "Robert, can you have someone show us to our rooms?"

"Yes, of course, my dear." Fiender pulled out his VPad and summoned a clerk.

A small woman who spoke no English escorted Chase and Kerstin to another building. The woman used an automated translator programmed in the VPad that hung around her neck. The digital voice came out feminine, with a slight Mexican accent, perfectly suited to the woman it represented.

Between the buildings, Chase stopped. The solar shafts were powered down, except for the one directly in front of the building on the right. He lifted his face to the dark sky and examined the stars.

"Chase, what are you doing?" Kerstin didn't waste time getting to the door of the guest quarters. "You look like you've never seen the sky before."

"It's been a long time." He continued his star gazing. A coyote bellowed in the distance. The smell of the desert brought burned toast to mind. But it was good to be outdoors. "Just let me enjoy the night air for a few minutes."

"What can you see?"

"I see what you see. A black night. No moon. A million stars. It's glorious, isn't it?"

"Power your night vision."

"No, I just want to see it like it is. Robert thought this place might be therapeutic. I can see why."

"Just do it, Chase."

He turned his gaze to her. She stood near the door of the building, her arms folded. "Are you afraid of the coyotes?"

"Not at all," she answered. "They'd never make it past the guards."

Chase powered the night vision and looked beyond the ten-foot fence. Every few feet, a cyber-guard with a laser gun looked back at him.

"You really don't trust me, do you?" He followed Kerstin into the building. "So you put a whole unit of mindless robots out there to watch me. Don't you think I could outsmart them with my augmented brain?"

"I didn't ask for the guards. That was SynVue's idea." She walked behind the computer-voiced girl.

Chase took in the plain décor. A desk with a data screen and a couple of chairs were spread on a beige rug. Paintings on the walls brought a little color to the place.

"Why is it that I haven't been visited by any of the execs? Not that I ever saw them much before. Now that they own me, you'd think they'd come around once in a while."

"They're busy men, Chase. They run the country, you know."

The Mexican girl took the hallway that shot off from the lobby and stopped at a door.

"Your room, Señor Sterling," she said in Spanish. The translator spit it out almost in unison. The door to the left came open at the wave of her hand. "Your room, Señorita Bennett." The door on the opposite side of the hall opened. The girl smiled and walked away.

Chase stood there for a moment, looking at Kerstin. His room was behind him. He turned and went inside, waved his hand, and smiled as the door shut. Then he waved his hand again and the door opened. He laughed.

"What so funny?" Kerstin asked, her arms folded.

"I can go in and out of my room. First time I've been allowed that privilege since—"

"But you may not leave this building. Not until morning. Don't even try it."

"Are you sure you don't want to join me in my room?" he asked. "In days past, we would have never gone on a trip and stayed in separate rooms."

"You're not serious."

He wasn't—that was the truth. "Things have changed between us, I know. But the kiss the other night…"

"Nothing has changed. Not on my part. I feel for you what I have always felt." She came near him and put her hand around the back of his neck. "After tomorrow's exam, perhaps." She kissed him lightly on the lips.

"What happens tomorrow?"

She left him and entered her own room. "Good night, darling." Her door slid shut.

25

Chase dropped to the soft bed. A Picasso hung on the wall above a gray settee. The painting was an early one, pre-1907. Chase remembered it from his studies in college. *Science and Charity*. A woman lay ill in her bed, a doctor on one side, a nun holding the woman's child on the other. If it wasn't the original, it was a very good reproduction.

Chase wondered if anyone viewed the painting through his eyes.

"Kerstin, do you like Picasso?"

Ten seconds passed. His VPad chirped, and he swiped his finger across the screen. Kerstin's face appeared.

"It's not a Picasso, Chase. He painted abstracts."

"He painted this when he was sixteen, before the abstracts."

"I don't believe you."

"Look it up, Kerstin. And turn off the monitor. I need a shower, and I'd like some privacy."

She smiled. "Maybe I'll leave it on."

"Then I'll never shower again."

"You know it wouldn't be the first time you've been monitored in the shower."

"That's why I never look down," he said with a grin.

She laughed, and the sound of it brought Chase back to days of success and routine and control of his own life. And love. "Please," he said.

"OK, Chase. But don't think I won't check on you as soon as I wake up."

"Thank you." He ended the call and put the VPad on the nightstand. His suitcase waited on a small table. He opened it and pulled out flannel shorts with a drawstring.

The bathroom had a huge tub with jets, and Chase opted for a hot bath instead of a shower.

The big bed welcomed him and sleep came quickly.

At four seventeen, his eyes flew open. He knew the time without thinking about it—the clock in him worked consistently now, and he never shut it off. The room remained dark and quiet. He sat straight and propped a pillow behind him. He powered the night vision and was surprised to find his door wide open. Kerstin's door across the hall was shut. A black t-shirt, jeans, and loafers waited at the foot of the bed. They were his, but he hadn't pulled them from his suitcase. Someone had come in.

Someone wanted him to come out.

He pulled on the shirt and slid the jeans on over his pajama shorts. He grabbed the VPad and dropped it in his pocket and then stepped into his shoes.

The hall was empty. No one waited in the lobby. The front door stood wide open.

Chase walked outside. All the solar shafts were dark. He could see only three guards now, as opposed to the dozen he'd seen before. They walked fifty feet apart, and soon they were all at various points at the rear of the compound. They didn't seem to see Chase, but he knew they must have night vision. No doubt, they could power the solar shafts. The black limo waited in front of the building that housed the laboratories. The ten-foot gate at the front of the compound was open.

Chase walked to the big vehicle. Knowing he couldn't possibly escape, he put his hand on the car's door. He shouldn't try it. They'd be after him in seconds. Why would he even want to run? They'd done amazing things to him, and they must certainly have an amazing life planned for him.

Why did he want to escape?

He opened the door and slid into the driver's seat. Everything in him, original and augmented, told him to get out of the limo and go back to bed. Why would they lead him out here? It was a test. Or a trap.

The small party of guardsmen came around the square of the compound and walked the front quadrant. They did not stop to shut the gate. Their heads did not turn toward the interior of the fence.

Chase powered his hearing. He hadn't done it since the night it had caused such pain and agony. This time he knew he could control it.

The only sound was a voice coming from inside one of the buildings. Fiender's voice. "You can leave, son. The guards will not stop you. But you must leave now. Soon it will be too late."

Chase waited. The message repeated. They had it on a loop. This was a trick.

But if the doctor didn't know when Chase would hear the message, he'd program it to repeat. Maybe he really was trying to offer release from the whole outlandish plan.

Why would Fiender help him escape? Regrets about what he'd done?

Fiender and his team had made a prison for him —

one monitored by his own eyes and ears. Running wouldn't do him any good. He thumped the steering bar with his finger. Once. Four times. Twice. The code from Fiender—142. Maybe. Chase didn't have that many processors. But he had thirty-three.

He searched for the one programmed as number fourteen and found it in halfway down his spine. He concentrated on the fourteenth processor, and with a mental tug, he drew out the number two. Like a dying man might envision his life, Chase saw the day's events in his mind. He saw the compound as he entered it, the scientists greeting him, the Mexican girl leading him to his room, the painting on the wall. He viewed these things and mentally replayed the sounds occurring from the time he arrived at the compound until he closed his eyes in the guestroom bed.

Only the blackness and silence of sleep remained. And that's where he set the COP. He didn't know if it worked, but he was sure this was the lesson Fiender had tried to teach him days earlier. He could set the program to replay recent past events rather than report in real time. Anyone checking on him, he hoped, would assume by what they saw and heard that he was asleep in his bed.

Maybe Fiender *was* helping him escape.

But even the man in charge couldn't get away with releasing Chase. And maybe it was the doctor who tested him, a game Fiender played with him. Still, to be free, it was worth taking this chance.

Of course, the limo wouldn't start for just anyone. He tapped the starter on the control panel. The electric engine quietly fired. Chase smiled. The guards should be coming back around, but they weren't. Maybe he'd missed them as they circled, and they were already at the rear of the compound.

He eased his foot onto the pedal.

"This is stupid," he said. "They'll kill me."

But he knew they wouldn't—he was too valuable. He drove the limo slowly past the gate and into the desert.

Increasing his speed on the narrow dirt road, he let out a whoop. He laughed as he passed a mile marker, then another. A few lights from the nearest small town came into view. He increased his speed.

But then the limo slowed and came to a stop. It shut down. He touched the start panel. Nothing. He pounded on it with his fist. The doors locked.

"OK, you got me." The trick with the COP didn't work—they must be monitoring.

"If you expect me to walk back you'd better let me out."

A thin stream of white smoke, or something, came through the air vents. An acrid smell filled the limo.

"Let me out," Chase screamed as he pulled on the door, and then turned to open the window between the driver's seat and the passenger area. It did no good. He could not hold his eyes open. They'd find him dead.

"I can't believe you're doing this." Darkness swallowed him.

26

Chase opened his eyes, but the pain in his head drew them shut again. He couldn't move. Someone came near. "Things will change now." The voice was Fiender's. "The COP is deactivated—no one can hear me except you. No need to monitor you while you're in this condition. You learned this morning that there are ways to override the system. You can do it again, son."

Then silence. Hours must have passed as consciousness came and went. A chemical taste remained on his tongue. He wanted water. No one offered.

Sometime later—he didn't know how long—Kerstin spoke to him. "I knew you would run."

Chase struggled to open his eyes. "So you tested me?"

"What are you talking about? There was no test. You shut down the cyber-guards and took off. I didn't know you had the capability to turn off the guards."

"The guards surrounding the compound? I didn't do anything."

"Chase, don't pretend with me. You said you could outsmart them, and you were right."

"But you programmed the limo to let me escape."

"No one here *let* you escape. I don't know how you got it to start, but it's equipped with an anti-theft device. That's what knocked you out. Under normal circumstances you'd be in a WR holding house now."

"What are you going to do to me?"

"That's what we've been discussing. Our plans have changed."

Chase couldn't hold his eyes open. The muscles in his arms and legs twitched. He struggled against the restraints that had his wrists bound to the gurney. "What *were* your plans?" he asked.

"To add a state-of-the-art tracking device, in case you learned how to shut down the COP. I'm impressed that you figured out how to use the replay option. But I'm not surprised. I always knew you were too smart to be a game-show host."

Now that I've tried to escape, you're not going to add the tracking device? Doesn't make sense."

"You've shown yourself to be completely uncooperative, so we've decided on something a little more fail proof."

"You're going to turn me into a puppet."

"I'm going to make you manageable. I can't have you taking off."

"Why not go through with your other plans? Why not add the tracker?" He knew the answer.

"I don't want to waste the money. When we're through with you, darling, you won't want to run."

He pulled his eyes open again. Her smile was cunning. Her eyes sure. She kissed his forehead.

"I won't run again, Kerstin. Please don't do this."

"It's already set in motion. Just go with it, Chase. It doesn't have to be difficult."

He clenched his fists, turned on his strength sensors, and broke free from the restraints. He sat straight on the hard gurney. A blanket covered his legs, and he pitched it across the room.

"Chase, there's nothing you can do." Kerstin

backed against the wall.

He lunged at her and pinned her arms. "You said you knew I could break you in half. It'll be the last thing I do before they destroy me."

"They are not going to destroy you," she screamed.

Fear showed in her eyes, and that was all Chase wanted. He let her go. "They're going to try. But they won't succeed."

A few orderlies rushed in. Before he could verbalize his surrender, a needle slid into Chase's shoulder. The effect was immediate, and he needed help climbing onto the gurney. "Where is Fiender?" he asked.

"In a virtual conference with network execs," Kerstin told him. "He has some explaining to do." The fear was gone from her voice.

"About how I turned off the guards?"

"Yes."

"Kerstin, I didn't turn them off."

"Hush now. When you wake up, everything will be fine. You'll go home to SynVue Estate and get ready for your big debut."

"I want to go home to my own…" He could not form the word. His eyes fell shut.

"Soon, Chase. But not to your old townhouse. You have a beautiful new house in the country waiting for you."

"A new house? Am I the winner?"

She laughed. "We *have* changed your life, haven't we?" She laughed again.

Wheels moved under him and the air cooled around him. Did they know he was still conscious?

Dr. Fiender's voice melded with others. The sound

seemed distant, but a hand came to rest on Chase's arm. "We'll begin in a few minutes," the doctor said. "All of you go up to the observation deck, and let me prepare my subject."

Footsteps. A door slid open and then shut.

Fiender came so close that Chase could feel his breath. He smelled like an old man's aftershave.

"I can't stop this from happening, but I'm programming a code into the exoself that will help you. Like the one for the COP. Use it to override the system."

The door slid open and the hand released its grip on Chase. "Start the drip now. We'll begin in five minutes."

A warm sensation came through Chase's hand and up his arm, and the consuming darkness returned.

27

"Charles, what do you see?"

He was back in the game. Who was the man behind that voice? The first time, Chase thought he was a director, but they all swore there was no regression game. They didn't know what he was talking about.

And yet here he was again.

"Tell me who you are," Chase said. "Are we going to watch old movies again?"

"Answer my question. What do you see?"

Like before, Chase couldn't see anything. "A black hole and I'm falling in."

He felt beside him and found the nightstand, like before. The metal bowl rested there. Everything was the same.

"Show me the movie screen," Chase said. "Let's see what you've got."

The screen lit up.

Sunlight and blue-gray water filled Chase's vision. His father stood on the beach. Dad's hair was brown and full, his face free of the lines brought by life and time. The Gulf's placid waves lapped the shore. Gulls flew past.

And there Chase was in his blue bathing trunks and a tank top with that big yellow bird on the front. He lifted his face to the sun and pushed long bangs from his forehead. When he smiled it became clear he was very young—he still had baby teeth.

"Charlie, not so far," Dad called. "When the waves touch your belly you've gone far enough."

Chase turned to his young father. The salty smell and the heat on his shoulders pulled him in, and it was no longer a game or a dream. It was real.

"OK, Daddy."

His dad took a few steps and picked up his fishing pole, being careful not to cast too close to Chase or others frolicking in the water nearby. He walked a distance down the shore and then looked back and waved. Chase waved in return.

Chase bent to scoop a handful of wet sand and let it sift through his fingers. Two tiny shells were left in his palms. He rubbed them carefully to remove the grit, examined them, and tossed them back into the waves.

He looked to see if his father was still there. Of course, he was. Chase marched through the water, splashing as he went.

"I don't think I'm gonna find any good shells today," he said when he reached his father.

"We should have come earlier," Dad said. "I don't think I'm going to catch any fish."

But the line pulled tight. "I got one, Charlie." He gave the pole a yank.

"You think it's a big one, Daddy?"

"I hope not."

"Why? Mr. Sauder next door is always talking about catching a big one. Don't you want to catch a big one?"

"No, and I'll tell you why, Charlie. If I catch a big one, I'll be tempted to take it home. And your mother will ask me why I brought that awful thing in the house. She'll send me out in the yard to cut it up. Then she'll complain about the mess anyway, and she'll want to know who's going to cook it. And I'll end up taking it over to Mr. Sauder to cook, because I really don't know anything about cooking fish. Then I'll have to listen to Mr. Sauder's story about how the last one he caught was twice the size of the one I caught."

Chase tried to follow all this. "So, you want to catch a little one? Like last time?"

"Exactly." He smiled. "Do you remember what I did last time?"

"Yep, you threw it back." Chase watched the line as he reeled in his catch. "If you don't want to catch a big one, and you're just gonna throw back a little one, why did you want to go fishing?"

"Guess," he said.

Chase thought about it. "Beats me."

"To spend the day with you, Charlie."

Chase smiled and wrapped his arm around his dad's leg. "Cool."

"Hey, look at that. It's not a fish at all."

Chase watched as he reeled in a gray bottle. He wrapped his hand around it, and they rushed to sit on the shore.

The glass bottle, maybe eight inches long, had a cork stopper. A metal handle protruded on one side. The color was not solid—the glass was smoky. Chase could see inside.

Something's in there, Daddy."

"Well, sure something's in there. When you throw a bottle into the ocean, you put a note inside. You send a message."

"To who?"

"To the person who finds the bottle."

"I don't get it."

"It's kind of like a game. You put a message in the bottle, then you toss it into the ocean and hope somebody will find it and read your message." He removed the fishhook from the metal handle and pulled on the cork. "Of course, somebody could be sending out an SOS. But I doubt that really happens. Only in the movies."

"What's an SOS?"

"A call for help. Suppose someone was stranded on a desert island, or being held hostage on a ship. They'd try to get a message to someone to help them."

This struck something inside Chase. "We've got to help them."

"Like I said Charlie, that probably only happens in the movies."

But Chase had to know if somebody needed help. "Hurry, Daddy. Open it."

The cork came loose, and Dad stuck his finger into the crusty bottle. He pushed the paper against the inside of the glass and tried to slide the note out. But it wouldn't come.

"Here," he said. "Your fingers are smaller. You try it."

Chase poked his finger into the bottle, but he couldn't grab the edge of the paper. He turned the bottle upside down and shook it. The note fell forward a bit, but he still couldn't get hold of it.

"I hate to break it. It's a beautiful old thing," his father said. "Let's take it home and work on it. I bet your mother can get it out."

"But, Daddy, somebody could be in trouble!"

"Come on, son. Nobody's in trouble. Some kids in Mexico probably put the message in there."

"Let's go," Chase said. "We have to make sure."

They gathered the tackle box, the cooler, and the towels, and climbed into the station wagon. Chase fretted all the way home, wondering if someone was trapped on a boat with a pirate or hiding from headhunters on an island.

"Daddy, what's a headhunter?"

He laughed. "Where did you hear that expression?"

"On TV."

"Long time ago, I guess, natives in the jungle would cut people's heads off. Now it's just the name of a jazz band. It's nothing to worry about, Charlie. Whoever wrote that note is not running from headhunters."

Chase hoped Dad was right, but he was still worried.

At home, Mom took the bottle and cooed over it for a while. Chase tried to be patient, but somebody was in trouble. He just knew it.

"Mommy, get the note out."

"OK, Chase. Expecting a message from a little Mexican girl?"

"I gotta know what it says, that's all."

She went to the drawer in the kitchen—the one with all the junk in it—and pulled out long tweezers.

Carefully pushing the tweezers into the bottle, she grabbed hold of the paper. It stuck at the mouth of the bottle, but Mom turned the tweezers until the paper rolled into a narrow tube, and it came right out. She unrolled the note and read it, and then shook her head. "Makes no sense."

Dad took the note and read it out loud.

"'You will become a helper of those in need. 32-7'"

He handed Chase the wrinkled paper. "See, I told you nobody was in trouble," he said. "Sounds like something out of a fortune cookie."

Chase looked at the writing. He took his father's word for what it said. The numbers, Chase could read for himself. He could count to a hundred. "Man, I thought somebody needed help," he said. "I was gonna rescue them."

Mom pushed the bangs from his face. "And how would you do that, little man?" She smiled. "Let's clean you up and go to the barber shop."

"I *could* help." Chase looked at his father. "We could do it, couldn't we, Daddy?"

He took the note from Chase and studied it. "I wonder what it means."

"We'll never know," Mom said. "But the bottle is pretty. Prettier than some old dead fish." She smiled at Dad, and he kissed her.

"You're welcome," he said. He laid the note on the counter, and Chase picked it up and stuck it in his pocket. He walked to his bedroom and climbed on the bed, sandy swim trunks and all, and closed his eyes.

"Twenty minutes, Chase," his mother called. "You want to go to Jo's for lunch?"

Chase didn't answer her. Soon he fell into a dream of saving a poor little Mexican girl from headhunters.

28

"You were four when that happened."

Chase woke at the sound of the voice and found himself back in the bed in the darkness. "I don't remember."

"Do you remember the bottle? It remained a part of your mother's collection of knickknacks and dishes. Third shelf down in the curio cabinet."

The cabinet came to mind, and Chase saw the smoky gray bottle there. "Yes."

"You kept the note until you were ten. One day your mother sent you to clean your room. You dumped the contents of your desk drawer into a trash bag, and that was the end of the note."

"How do you know that?"

"Remember the note?"

"Yes, but it was gibberish," Chase said.

"You grew up to be a helper to those in need, didn't you?"

Change Your Life filled his thoughts. He remembered every contestant, every prize. Kerstin telling him what to do and when to do it. Directors making every decision that Chase presented to the world as his own. He told himself he made a few lucky people rich. He made them healthy. He made them beautiful. But it had been a sham.

"I've never helped anyone."

"People consider you a great man, influential, a

friend to the downtrodden."

"They're wrong," Chase said.

"How will you fulfill your destiny?"

"There is no destiny."

"You will become a helper to those in need."

"That note apparently got thrown out a long time ago. Now I'm ready to throw out the dream. I'm not going to help anybody. Not like this. I don't want to be a super hero."

"Don't forget the numbers."

"Thirty-two, seven," Chase said. "It was just some stupid game somebody played with an old bottle. Nobody but the person who wrote that note knew what it meant. And I don't believe the numbers were even there. I'm dreaming or I'm playing some stupid game. That's all." The numbers sparked something in the exoself. They split and ran down Chase's spine. "Processor thirty-two," he said. "Seventh factor."

"That's right."

"What's right?"

"Do you want to see Mel?"

"Are you going to show me when I met her? Did she give me some secret code I can't remember?"

"Not at all," he said. "We're through with the past. At least for now."

"What then, the future? That's ridiculous. You can't do that."

"Can I turn you into a four-year-old and send you fishing with your father?"

Chase didn't answer. The future—his future—was a scary place. The old movie screen came to life. Blue sky met a wide field. Hundreds of people stood in the openness. Smiles and laughter filled the place. And there Chase was. He needed a haircut. His shirt was wrinkled, and his shoes were scuffed. He didn't look like any super hero. A hand slipped into his, and he looked down at the small brown fingers wrapped around his calloused palm.

Mel.

That's when it became real.

"Hey, boss, you got those meals ready to deliver?"

"They're ready. Dinner for four hundred."

"You did all that?" She smiled.

"Me and a whole bunch of other people."

"We'll be headed for the meeting spot within the hour."

"Do you think it's safe?" Chase asked.

"Always a risk. You got your sensors turned on?"

"Yep. No drones nearby."

"That could change."

"I'll know if it does." He scanned the surrounding hills.

She squeezed his hand. "Have I told you how good it is to be working with you again?"

"Have I told you how much I missed you?"

Another voice spoke. "All right, you two, knock it off."

Chase's mother was there, a huge box in her arms. Gray hair crowned her delicate face. Laugh lines deepened when she smiled. She was so beautiful.

"Let me help you," Chase said. He took the heavy box and lifted it easily over his head.

"Show-off," Mom said. "Get your augmented self over there and load that truck."

Chase laughed as he headed for the moving van they'd turned into a kitchen on wheels.

A big guy came alongside him, and Chase asked him if he knew the location of the meeting place.

"Processor thirty-two, seventh factor," he said.

Chase stopped walking.

The man looked at him.

"What did you say?" Chase asked.

"House thirty-two in the seventh region."

"Oh. Yeah, OK. That's sounds right." Chase kept walking and then turned to watch Mel. Black curls fell to her shoulders. She and Mom were loading another box. They both looked up from the task and smiled at him, and he went on to the truck.

His shoes were worn. His hands, as well. He knew there was no house in the country, no warm bed waiting for him. But life was good. He couldn't believe how good it was.

The nightmare began when he woke up.

29

"He should be waking soon." The doctor's voice was back and distant as before.

Chase struggled to move his lips. "I remember," he said.

"What do you remember?" Kerstin's voice was much closer.

"No, no, kitten. Secrets will not be shared today." Chase opened his eyes and gave her a weak smile.

"Darling, how are you feeling?"

"Different. Better."

"Rest now. We'll leave for Chicago in the morning. Only three days until your primetime special. The world is abuzz." Chase smelled her perfume. A strand of her silky hair fell on his neck.

He lifted his hand and spread his fingers across the back of her head, weaving his fingers into the black tresses. Pulling her close, he kissed her. "I don't care about the show, Kerstin. Let's just go home."

"Not yet, Chase."

"Can I still see in the dark and all that stuff?"

"Nothing has changed."

"I can't wait to show it off. Are you going to turn out the lights in the studio?"

"If that's what you want. Maybe we'll let Larin hold a sign with a message, and you can read it in the dark."

"Can I lift the old boy over my shoulders and toss

him into the crowd?"

"You mean like in the days of the mosh pit?"

"Or the trash pit." Chase laughed.

"That's not very nice," Kerstin said.

"What do *you* care?"

"I care about perception. You do know that, don't you?"

"Of course, kitten. I'll do nothing to embarrass the network."

"The last time you referred to me as a feline I found it rather offensive. Now it's kind of sweet. You may continue to call me kitten."

"Whatever you say, kitten." He smiled. "Where's that crazy old doctor?"

"Robert? He right here. He hasn't left your side."

"Bob, old boy," Chase yelled. "Get over here."

The doctor came across the room and stood beside Kerstin.

"I'm glad you're awake, son," Fiender said. "I was beginning to think we'd have to load you onto the jet unconscious."

"I just wanted to apologize to you both for any problems I've caused. I intend to be a good boy from now on."

"What is it that you've done?" the doctor asked. "Tell me."

"I think I…"

"Don't you remember?"

"I don't think so." Chase closed his eyes and rubbed his face.

"Do you remember taking the limo and racing into the desert?" Kerstin asked.

"I would never do that."

The doctor cleared his throat. "Do you remember

shutting down the security force?"

"Security force?" Chase opened his eyes to find Kerstin pulling the doctor to the other side of the room.

"I don't think he remembers the trouble he caused. He seems almost, I don't know," Kerstin said. "Drunk."

"It's the drug. It'll wear off," Robert told her.

"People, I turned on my super ears," Chase said. "I can hear you."

They came to his bedside.

"Never mind," Kerstin said. "Go to sleep. Robert and I will get everything ready for the trip home."

"I don't know how to shut down a security force." Chase looked at the doctor. "Bob, do you know how to shut down a security force?"

The doctor grumbled and shook his head. "That's enough, son."

Kerstin pulled the doctor away again. This time she took him out of the room. "I just wanted him manageable, Robert. I didn't want you to turn him into a blithering idiot."

"I can still hear you," Chase said.

❦❧

By morning the haze in Chase's head had cleared. Anxious to get back to Chicago, he returned to his room in the guest quarters, under close guard, to shave and shower and pack his things.

Halfway through his shave, Kerstin came into the room. She seemed out of breath when she stopped ten feet from the open bathroom door.

She smiled. "There you are," she said. "Those peons in the lab shouldn't have moved you without my permission."

"You told me we were leaving, and I wanted to get ready." He finished the shave and put down the laser razor. "I can't wait, kitten. I long for the crowd, the celebration. I want to move on, to embrace the new ways of changing lives." He rinsed his face and came out of the bathroom. "And I can't wait to see Larin. How's he doing? Is the new kidney functioning properly?"

"Yes, he's fine. You'll be surprised though. He looks quite different."

"I'm sure. We can't put a sick old street sweeper in charge of a new show."

"You really are interested in the network's plans now, aren't you?"

"I've always been interested, kitten. Nothing else matters." He came to her and put his arms around her. "Almost nothing."

"Chase, finish getting ready. I'll see you back in the lab in a few minutes."

"Yes, kitten. I'll get my shower now."

"You are feeling all right now, aren't you?"

"Never felt better in my life. Whatever adjustments Robert made to the exoself, the old me appreciates it tremendously."

"Wonderful. I'll see you in the lab."

She left him, and he returned to the bathroom and showered. He dressed and packed his bag. Walking across the compound, he had the urge to stop. The open desert stretched beyond the fence and the air was still and hot. A cloudless sky covered him. He paused for a second. "No time for idle pleasure." It was up to him and him alone to tell the world how marvelous life could be with a little augmentation. No one would become like him, of course. But everyone deserved the opportunity for a better life. A life improved by the innovations made possible by the Helgen Institute. And SynVue, of course.

He entered the laboratory and greeted Robert with an outstretched hand. "My friend and savior. How are you this fine morning?"

"Chase, son, how are *you*?"

"Never felt better. I remember figuring out how to turn off my crypt offloading program. Don't know why I would want to do that. I want you to turn it back on."

"Do you recall how you turned it off?"

"Nope, not at all. I doubt I'll be able to do it again. And why would I want to? It's good to know someone is always watching out for you."

"Do you recall anything about a code?"

Chase smiled and put his arm around Robert's shoulder. "Nope. You look worried, Bob. Not me—I have a feeling you programmed all my worries right out of me."

"I see."

"Why the glum face? You seem disappointed. Things are moving in the right direction now. You told me we would take on the world. Well, I'm ready."

"*That* you remember."

"You bet I do. Let's get to it. No more changing one life at a time. I'm going to change the world."

30

Throughout the flight to BHO, Chase wondered what was on the screen Dr. Fiender studied with such determination.

"Are you monitoring me, Bob?" he asked when the doctor looked up from his VPad.

"Not at all, Chase. I'm working on the network's next project."

"What are you talking about? You're still going to take care of me, aren't you?"

"Life goes on, young man. I only came along on the flight in case you became anxious. I thought your phobia might interfere with your new programming."

"I appreciate that, Bob. Don't like to fly. Can't you do something about that?"

"No, son, I can't. Fear runs too deep." The doctor swiped the VPad and dropped it into his shirt pocket.

"You will stay with me for a few days, won't you, Robert?"

"I must hurry back to the desert. So much to do, you know."

Little else was said between the two for the duration of the flight.

The jet pulled right up to the terminal in the daylight. No hiding this time. Chase emerged from the plane surrounded by armed guards. Kerstin walked in front of him, and she turned to give him a smile as a group of reporters approached. These were some of the men and women who for years had waited backstage after episodes of *Change Your Life*. The ones his assistant would gather into the press room for reports of how the network managed such incredible feats for their contestants.

And now his life was the one changed.

The media reps didn't run to surround him. They didn't hammer him with questions as soon as they saw him. Instead, they stood in awe. And silence.

Chase stood almost behind Kerstin and whispered in her ear. "My debut, kitten? I didn't expect this. What do I tell them?"

She tilted her head toward him. "Tell them the truth. It's the right time, Chase. They will prepare the public." She addressed the crowd. "Thank you all for coming. As you can see, we have a great revelation. Our own Chase Sterling has not only recovered from his injuries, he is ready to step back into the public forum. His fans—and who in this world is not a fan-- should know…" She stepped to one side and pulled on Chase's arm. "His recovery is not only complete. It's miraculous. The world will soon know how far science has come. How vast the possibilities. And the man who will reveal these great things is standing before you."

She moved behind Chase.

"It's so good to be back with you all. I am, as you can see, fully recovered."

A hand went up. Chase couldn't recall a time when these people had raised their hands. He remembered the man as the one who had made him stop backstage after Judy Bamber's win. The reporter had commented that Chase must be running out of ideas. Chase never knew the reporter's name, just his face. But now, somehow, he knew.

"John McKent. Question?"

"Yes, Mr. Sterling. The night you were injured, I thought...We all thought you must certainly be dead. What happened to you?"

"If any of you have done your job as a reporter, I would also like to know what happened to me. Someone must know who sent that M-snipe into the studio."

Kerstin poked her fingernail into his back.

"Of course, that has nothing to do with my recovery." Chase smiled. "I was mortally wounded, and yet I recovered. And not only did I recover, I became more than I was."

"How so, Chase?"

"Julie Hill, so good to see you again," he said. "The organs blown away that terrible night were replaced with new ones. My heart and lungs, among other things, were manufactured at the Helgen Institute. I was put together by a team of scientists led by my friend, Dr. Robert Fiender." Chase turned to see if the doctor was behind him. Kerstin shook her head, and Chase returned his focus to the reporters.

"We'll introduce him another time."

"Chase, I saw you," a man in the crowd said. "You had a hole—a big one—blown clean through you."

"I'll take your word for it, Blain."

The reporter continued, "When they said you were alive, we all thought your brain must be hooked to some new kind of life preserver. We never expected you to come walking into an airport terminal."

Another of the media reps cut in. "Have you been at the Helgen Institute the whole time?"

"No, Karl. I've been right here in Chicago, at Synvue Estate."

Questions came fast then, but Chase answered them, filling in details as much as he could. What he didn't know, Kerstin seemed able to answer. It satisfied the reporters. Chase wondered why the doctor wasn't present. Where was he? Still on the jet? At some point during the rapid-fire Q&A, Chase looked behind him, to the runway. The jet was gone.

Kerstin wrapped up Chase's meeting with the media and gave a preview of the upcoming SynVue special. "In two days," she said. "The world will see what this man can do."

In what seemed to Chase an afterthought, she spoke of the new show—the one replacing *Change Your Life*.

"As part of the program, Chase will interview Larin Andrews, host of the upcoming new show, *Reach Your Destiny*."

She dismissed the reporters, and the guards surrounded Chase and hurried him through the terminal. A crowd had gathered during the interview—obviously, the word was out. Throngs of people lined the narrow terminal. They cheered, clapped, and reached for Chase. Chase only smiled. He gave an occasional wave but didn't speak. These were the common people. Of course, they adored him. They wanted to be like him. He'd see to it that some of them got a little boost to what God had given them.

But he was a one and only. There would be no one like him.

☙❧

Back at SynVue Estate, Chase was taken to a new room. This one was larger, less medical. More like a suite at a luxury hotel. "I don't remember this room," he told Kerstin when they entered. "I think my recall was compromised by the latest procedure. I want to talk to Fiender."

"Robert has returned to the Helgen Institute. You don't need him anymore. As far as the room is concerned, you don't remember it because it was remodeled just for you." She reached into the leather satchel she carried at her side. "Here." She handed him a coded tag on a black string. "Hang it under your shirt. You are free to come and go from this room as you please."

"I can leave the estate?"

"No, not just yet. But you may walk to the cafeteria or wander the grounds."

"What else needs to be done to me? If you're going to continue to keep me here, I think I should be under the care of my doctor."

"No other procedures are required, Chase. We're keeping you close to make sure you have healed properly. And there are plenty of other doctors here. You know that."

"Dr. Fiender told me I couldn't survive without him."

"Sometimes geniuses are grandiose. You most certainly will live on without his presence. You'll outlive all of us."

"I met an old woman in the desert. A doctor. You seemed to know her, kitten."

"That crazy old dermatologist?"

"Right. Gaha, wasn't it? She's a hundred and ten."

"What about her?"

"Will I live to be that old?"

Kerstin laughed. "You'll still be a young man

when you're that age."

It should have been good news, but something inside Chase ate at him. "How old is Robert?"

"Why do you ask?"

"He's the one to come up with all this. Body parts that don't wear out. Augmentation. He's the doctor. He made me." Chase sat on a blue sofa. A huge window overlooked the pond behind the estate. "This place is very nice, kitten. Will I be here long?" He settled back to enjoy the view.

"Are you all right, Chase? Don't you want me to answer your question?"

He looked up at her. "Question?"

"Robert's age."

"His age?"

"Chase, you just asked me how old the man is."

"Right, how old is he?"

"Ninety-four." She seemed to study Chase.

"Wow, I would have never guessed. I thought he was in his sixties."

"A lot of people are older than they look, thanks to medical advancements." She smiled. "Of course, the new ways will leave modern medicine in the dust."

"Robert is augmented like me? He didn't tell me that."

"He's nothing like you. He's got a new liver and kidneys, and some arteries or something."

"There's no one like me," Chase said. "I don't need Fiender."

31

Chase spent most of the next day looking at his own reflection. The people who'd made him should have done a little more to improve his appearance. Not too many years would pass before he started showing signs of aging.

When he grew bored of calculating the time it would take to wrinkle, he left his room to stroll the grounds. Exercising his organic parts would surely help keep him young. He jogged awhile on a mulch path. Recognizing the rosebush that grew outside the window of his former room, he stopped to sit on the ground beside the red blooms. The black cat he'd observed with his night vision stared at him from the low limb of a laurel tree.

Chase held out his hand. "Kitten, come here."

The cat jumped from the branch and hurried to Chase's side.

Chase wrapped his hand under the cat's belly and lifted it onto his lap. Rubbing its head against Chase's hand, the little cat purred.

"That's my kitten." He stroked its back and rubbed its ears.

Chase opened his eyes wide, giving the COP monitor a good view, and then he wrapped his hand around the cat's neck.

That night Chase and Kerstin dined in his suite.

Kerstin poked at her steak. "Why did you kill that cat?"

"You don't seem very hungry."

She stared at him, silent, from across the table.

He shrugged. "I don't know. Maybe just to see if anyone was watching. Was it you who witnessed the murder?" Chase smirked.

"No, it was a nurse monitoring your COP. She was quite repulsed. She called me and every doctor at the estate to come at once to address the issue."

"And what did the competent minds behind the great Chase Sterling conclude?"

"Nothing—that's the problem. We installed a program that should tell us what you're going to do just prior to the time you do it." She paused. "Chase, don't you find it amazing that we could do such a thing?"

"It's been in the works for years."

"At any rate, it seemed to be working, until the cat. The sensor only indicated you were going to pet the cat, not kill it." She sipped her wine. "I think you need some more work done."

"I was fond of the cat. It used to play outside my window when I first began to use my night vision. How long ago was that, kitten?"

"It's only been a few weeks. You know that, don't you?"

"Time seems to have stopped for me. And yet I always know what time it is."

"Chase, don't you have anything to say about the prophecy sensor?"

"The what?"

"The new program that tells us what you're going to do before you do it. I expected you'd launch one of your objections when you found out about it."

"Do you know what I'm going to do right now, kitten?"

Kerstin lifted her fork and took a small piece of meat between her lips. She chewed slowly and swallowed as though the bite stuck in her throat. "Before you killed the cat, you called it the same thing you've been calling me these past few days—kitten."

"I did?"

"I think you should talk to one of our psychiatrists."

"Or Robert could just adjust my sensors."

She dropped her fork onto the plate and stood. "Is that what this is about? You're trying to get me to bring Dr. Fiender back here?"

"Kitten, don't be angry. I'm sure a little adjustment is all I need. Any one of Robert's protégés could handle it. We brought someone back with us from the Helgen Institute, didn't we?"

"We've brought in four of their doctors to remain on staff. I'll see to it that one of them examines you tomorrow morning."

"Don't look so worried. I'm sure there are no other cats on the premises." Chase smiled.

Kerstin took her seat. Her eyes remained fixed on him.

"Why do you stare, kitten?"

She turned her eyes away. "We mustn't give the public any reason to doubt your integrity. Violent outbursts, if that's what happened today, can't be permitted."

"Do you really think I would hurt someone? I tried

out my strength sensors on a cat, that's all."

"Anyone could snap the neck of a small cat, Chase."

"Are you saying I'm nothing special?"

Fear barely sparked in the back of her eyes. "Of course not." She smiled. "You're special, Chase."

"That's right, kitten." Chase cut a hefty bite from his tenderloin.

❧❦

The next morning Chase found himself stretched bare on a gurney, covered by a thin sheet. The man in charge seemed too young to be examining the greatest scientific wonder in the world.

"Robert turned me into a prime example of augmentation," Chase told the fledgling.

"We all worked on you, Mr. Sterling. I actually positioned your new organs in the rebuilt body cavity."

"Can you call Robert? He should be watching what you're doing. He can do that from the institute, can't he?"

"Yes, of course, he can. But there's no need."

"Who are you? I don't remember you."

"Dr. Bentley."

"First name?"

"Jack."

"Jack, why are you sticking that probe in my auricle? Something wrong with the hearing enhancer?"

"No, your left ear is where the neuroprosthesis was installed. I'm trying to determine if there's a problem."

The small instrument caused pressure in Chase's

ear, but no pain. "Is that the personality alteration thing? Does Elaine Jenz have one?"

"As far as altering your personality, I suppose it does, in a sense. As far as Elaine Jenz is concerned, I have no idea what type of device they used on her. It was probably a simple EWB."

"What's that?"

"Emotional Well-Being Enhancer—a chip in the brain."

The probe went deeper, and Chase winced.

"Sorry about that." The doctor pulled out the metal implement. "Doesn't seem to be any problem."

"Robert made Elaine Jenz manageable. Takes more than a chip for depression to do that."

"If you say so, Mr. Sterling. I was at the Helgen Institute when Ms. Jenz was worked on."

"What's wrong with me? I'm not causing any problems. Am I?"

"Have you experienced forgetfulness?"

"I don't remember," Chase said with a grin.

"Any confusion?"

The smile left him, and he clenched his fists. "I can't get these numbers out of my head. And I'm having dreams."

"Everybody dreams," the doctor said. "Are yours troubling?"

"The numbers run through my head all the time. They repeat in my sleep."

"Maybe your sensors are having trouble accepting code from the NP."

"NP?"

"The neuroprosthesis—the thing in your ear."

Chase pulled on his ear and rubbed his head. "Can I see Dr. Fiender now?"

"Sir, he's not here. Remember?"

"Kitten says he's not coming back. I don't need Fiender."

"I'm beginning to think you do. I'll consult with the team, and one of us will give him a call. I can't believe they're going to put you on live tonight. Maybe Dr. Fiender can get here before the show."

Chase grabbed the doctor's arm. "Did you know I can make a diagnosis of your health simply by touching you?"

The man pulled away. "I was there when Fiender installed the Wilberton sensor."

"What's the matter? Don't you want me to tell you what's wrong with you?"

"Mr. Sterling, I'm a doctor and you're not. I consider—I've always considered—putting that device in you something of a circus act."

"Like the super hearing and the night vision and the upper body strength of a gorilla?"

The doctor huffed as he walked across the white, sterile room. He stroked the screen of a full-size VPad monitor mounted to the wall.

"Why can't I run like Steve Austin?"

"Who?"

"Can you put in a sensor to make me run fast?"

"No, Mr. Sterling, I can't."

"Robert could do it."

"So, if you want to run like you're a superman, tell Fiender."

"Steve Austin."

"OK, Mr. Sterling. Next thing you'll want to do is fly without a personal flight pack."

"I wouldn't fly *with* a flight pack. Robert says I have a phobia."

"Somebody like you, with all the money and privilege of a prince, doesn't use a flight pack once in a while? I bet we can program that phobia right out of you."

"Robert said that wasn't possible. Anyway, do you know how many people die on those things every year?"

"More people die in those so-called crash-proof Selfdrives. Why are you worried about dying, anyway? We brought you back from the dead once. We could do it again."

"I have a Selfdrive. But I don't know where I put it."

The doctor mumbled something and left the room. Chase pushed away the sheet, rose from the gurney, and put on his clothes. He held up the tag on the black string in front of the door. The door slid open, and Chase draped the string over his head and pulled the tag under his shirt. "Program away a phobia," he said to no one. Or to anyone monitoring his COP. "Jack can do it. Then he could make me fly."

His stomach—the only thing left in his midsection that was truly his –beckoned him to find some lunch. Walking to the cafeteria, he was approached by a nurse. The dark woman in green scrubs matched Chase's stride. She put her hand under his elbow, turned him toward an empty hallway, then squeezed herself into a corner and pulled Chase close.

"What do you think you're doing?" Chase asked.

"No cameras here," the woman said.

"Doesn't matter. I have cameras in my eyes. Now what do you want?"

"I managed to disabled your COP, but we only have a minute or two before someone notices."

Chase started to turn and run, but the woman grabbed him by both arms. "If you know about the COP, then you know I can get away from you," he said.

"Don't you remember me, Mr. Sterling?"

He studied her. "Nurse Patty."

She let go of him. "I asked about you," he told her. "They said you got reassigned."

"Got sent to a mental ward in Minneapolis."

"Well, they must have needed a good nurse."

"I didn't get sent there as a nurse, Mr. Sterling."

He paused a moment. "Oh."

"I got caught contacting the underground."

32

"What has that got to do with me?" Chase asked the woman.

"You asked me to contact Melody. I found her in New York, and I sent a message to her. She replied back to me. She told me some things. I wanted to know more, but before I could get in touch with her again, she went underground. So I called the main church house in New York. I only got as far as the contact man."

"That's how you got caught?"

"Yes. Two weeks in a facility—first time offender. My contact disappeared. Thrown in prison, or worse."

"Two weeks, that's it?"

"Enough time for some attitude adjustment," she said. "Didn't work—only made me stronger. Now I'm out of the system. No new assignment, no income, no WR insurance. But I don't care anymore."

"Why are you here?"

"You need to know what Melody told me."

"I'm the greatest example of technological augmentation in the world. I don't need an assistant anymore. You didn't need to come."

The woman's eyes got even darker, and she pushed Chase against the wall. "I just got out of a mental ward. I wasn't crazy when I went in, but I must be now. To think I'd come sneaking back in here.

Melody was wrong about you." She turned to leave.

"She was my friend." Chase pulled up his COP sensor as he reached for the woman. News of Mel seemed to clear his thoughts and untangle the knots between him and the exoself. "I think she was my only friend. She'd do anything for me."

Patty faced him. "You have no idea."

"Don't go. Tell me what she said."

"No time—we'll get caught. Your COP will be back on. I should never have tried this."

"It's not coming back on. I just left an exam room, and I set the program to show I'm still there waiting for the doctor."

"You can do that?"

The feat surprised even Chase. After what happened at the institute, he was sure he couldn't do it again. "Yes, and I turned off that camera." He pointed to the tiny lens at the end of the hall. "I didn't know I could do that, but I'm sure I just did."

"They'll come looking for you," she said.

"Not for a while. Talk. Where is she?"

"Melody had to go under. I heard she's in the Southeast Territory. Atlanta."

"What did she tell you?"

"She put some information trails in you. In the exoself. If you can tap into her programs, you could be a great help to a lot of people."

"*She* put them in? What does she know about such things?"

"She studied AI in college."

"Artificial Intelligence? I never knew that. At least, I don't think I did. Things from the past are a little fuzzy."

"She didn't want to be put to work in the field.

The WR doesn't care what you study anyway—they just put you wherever they want. But she didn't want to take any chances, so she kept it quiet. She decided it was wrong to mess around with the created order."

"That, I knew. I think." Chase remembered his assistant touching the nodding head of a ceramic figure. "But she just fed some poor people—stuff like that. She wasn't in the Underground Church."

"Trust me, she's gone under."

"Why?"

"After you called her office in Brooklyn, WR detectives started following her. They found her group supplying the underground. Most of the group got caught. Melody and a few others escaped, but there was no going back to their old lives."

"It's my fault."

"No." Patty put her hand on his arm. "Those of us still functioning in the system know it's only a matter of time."

"I don't understand."

"The government leaves us alone, lets us do our religion thing, as long as we remain loyal to the WR. Or appear to anyway. But we're not loyal to anyone but Jesus, and eventually, that gets us in trouble."

"And then you go under."

"Right."

Chase barely remembered making the call to the WR office in New York. "I couldn't get through to Mel. The woman in Brooklyn said Mel thought I would never recover. She had to have known differently if she worked on me."

"She was never allowed near you after the shooting. I know, I was here, too. She asked if she could work on the systems that might be used if the augmentation was a success. And she hid things in you. No one, not even Fiender, knew it. But after a few weeks Ms. Bennett got suspicious. *She* told Melody you wouldn't recover, that the whole thing was a waste of time. And then she sent her to Brooklyn."

"Fiender let me call there. He didn't mention he had worked with Mel, or that he knew her at all."

"So many people come and go in this place. He probably just didn't put two and two together. The guy's a little absent-minded if you ask me."

"And confused about where his loyalties lie," Chase said.

"What do you mean?"

"He told me how to find Mel. He taught me how to mess with the COP. I think he might have even helped me escape in the desert." Chase crossed his arms. "But then he turned me into a puppet."

"Mr. Sterling, I don't know about any of that. I'm just here for Melody. She went to so much trouble for you, I had to come."

"How did you get in?"

"I still have friends here, and so do you. Remember Jimmy?"

Chase thought about the young man who'd put him in touch with Patty weeks ago. "He let you in?"

"What with the live show tonight, more workers than usual are coming through the estate entrance to get to the studio. Jimmy got me a tag. Getting in was pretty easy. Getting out might not be."

"I remember something in my data bank about church locations. Mel did that?"

"And more, Mr. Sterling. She's got you wired to church houses and sympathizers all over the world."

"Why? Why would she do that? Hoping I'd come

over to the other side and start saving souls? Don't you people have your own computer systems?"

"We don't use tech methods underground—too dangerous. Believers still in the system have access to aid and encouragement and warnings, but those underground get by with messages passed along by word of mouth. Sometimes it works, sometimes it gets us caught. Or else we end up lost in a maze of misinformation. The data bank locked in your head is one of a kind. You could help us. If you wanted to, that is."

"When I said Mel was my only friend, you said I didn't have any idea. Sounds like she wired me to help her *other* friends." Chase felt something spark in his processors, and he reset the COP to repeat the scene with the doctor again. Someone would notice soon that he wasn't where he was supposed to be.

"Accessing her trails could be just as helpful to you as it would be to us," Patty said.

"How do I do it?"

"I wish I knew, Mr. Sterling. I lost touch with Melody before she could explain it all. I don't have any idea how to get to all that stuff in you."

"Time is up," Chase said. "You need to go."

"One more thing. Puppets don't know they're puppets. Fight it, Mr. Sterling. Fight what they did to you." She looked to the floor, covering her face with her hand, and walked away.

Chase remembered the second call he'd made—the one to Mel's VPad. "My mother." He started to call after Patty, but she was gone. He didn't dare follow her. He set the COP to real time and walked to the cafeteria. Maybe no one was watching all that time he'd had the program playing reruns. Maybe he got away with it.

He prayed Patty could do the same.

33

Chase ate his lunch listening through walls, expecting conversation that would let him know he'd been caught misbehaving. He heard nothing except a nurse getting hit on by one of the surgeons the network had moved in from the Southwest Territory.

He returned to his suite, sat on the plush sofa, and spoke the big GV into operation. Elaine Jenz appeared on the screen and gave a report of the evening's upcoming events.

"Chase Sterling, in his international debut, will not only show the world some of his capabilities, he'll come face to face, for the first time, with the final contestant of the canceled program, *Change Your Life*. Larin Andrews's future is certain as he and his new show, *Reach Your Destiny*, replace Sterling and the old program. But Chase's future is not so sure. The network is trying to figure out what to do with their over-budget guinea pig."

"Off," Chase said. The GV continued as Elaine Jenz announced to the world that Chase Sterling may not be worth the investment.

"Off!"

The screen went dark, and Chase stretched out on the sofa and buried his head with a gold-tasseled pillow. He listened for sounds of interrogation or an arrest being made on the grounds. He heard nothing. Patty made it out, he hoped.

For an hour he thought about his future, about what Elaine Jenz said in her news report. He drifted in and out of sleep and dreamed of being a little boy on the beach in Florida.

"It's a beautiful old bottle," he heard his father say. "Let's take it home. Maybe your mother can—"

"Chase, wake up."

He opened his eyes to find Dr. Fiender standing over him.

"Bob, old boy. Good to see you."

"You've been having some problems, I hear."

"Confusion." Chase sat up and wiped his face. "But I think it's clearing."

The doctor pulled out his VPad and stroked his finger across the screen. "I'm shutting down some of your systems," he said. "COP monitor, please do not interfere. I will need some time to examine Chase with no programs running. I'll power him back up in an hour or so."

"I really don't think anybody's watching today." Chase ran his fingers though his hair and relaxed into the sofa.

"What makes you think that?"

Chase didn't tell him about the nurse's visit or that he'd rediscovered how to play tricks with the system. "That boy doctor, Jack, did he call you?"

"He's nearly your age, Chase. And very smart."

"I'm having some memory issues, I guess." Chase looked Fiender in the eye. "But I remember the desert. I was allowed to escape. Did you do that?"

"Yes. I'm sorry—I knew you would get caught. There was no way you could make it."

"Then why'd you do it? Why set me up like that?"

"It gave me an excuse to add the new device."

"The NP?"

Fiender's bushy eyebrows lifted. "How much do you know about it?"

Chase stuck his finger in his left ear. "Boy-doctor told me some things. He thinks it's not working properly."

Dr. Fiender smiled. "He's right. If it worked, you and the exoself wouldn't be at odds. But you're struggling, aren't you? Trying to hold on to your—"

"To myself? To my soul?"

"Yes."

Chase stood and walked to the window. He put his hand on the frame and then made a fist and slammed it completely through the wall. "I don't understand. Do you want me to lose my mind? Because that's what's happening. I can't be your magical creation and be Charlie Redding at the same time."

"You used your real name."

"Chase—I'm Chase Sterling." He fell against the wall and gripped the sides of his head. "I've been having dreams. Well, some of them are so real, they're more like, I don't know, visions. Real live visions of my past. Things I'd forgotten. But then there are things that never happened, and they're just as real." He came across the room and sat in a chair directly opposite the doctor.

"You've been dreaming about your life as Charles Redding?"

"He was a nobody."

"He's you. Your memories, your roots. It's only natural to dream of that life from time to time."

"You gave yourself good reason to mess with my personality, and then you secretly junked the system?

Why did you do it, Robert?"

"They were going to do it anyway—alter your personality. They planned to do it without me. Then you'd be gone—there'd be nothing left of Charles Redding *or* Chase Sterling."

"Why did they send you back to the desert?"

"To plan the next phase. The government plans radical augmentation of a select group, then a larger group. You were only the beginning, Chase. When they thought I had you under complete control, they put you in the hands of others—my protégés—and they gave me a more extensive assignment."

"You left…holes in the NP. Holes I could come back through."

"In a manner of speaking, yes."

"Didn't you know it would drive me insane?"

"You will not lose your mind, Chase, or your soul. I'll help you escape the NP."

"It would have been better to let me die the night I got shot."

"I must do what I can to avert death," the doctor said. "I saved you, Chase. But I am no god. I don't want to do this anymore."

"I think I've been talking to Him in my dreams, or whatever they are."

"Talking to whom?"

"To God."

The doctor rose and came near Chase. "I'm sorry, son. I'll completely remove the NP and no one will know the difference. I'll teach you how to fake it."

"You think the NP is responsible for me having conversations with God?"

"I don't know, but something's not right."

"It started when I was first unconscious, after that

night with Larin."

"You mentioned a regression game, and we told you there was no game. Is that what you're talking about?"

"Yes."

The door to Chase's suite slid open and several men came through, including the young doctor, Jack. Kerstin came in last, her eyes making demands before her mouth spoke the words.

"Robert I won't allow this," she said. "You will not come in here and examine him without supervision. No one person can control this situation. It requires a team." She held her hands open before the men who'd taken position on either side of her. "Here is your team. You will work with them. *Not* without them."

Fiender slumped into the chair. "My apologies, Kerstin. I didn't mean to overstep. He stood. "But he is *my* creation. I only came to help him. Something isn't right."

"What isn't right is that you think you can come in here and take over," she said. "Jack told me that he called you in to *consult*. Your time as head of this operation ended when we brought Chase home. You know that." She looked to Chase and fixed her eyes on him.

"It's all right, kitten. Bob and I were just talking. He's done nothing to me."

"He should never have been allowed to enter your suite, just as you shouldn't have been left in Jack's examining room for an hour unattended."

Jack took a step forward. "But I—"

"Never mind," Kerstin yelled. "And you shouldn't have called Robert. I am the one who will make decisions about Chase's care."

"I told him not to call Fiender. I knew you wouldn't like it, kitten."

"You wanted me to get him here. To program you to run like..." Jack crossed his arms. "It doesn't matter—you need a complete exam."

Kerstin waved her arm in front of the young doctor. "So give him a complete exam. Or are you incompetent?" She turned to Dr. Fiender. "Robert, you may accompany the team to the exam room. See if you can fix this. The NP turned him into a clown, and the prophecy sensor is completely unreliable. So do something. But make sure he reports to his personal presentation assistant in one hour."

"Nanette?" Chase asked.

Kerstin whipped around, her eyes full of fire. "How would I know? Just make sure you get there, Chase. You will not ruin this night." She went out the door and down the hall.

The doctors—Jack and Fiender and the rest of them—surrounded Chase. They walked in silence to the exam room. The examination resulted in nothing. No conclusion was reached. No adjustments were made. Chase faked the good cyborg.

"Kitten is very excited about the show," he said. "And so am I. The world will be astounded at what I can do." Stretched naked on a gurney, he stared at the monitors surrounding him. They meant nothing to him, and the doctors seemed unconcerned about the numbers and lines of computer code.

Jack spoke to Fiender in a hushed tone. "Sorry, Robert. I may have wasted your time. His readings show compliance. This morning he seemed about to pop."

"What does that mean?" Chase asked.

"It means I wasn't sure proper management could be maintained. But you seem much better now, Mr. Sterling. Less confused. More sure of yourself."

"I'm sorry I troubled you, Jack. I feel fine now. Quite fine. I and my exoself are in perfect harmony."

"Good," Jack said. "So you're ready for this? For tonight?"

"It'll go off without a hitch, Jack." Chase pushed himself up on the gurney. "Somebody get my clothes. No time to waste. It's nearly show time."

Robert reached for Chase's pants and shirt. "Perhaps you and I could get some dinner before the show." He looked to the other doctors. "Is that permitted? You can monitor everything I say and do, of course."

No one seemed to care.

"Fine with me," Jack said before he left the room.

34

Dinner was two sandwiches delivered to Chase's suite. He easily set the COP to show that he'd spent an hour waiting patiently for Nanette, though it was only a few minutes. Now he played it back so that he and Fiender could speak privately.

He wanted the doctor to set him free from the programming right now, and he wanted to take off and never look back. At least part of him wanted it. But he longed for the crowd he knew waited for him at the studio. He wanted to hear the applause, to feel the love of his fans. They must have missed him. They must be anxious to see him.

Tonight he'd pick a few poor souls, touch them—they would love that—and tell them what kind of medical treatment they needed. He'd give a few fans the gift of a new assignment—jobs he pulled from his magic data bank. He'd bless a few more with better, but modest, housing. How did this happen so fast? Only a few weeks ago the people expected to see one lucky life changed outrageously. Now they'd be content with a few upgrades in housing? Chase knew it wasn't true. They'd despise him for giving them what they needed, and not what they wanted. Maybe Larin would be the one to bless them with new lives. But then *he'd* be the one they loved.

"Son, what are you thinking?" the doctor asked.

"I'm torn between wanting to run from here and

needing to return to my status as the most popular man in the Western Republic. I can't have both, can I?"

"Maybe neither. You can't run, Chase. No matter how you mess with the programs, you can't hide—not for long. They'd find you. As for your popularity, people are fickle. Give them something new to occupy their empty lives, and they forget what was."

"But I *am* new. I'm completely new."

"Will you embrace your role as the new Chase Sterling?" Fiender bit into his turkey-on-wheat. "Is that what you want, son?"

"What about you? Are you embracing your new role?"

"What do you mean?"

"You said earlier that you didn't want to do this anymore."

"I don't want to make techno sapiens. I thought I did, but really, I only wanted to heal people, to give them new organs. Maybe do a little brain-machine interfacing for the military. For the good of the people, of course. Not for world domination or forced evolution." Fiender dropped his sandwich to the plate and his hands to his lap. "This is my fault. I took the research too far, and now there's no going back. I only wanted to help people."

"Robert, what have they got you doing?"

"The next step is to turn prisoners into soldiers. No one will need incarceration in the future. Oh, they'll go to jail, but soon they'll be shipped to bases, fully augmented, completely under control of the WR."

"That's the select group you spoke of. After that?"

"People applying for reproduction permits."

Chase nearly dropped the coffee mug he held at his lips. "What on earth are you saying? What have they got planned?" He set the mug on the table beside him.

"Ovum coding," the doctor said. "Preconception genetic reconstruction."

"Who's doing this, Robert? Who's making these decisions?"

"The system," Fiender said. "The government. The network. The computer models say it's time."

"What will happen to the babies?"

"They'll be stronger, less prone to disease. And they'll be ready for programming. No NP needed—it will be inborn. Only one generation will need coding. After that, it will be part of the genetic makeup of the human...The transhuman race. Or posthuman, I should say."

"This will happen worldwide?"

"That's the plan, Chase. And I did it. Well, Naomi Helgen started it, but I perfected it." His face showed no pride in the accomplishment. Only regret.

Chase stood and faced the window. "What's my part in all this? Am I just a showpiece? You told me a few weeks ago that I was the firstborn of many to come."

"Yes. Starting tonight you will begin to bring the world on board."

"So I'm the spokesman for transhumanism. Not exactly my dream job."

"There is no way to get out of it, son. I can free you from the system, but you'll have to act the part. Even then it won't be long before they figure it out." The doctor covered his face with his hands. A guttural sound escaped his throat. "Perhaps I should have programmed you like they wanted. At least then you wouldn't know the extent of your misery. You wouldn't be fighting a war you cannot win."

"I'll play along, Robert. I'll be the hero the world needs. I'll show them the way." Chase turned to face the doctor. "But I'm getting out of this, first chance I get."

"There is no place you can hide, son."

"I know a place. You can come with me."

"What are talking about, Chase? You can't escape. I can't either."

"The underground. I have friends."

"Religious people? What do you know about such things? You'll bring death and destruction to the whole group."

Chase sat across from the doctor and looked him in the eye. "Not if I still have my exoself. Don't take it from me, Robert. Disengage the COP and the NP, but leave the super powers and the data bank alone."

"They can use it to track you."

"Not if we mess with the program. You can do it. If you can manipulate the evolution of the human race, you can program one man to hide from the bad guys."

Fiender let out a sick laugh. "I am one of the bad guys, Chase."

"You *were*, Robert. Not anymore." Chase smiled.

"Who are these friends of yours? How do you plan to join the underground?"

Chase sat back and studied the doctor. He had no choice but to trust him. "Do you remember a young woman, dark skin, pretty, who helped with the programming when you started the augmentation?"

The doctor raised his brow and looked at the ceiling. "She was a network employee who had some training in AI, as I recall."

"Do you remember her name?"

"Don't know that I ever knew her name. I didn't work with her directly. Seems like there was some sort of fuss from Kerstin, and I never saw the girl again."

"Kerstin didn't want my trusted assistant involved."

"Melody Reese? The woman you attempted to contact in New York?"

"That's right. She programmed all kinds of information in me about church houses and sympathizers. I haven't tapped into all of it yet. But it's there, and I can use it to hide. I know I can."

"I thought you weren't able to speak with the girl."

"I wasn't. Now she's gone underground. I don't know where she is."

"But you know that much. How?"

"Had a visit from a former estate employee, also in the underground now," Chase said. "If I can join up with the group, they'll protect me. I know they will."

"How do you know? You're not one of them. Are you?"

Chase felt a jolt in the exoself, and he knew time for this conversation was nearly gone. "No, I'm not one of them. But I need them, and they need me. With the exoself, I have a bargaining tool."

"But not me," the doctor said. "I would be most hated by a group of God-loving throwbacks."

"Time's up."

"Yes it is. Be careful tonight, son. Do exactly what's expected of you. Go on now. Reset your COP and head for the studio."

"Will you be there?"

"I think I'll stay right here, if that's OK with you, and watch the GV."

"If that's what you want."

Chase made a mental shift and set the COP to real time. "Dr. Fiender, thank you for stopping by. I'm sorry we couldn't have dinner together. Please, stay here and have a sandwich."

The doctor seemed confused, but he caught on and played the part. "Yes, yes, thank you, Chase. And good luck out there. I'll be watching."

Chase turned to the door and pulled on the black string hanging under his shirt. The door slid open, and he headed for the underground passageway that ran from the estate to the studio. He found a mini-drive waiting for him, his name flashing across the front bumper. Riding alone into the dark tunnel, hope sparked in him. Somehow, he'd find a way out of this.

But just as real as that hope was the anticipation of standing before an adoring throng of fans. Was it programmed into him to crave the audience? It would benefit the powers in charge of all this for him to continue gaining the praise of the people. But it was just like him—the real him—to think this way. Both of these deliberations, he knew, came from the self. The exoself was only a program. It was Chase who'd mastered the art of uncertainty.

35

Chase arrived backstage to find Kerstin ripping into some poor intern. He didn't even slow down to find out what the young man had done wrong, and Kerstin didn't seem to notice that he walked right past her and into the green room. He hurried through the door and found Larin sitting on the sofa. At least he thought it was Larin.

"Hello, Chase," the man said. His skin, his eyes, his posture, everything was younger. The graying hair was brown and lustrous. He'd put on a few pounds—just enough to look healthy.

"Larin. You look...well."

"Of course I do. What did you expect? A sick, aging man?"

"No. It's just that it's a bit of a shock to see you again. The last time we were in this place, both our lives were about to change radically. Only I didn't know it was going to happen to me."

Larin's eyes were hollow. And fearful. "I didn't know what they were going to do, Chase."

"But you knew something. Didn't you?"

"They only told me there would be a surprise ending to the show that night."

"Who told you that? Kerstin?"

Larin didn't answer.

"I thought so."

She came through the door and took control. "I see

you two are catching up. Here's what will happen: Chase, you will go out after the announcer introduces you."

"Kitten," Chase said, and he nearly choked on the word. "We've been all through this. I don't know why Larin and I couldn't rehearse together. Then maybe you wouldn't be trying to fill us in on every move right now."

"I didn't want you to rehearse together because I wanted it to be fresh. I wanted you to see him for the first time on stage. You were not supposed to come in here."

"Nobody told me not to come in here, kitten. I walked right past you, but you were so busy yelling at some kid that you didn't notice."

"No harm done. Just act surprised when you see him."

"There'll be a lot of acting tonight."

She crossed her arms. "What do you mean by that?"

He moved forward and kissed her forehead. "I didn't mean anything. Don't worry. I know what to do."

"I'm not worried," she said. "I had some concerns earlier today, but since then the doctors have declared that you're in perfect working order." She looked at Larin. "No one is to know that he required some last minute adjustments."

"Really, Kerstin, I have no idea what you're talking about. I'm just here to do my job. As if I had any choice," Larin said.

"Meaning what, Larin?" She went at him, her claws coming out. "You wanted this job."

"I still want it." He looked at Chase. "But it was

his."

"He's had the need for retribution programmed right out of him. He wouldn't hurt a pussycat." She paused and seemed to turn even paler. "Unless we wanted him to."

Chase couldn't help but smile. "That's right, kitten."

"Both of you get ready," she said. "Chase, go and wait behind the new digital wall. As soon as your name is announced, the wall will begin to fade. You'll step though it before it's completely gone."

"Yes, I'll walk through the wall."

She practically pushed him out the door. A hoard of studio grunts surrounded him, checking his hair and makeup, giving last minute instructions.

"I know what I'm doing, people. It's not like I've never been on this stage before."

A young woman lingered with him behind the digital wall. He could hear the low roar of the audience. The sound began to pull him in. "What are you doing?" he asked without really looking at the woman. "I've got this. You can go."

"I heard you can diagnose people just by touching them."

"This really isn't the best time."

"I've had a permit for a baby for almost a year, and it's about to expire. But now I've missed—"

"OK, OK," he said. He grabbed her arm and looked her in the face. "Yes. And you're lucky it happened now."

She smiled and gushed her thanks. "What do mean about me being lucky it happened now?"

The announcer bellowed his intro. "Ladies and gentlemen, at long last, Chase Sterling."

Chase motioned the woman to leave as the wall began its slow fade. Before the facade of solidity was gone, he stepped through. The audience cheered and then began chanting his name in unison.

"Chase. Chase. Chase." Small groups among the crowd began to rise to their feet. Soon all of the five thousand were standing. Chase accepted the adoration. He stood before a sea of people who loved him. He listened as their voices rose in unison and echoed through the great auditorium. After a few moments, he lifted his hands and motioned the crowd to settle. They dropped to their seats and waited.

The familiar set was gone. No longer gold, but translucent blue, the stage had the look of water. The tiered balcony no longer needed the darkened portal. Kerstin was behind him, he knew, and not watching from above. She would call no one to begin a new life. The flashing beams were gone, and what looked like soft gray mist lifted from the stage and floated over the audience. Shimmering gold and silver orbs flitted about the auditorium like pixies or angels. One swooped close over the heads of a row of fans, and they cried out in awe.

"Welcome, my friends," Chase began. "How I've missed you. I spent so many years on this stage changing lives. My plan was to carry on with that mission. Now I'm the one whose life was changed. As you can see, I have completely recovered from my injuries."

The people cheered, and some rose again to their feet but quickly took to their seats.

"Those injuries were impossible to survive. In fact, I was a dead man. But thanks to SynVue and a team of scientists from the Helgen Institute, I was awakened.

Now, I am not only whole, I am an example to the world of what technology can do for us. For the human race." He walked to the edge of the stage.

"No longer will mortal wounds mean the end of life. You, good people, will one day need reviving, rebuilding. And it can be done. Look at me." He spread his arms and laughed. "I am no longer a man of just flesh and bone. I am capable of more than you can imagine." He turned to the left side of the stage and made a request to the directors. "Turn down the lights." As planned, the whole place went black. A few people raised their voices in fear.

"Young lady in the fourth row, I can see you're in distress. Yes, you in the yellow blouse." Chase walked the incline and moved into the crowd. "Stand up, dear. I'm coming to take your hand."

The woman stood, confused and fearful.

Chase grasped her shaking hand. He pulled her from the throng and walked her through the darkness to the stage. "I have pulled from among you a woman with dark hair and blue eyes. She's standing beside me now. Please bring up the lights," he said, and the brightness returned.

The crowd seemed impressed but not overwhelmed. "Sir, I hear what you're saying." Chase looked to the right side of the audience. "You in the gray blazer and green shirt."

The man looked at Chase.

"That's right, you, my friend. I can hear every word. You said, 'They made him see in the dark. So what?' But they can do it for you, too. I'm here tonight to show you what's coming. No longer will we grant a better life to only a few. Now SynVue will give these same benefits used in my augmentation to as many as are deemed fit to receive them."

Applause filled the auditorium.

"Now, observe the technology all medical personnel will soon possess." He reached for the woman in the yellow blouse and firmly wrapped his hands around her forearms. He knew as soon as he touched her that she was numbered in the hundred with cancer, and it was bad. Choosing someone at random was Kerstin's idea. Now Chase didn't know how to handle it. No one told him what to do if he tried this trick and found serious illness.

"Soon illness will become a thing of the past. Please take your seat." The woman's bewilderment showed, but Chase prodded her off the stage as some in the crowd verbalized their frustration at how things were going.

"Please, my friends, we have so much to do before we bring out the host of our new program. I have good news for seven among you. Within me is a storehouse of information that will benefit you this very night." Chase called the names of the lucky seven, chosen beforehand by Kerstin and the directors. He brought them on stage and told them about their exciting new job assignments or housing upgrades. The selected showed some enthusiasm. The fans clapped. They shuffled in their seats and whispered complaints Chase wished he couldn't hear.

The seven took their seats, and Chase moved to center stage. "Now, as you all know, the last contestant from *Change Your Life* is the host of SynVue's brand new show, *Reach Your Destiny*. Let's give a big round of applause for Larin Andrews."

The fans showed their pleasure. A spotlight lit a darkened corner, and Chase walked to Larin and shook his hand. The two settled into comfortable chairs. The set looked much like the one from the last time the two sat together in this place.

"Doesn't he look wonderful?" Chase asked as he faced the crowd. They responded with cheers and applause. Larin smiled, his shiny new teeth catching the light.

"But look at *you*," Larin said. He turned to the fans. "This man had a hole blown clean through him. Everything in his mid-section was rebuilt using the latest technology. He is closer to being immortal than anyone outside of the movies has ever been."

Someone in the crowd muttered loud enough for more than just Chase to hear, "So he's got a computer in his head, and he can see in the dark. Nice perks if you can get them. Hand out the goods to all of us—that'd be a big deal."

Chase stood and faced the stranger. "It's coming, buddy. But you won't get it, *it* will get *you*."

Larin grabbed Chase by the arm and laughed a bit. "Now, Chase, let's get on with the night's programming."

Chase jerked free and took his seat. "Yes, Larin, let's do that. Tell me about your new show."

"It's simple, really. Thanks to what we've learned in just the past few weeks, we can offer what's called auto-educational implementation to anyone. These lucky souls will not only gain years of education in a matter of hours, they'll be put in the best positions possible and their knowledge will benefit us all."

Chase had not been given the privilege of hearing any of this ahead of time. He could only imagine what they would cram into people's heads and what those *best positions* might be. He searched his exoself for any information on the real purpose of *Reach Your Destiny*. He found nothing. He had to go along. "Tell me, Larin, how are these lucky souls, as you call them, chosen? And what will they do with their new super brains?"

"That is the question, Chase. The only thing we need to know tonight is that the seven you chose already—the ones who just left the stage—will be the first to receive this marvelous gift." Larin stood and lifted his hands. "Please return to the stage, and to Destiny's Road."

Five stood right away and moved through the audience to the aisles. "Where are the other two?" Larin said. "No need to be afraid."

Chase stood and came beside Larin. "Tell them what's on that road, Larin. What is their destiny?"

"To usher in a new world. To become a building block in the government's infrastructure. That's right, those of you receiving this marvelous gift tonight will go to work directly for the WR. The melding of the internal man and the external program will lead us to a world without end. No one can stop us." Larin's appearance and the audacity of his speech brought an ovation from the crowd. They were coming on board.

But to the right of the auditorium Chase could see two people—two of the seven—slinking out an exit.

They didn't get far.

Soon all seven of the night's *contestants*, as Larin now called them, were back on stage. Three seemed genuinely excited about what would happen. Two appeared nervous. And the two who'd tried to run now stood among the others, captured. Guards waited just out of view of the crowd.

The exoself told Chase this was the future and that it was not only acceptable but something to be embraced. The world would be a better place. Less sickness, boundless knowledge. Death suspended. Soon people would live as long as…

"Who decides?" Chase asked.

Larin stopped his sales pitch. "Who decides what, my partner?"

"Partner? I'm only here for the night, Larin. After that, who knows? Who decides where I go from here? Who decides who is augmented and who is not? How long will people live? How adaptable must a mind or a body be before it's determined worthy of this new life?"

Larin fumbled for words. The audience grew restless.

"People, just a few weeks ago you wanted new cars and bigger houses and more beautiful faces and bodies," Chase said. "I was glad to deliver. But things have changed."

"Things have changed indeed." Larin stepped in front of Chase. "Life improvement is no longer about mansions and flawless skin and car dealerships. It's not about organ transplants and dream jobs. It's about the continuance of our race. Now nothing can destroy us. Not pollution or poor health or stupidity. It's only lack of knowledge that brings us to our end. Now knowledge knows no boundaries. We have become invincible."

"*You* are not there yet, partner." With one arm, Chase grabbed Larin around the middle like he was a misbehaving toddler and hauled him off the stage. The crowd roared. Some laughed. Some protested. The backstage crew scattered like ants. All except for Kerstin. The queen stood still in the center of the disturbed mound. Chase stopped before her, Larin flailing and screaming in his strong grip.

"Shut up, Larin." Kerstin's temples seemed to bulge under her black hair. "Chase, put him down."

"Not until you tell me what's happening here."

"Isn't it obvious?"

"Put me down, Mr. Sterling," Larin said, his voice shaking.

"You know I can break him in two. Tell me who started all this. It's mad, Kerstin. I won't be a part of turning these people into—"

"Into what, Chase? Into augmented specimens of the new human race? Like you?"

Chase tightened his grip. Behind him, the audience stomped their feet in unison and yelled for Larin to return. The chosen seven came backstage. Three of them rushed to Larin's aid, but Chase, still holding Larin with one arm, wrapped his other hand around Larin's neck and the three backed off.

"Chase, you can't just snap a person's neck the way you did that cat," Kerstin said.

"Of course I can. You programmed me, remember? I can do all sorts of marvelous tricks."

"No, let me go," Larin cried.

"Shut up," Chase said.

"Just put me down. Please."

"Only after you tell me the truth."

"About what?"

"About the night I was injured." Chase tightened his grip on Larin's scrawny neck.

"I didn't know they were going to shoot you. I just knew I was getting assigned to host a new show. That's the truth, Chase. I tried to save you from the M-Snipe but it was no use." Chase dropped him to the floor, and the three eager ones of the seven helped him to his feet. Larin shook himself off. "What do I do, Kerstin? Should I go back out there?"

"Yes," she said. "But the show is over. Tell the people we've had some technical difficulties. Tell them they'll each receive an external prep transmitter."

"OK." He straightened his clothes and looked at Chase. "I'm sorry, Chase. I don't know what they did to your brain, but they'd better work the bugs out before they do it to anyone else." He turned toward the stage and then looked back. "Kerstin?"

"Get out there, Larin."

"But I need to know—"

"What is it?" She screeched.

"What's an external prep transmitter?"

Kerstin balled her fists. "It will help them prepare for augmentation."

Chase breathed deep and flexed his shoulders. "What if they don't want it, kitten?"

"Larin, tell them they've all been chosen as potential candidates. We will usher them into the future. Tell them you've already received your augmentation, and it's changed your life like nothing else."

"I'll tell them, Kerstin," he said, and he pointed at Chase. "But you are not doing *that* to me. Poor man doesn't know if he's coming or going." Larin turned to the stage.

"Watch out, Larin," Chase said. "Someone out there might blow a hole through you. Then you'll wake up like me whether you like it or not."

Larin slowed for a moment, but then he kept going. The audience applauded. The backstage crew and directors hurried to their posts to terminate the night's ruined show. But Chase wasn't finished.

"Kerstin, what happened to us?"

Emotion showed in her eyes but only for an instant. "The future has captured our imaginations and altered our beings."

"Your imagination, *my* being. Please, please explain it to me. You've wrapped me tight in your new world, and I don't understand it."

"It's all there. Can't you feel it deep down in your—"

"In my exoself? Yes. But it doesn't make any sense, and I want out."

"*That* is what doesn't make sense." She pulled her VPad from the pocket of her silk blazer. "Fiender is incompetent, and you are a disaster."

"What are you doing?"

She swiped the screen. Chase fell to his knees.

"Kerstin, you can't control me. I'm a human being."

"But darling, I can control human beings." One more time she ran her finger over the screen.

Chase's face hit the floor, and everything went black.

36

"Charles, I have something to show you."

Not again. As glad as he was to escape his real life, this game world was just as beyond Chase's control. He didn't want to get sucked into the movie screen and relive the past. Of course, the voice had told Chase the last time that they were through with the past. Chase thought about Mel and his mother in that field under a blue sky. The voice said it was his future.

"Can I see my mother again? Is she with Mel?"

"In good time. Right now you're going to have a talk with your father."

"You said we were through with the past."

"Don't alter my words, Charles. What I said was, 'We're through with the past, at least for now.' This is a new day."

"But I want to go back to that place—the open land and all those people. They seemed so happy. It was beautiful."

"Not so. It's a place of persecution. Now watch the screen."

The blindness didn't bother Chase anymore—he knew he'd see soon enough. He felt beside him. Everything was there—the nightstand and the metal bowl. He dipped his fingers into the cool water and turned his face upward in the darkness. The screen filled his vision.

Chase's father appeared older than the last time

he'd seen him—the day they'd found the bottle on the beach. Trouble showed on the man's face. He stood on the back patio of their old house in Bradenton, and he looked right at Chase. "Son, come here," he said. "Let's have a talk."

Chase saw himself walking out the open sliding glass door and stepping onto the patio. He knew by the cut of his jeans and his soured expression that he was sixteen.

Dad put his arm around Chase's shoulders. That's when the dream became real.

"I know we've had our differences lately," Dad said. "I still love you, Charlie. You know that, don't you?"

"Yeah, sure, Dad. Whatever. When are you gonna stop calling me Charlie? Nobody else calls me that."

Chase's father dropped his arm to his side and looked across the backyard. Chase turned his eyes as well, and they stood there watching two mockingbirds fly from tree to tree. The grass needed mowing—something Chase should've done days ago. But his dad didn't say anything about it.

"I wanted to tell you something," Dad said. But he just stood there.

"Dad, we've had this talk before—the one where you pull me outside and we look at the stars or the birds or something. And then you talk about life and my future or whatever."

Dad lifted his shoulders and huffed. "There's more to this world than what we can see right now, Charlie. Do you ever think of the bigger picture? The meaning of it all?"

"Nope. Never."

"*I* think about it. I've got things settled in my

heart."

"Dad, seriously, are you dying or something?"

"Sooner or later."

"And you want to tell me something before it happens? Just wait awhile if you're not gonna be pushing up daisies anytime soon."

His father laughed. "Sounds like something my grandmother would say. Where did you hear that?"

"Me and some guys in my language class did a report on clichés, and I found all these stupid old ways to say somebody died."

"Tell me some more," Dad said with a wide smile.

"I don't know. There was kicked the bucket, crossed the river, gone to glory. Or you could say somebody went to meet his Maker." Chase scuttled his flip-flops on the sandy patio. "I don't know."

Dad nodded. "Yeah." He cleared his throat. "When you meet your Maker, what will you say to Him?"

Chase had no answer for this absurd question, so he just shrugged his shoulders. They watched the birds a little while longer, and when he'd had enough Chase turned to his father to let him know he had better things to do. But when Chase looked at him, his father had changed. His eyes were bright, and his hair wasn't graying like it was only a few seconds ago. The lines on his face were smoothed away. He looked at Chase and smiled.

"Dad, what's happening?"

The smile faded. "I came to believe some things, Charlie, when you were a boy. But the world was a confusing place and nobody, well hardly anybody, made a habit of talking about life and death. Even if they knew the truth."

"You're not making sense, Dad. And what happened to you? Why do you look different?"

"I look different? *You* look different. You're a man. I never got to see what became of you."

Chase looked down. By his designer shoes and suit Chase knew he was grown, successful. The host of *Change Your Life*. And he was talking to his dead father. The tears would not be stifled.

"Dad, I can't believe this. I've missed you." Chase hugged him hard and then backed away and looked into his father's young face. "Tell me now what you wanted to say a few minutes ago. I mean, when I was a kid."

"You can't learn the truth from a dead man."

"But you're not dead; you're right here. Just like I'm not messed up with all that stuff they did to me. I'm just me—Chase Sterling."

"Chase Sterling is no more, son. In fact, he never was."

"Yes he was, Dad. I changed—they changed—my name. I became a great man. I helped people. Then they messed me up." Chase thought he was back to his old self, before they'd blown him apart and put him back together. But then he knew the sensors and processors were all there, and the organs in his body were manufactured. "No."

"What is it, son?"

"I didn't feel it at first, but the new stuff is still in me. I'm still wired. 'The first-born of an evolutionary leap.' I hate it."

"Everything happens for a reason, Charlie."

Chase bent his head and cried again. His dad put his arms around him. "Look, son," he said as he let go.

Chase turned his eyes to the yard, expecting the

birds would be there on the overgrown lawn. But an open field lay before him. The sky was so blue—bluer than he'd ever seen it. And his mother and Mel were there, arm in arm, walking among the others.

"I can't believe this," Chase said through his tears. "I can't believe any of it."

"These are the ones to tell you what I never did," my father said. "But they're not much better at it than I was. They've been hiding too long, and they're running scared. Find them and use what you've got inside you to protect them."

"The voice—the one that makes me dream these things—said this was a place of persecution. What did he mean by that?"

His father looked at him and smiled. "You think you're dreaming?"

"Dad, we look like we're the same age, and we're standing on our old patio. Of course it's a dream. But that voice—who is he?"

"You know that much, son. Everybody knows."

Chase did know. Not in the exoself, but in his soul. "He made me. Not Fiender or any of the rest of them."

"That's right, son."

Chase looked across the field again. S-drones came over the horizon. He wanted to warn the people, but there was nothing he could do. The drones fired. Screams filled the open field and the cloudless blue sky. Mom and Mel disappeared before he knew it. Most of the crowd seemed to run straight into hills surrounding the place. But some lay dead on the ground.

Only they weren't dead. They woke up and flew away. No flight packs. No angel wings. They just took flight and disappeared. "Amazing," Chase said, and he laughed. "Flying doesn't seem so scary anymore."

"Good, son. Don't be afraid."

"How did they do that?" Chase asked. "And where did they go? Dad, this is considerably more bizarre than the other dreams. I don't know what to make of it." Chase turned to his father. But he was gone.

"Dad?" Chase spun around to look inside the house. It was gone too. He looked back to the field, but there was only the movie screen, dull and lifeless. Just two numbers remained there like some final cryptic symbol at the end of the show. 32-7. Then he was blind. He fell backward onto the bed and wept himself to sleep.

෴

"Do you understand, Charles?" The darkness remained when the voice woke him. Chase didn't understand at all, but he couldn't answer. He had no right to speak to his Maker. He buried his face in the sheets.

The voice didn't push Chase for an answer. But He said something else.

"You are still Mine."

37

Even before he opened his eyes, Chase knew by the parched air that he was back in the desert. Every muscle in his body protested consciousness. Two numbers rolled through his mind as clear as the date of his own birth. Everything else was a mix of memories and images he was sure he'd never actually witnessed. The room was dark, but the Picasso filled his vision. His enhanced hearing picked up Fiender's voice, but he couldn't understand what the doctor said. "Hey, Robert, or somebody. I'm awake. Come in here, and tell me what's going on." No one came. Chase drifted back into sleep. When he woke again, sunlight filled the room. "Somebody...I'm hungry and I want to know what's happening."

Half an hour must have passed. Chase had no idea what time it was. "Something's wrong," he said. "There's no clock in me." He began to scan the exoself for information. But all he found was his own limited intelligence.

"What's going on?" He said it loud enough to be heard, even if no one was monitoring the COP.

The door slid open, and Fiender walked through. He looked a mess—unshaven, his hair knotted. His clothes showed as many wrinkles as his face.

"Son, you're awake." He sat on the edge of the bed. "I'm so glad." He barely smiled.

"I've been awake a couple of times. Why didn't

somebody come earlier?"

"I'm sorry." The doctor pulled an old-fashioned penlight from his pocket and flashed it into Chase's eyes. "I didn't hear you until just now."

"So turn on the COP, Robert. And tell me what's going on. Why are we back in the desert?"

"Do you have any pain, son?"

"No, I don't have any pain. Answer me."

"I brought you here for some re-augmentation."

Chase pulled up on his elbows. Pain shot through his shoulders, but he said nothing about it. He noticed the IV in his left forearm. "Explain."

"Do you remember the show?"

"Yes." He dropped onto the pillow and covered his eyes with his hand. "I'm sorry. I tried, Robert. I tried to play along like I was fully in support of the whole thing and under the control of the NP. But it was all so ridiculous." He looked at the doctor. "I lost my temper."

"The network feels you are not viable. Their experiment has failed." Robert rubbed his face. "*I'm* the failure."

"No, you're not. You could have programmed me to be exactly what they wanted. Undermining their plans doesn't make you a failure. It makes you an honorable man."

Robert brought his hands over his face, and his shoulders shook as though he quietly laughed. Or maybe he cried. Then he balled his fists and rested them on the bed. "How can you say that? I loaded you with all sorts of experimental programs when the only thing I was sure of was the organs I made. That's all I wanted to do, Chase. But they convinced me to charge into the future, and I completely remade you."

"I'm not blaming you." Chase covered the old man's hand with his. "Tell me what's left in me that still works. What happens now?"

"Everything is still there—the organs, of course, and the sensors and processors. The simpler systems still function. The hearing enhancers and the night vision and strength sensors are all in working order for now, just as the heart and lungs and the other organs. Even the Wilberton is still operational."

"What about the systems relying on outside programming and the information trails in the exoself?"

"Wiped clean. The COP is gone, and the data bank."

"You did that? Robert, we talked about this."

"My team at SynVue Estate did it. I only observed. All they had to do was delete some code and everything was lost. I couldn't stop them from following their orders."

"Then they sent me here with you for some re-working?" Chase had a sick feeling in his stomach.

"I asked if I could bring you back to my own laboratory to remove the internal devices. I told them it would be easier. Of course, I had to bring the team with me. The network insisted."

"You're going to pull out my insides? So, by *re*-augmentation, you mean *dis*-augmentation. Robert, I'll die."

"No, son, we will only remove the sensors and processors. The organs are yours to keep. You won't die."

"Well, thanks for not ripping out my heart. Never liked being a superhero anyway." Chase envisioned the open field under the blue sky—a place he'd never been. He shuddered. "But I have a feeling I'm coming out of this with all my new parts in working order."

"You have a feeling? Have you been off talking to God again?" The doctor walked to the window and stood with his back to Chase.

"Yes, Robert, I think I have."

"Must have happened before the code deletion. You should be thinking clearer now."

Chase pulled himself up again. "Why do I feel like I've been flat on my back for a week?"

The doctor turned around and came to the bedside. "You are in pain, aren't you?"

"A little. How long have I been out?"

"Ten days. They programmed you to remain unconscious until the surgeries were complete, but I reset the sensor to wake you up before the extractions."

"Why did you do that, Robert?"

"I thought you should know what's going on. You do have rights. I'll not go on with this as if you were a—"

"A lab rat?" Chase sat on the edge of the bed and put his feet on the floor. "Where's Kerstin? What's she got to say about all this?"

"In the Northeast Territory. She couldn't explain to the network execs how you got so far out of control. They sent her to the Brooklyn office—the one where your friend was—to do a study on public awareness of transhumanology."

"A desk job?"

"No, not exactly. She has her hands in the government's plans, and I'm sure she'll get plenty of recognition for it eventually. But they took away her show, and she's lost the prestige she earned as a GV producer."

"I bet she loved that. She doesn't know you're the one responsible for my lack of compliance, does she?"

"No, Chase. You're the only one who knows." He bowed his head. "But everyone knows the whole plan for practical augmentation was a failure. The network executives, the government higher ups, even the fans didn't get what they expected from the new show."

"What happened to Larin?"

"The network wanted him augmented—he told the audience it had already been done. But he took off. He's gone rogue."

"He's smarter than I thought," Chase said. "Nobody blames you for any of this?"

"As of yet, no. The science is still evolving, that's all. And this was just a misstep in the process. That's what they all think."

"So, not only did you screw up the plans of the network and the government, you covered your tracks. Pretty good for an old man. Let's see if you can do it again."

The doctor looked up, his bushy brows rising. "Who are you calling an old man?"

38

While Chase devoured a shrimp salad, Robert explained what had been decided by the other doctors. Young Jack Bentley and the rest of them showed little interest in what Robert had done with the subject of his failed government experiment.

"They told me to get the gadgets out of you, file my report with the WR, and send you back to Chicago. Minus the super powers, of course." The doctor folded his arms and paced. "They're busy with the military applications. They don't care what I do with my game show host—that's what they said."

"Do you believe them?" Chase asked.

"Why would they lie?"

"To catch you. Maybe the network execs are suspicious. I'm pretty sure Kerstin was."

"Catch me doing what? I'm not going to do anything other than what they expect."

Chase pushed the lunch tray aside on the bed and stood to his feet. "Of course you are."

Robert shook his head. "No, son, I'm pulling out everything but the organs. And you are going home."

"Home to what? What are they going to do with me? Reassignment?"

"Well, why not? People still admire the man you were. Maybe they'll revive *Change Your Life*."

"Come on, Robert, that will never happen, and you know it."

"Chase, what do you expect me to do?"

"I need a data bank. And I might need some other things. Can you do that without reactivating the COP?"

"No, Chase."

"Sure you can—you're my doctor. You made me, didn't you?"

"This is what you want? I've done enough damage already."

"It has to be," Chase said.

"What do you have planned? Will you exact revenge on the people who did this to you?"

Chase sat on the edge of the bed. "That never entered my mind."

"But you must despise us. All of us."

"No." He stood and walked to Robert's side.

"Then you must like being superior. A superman."

"Not at all."

"Then why, Chase?"

He smiled. "You can do it, can't you? You can put the exoself back."

"It isn't gone, Chase. Not really. The receptors are built into the processors and sensors. As long as they are in place, it's simply a matter of reprogramming."

"Then let's do it, Robert." He flung open the closet door, looking for something to wear besides the drafty hospital garb.

"Slow down, son. If you're leaving this room, you'll have to go on a gurney, unconscious."

"You're right. We don't want the others to get suspicious. Are they in the main lab?"

"I didn't say I was willing to help you with this foolish plan. But, no, they're in the rear of the compound, in the research lab. Regardless, they think you're still unconscious, and if you're leaving this room, that's the way you need to go out. You can't go walking into the operating room."

He briefly wondered if the doctor might put him under and go through with the original plan. But he had to trust him. "Tomorrow," he said. "Wheel me over there and put the stuff back. Will you do it?"

"Yes. I'll do it. But why?"

"You wouldn't believe me if I told you."

"Try me."

"I have to help people," Chase said.

"Why?"

"My father said so."

The doctor wouldn't understand. How could he? Chase didn't understand.

"Robert, I need to be able to know when S-drones are in any particular area. Can you do that?"

"S-drones—you mean the small drones developed a few years back?"

"I need access to deployment orders. If they're going on a hunt, I want to know."

"They're just little spy planes. Are you going to work for our enemies, Chase?"

"S-drones armed with weapons are killing unsuspecting citizens who've chosen a life apart from the WR."

"Who is doing this?" Robert asked.

"The WR's doing it."

"You're going rogue, aren't you, son?"

"You bet I am."

"I don't believe the WR would kill dissenters. They imprison them, yes, and soon, augmentation."

"They won't waste the money. They'll just kill them."

They stayed in the room with the painting, *Science and Charity*, for the rest of the day and into the night. No one came to ask about the doctor's plans. The staff of the Helgen Institute didn't seem to care what went on between the genius doctor and his unhooked, short-lived sensation.

They talked, but the Underground Church was not mentioned. Nor Mel, nor the mother Chase had not spoken to in months. Except for that once, perhaps, when she disconnected the call. He pictured her walking with Mel, arm in arm, in the field under the blue sky. Maybe he was crazy from all the programming and augmenting.

But he wasn't crazy. It was a real place. And he would find it, and his mother, and Mel.

"Son, I fear you've lost your mind. All of the things I did to you—it's no wonder. And now you're pulling me into your madness." Robert was on the settee across from the bed. "But I'll come along into your mad world. I'll do what you want."

"Then you can do it? You can add a program to help me track S-drones?"

The doctor nodded. "What else?"

"There were things in the exoself that I never accessed. Can you help me find them, even if you're not the one who put them there?"

"Only a few people fed data into the exoself, and I supervised."

"I told you before that Mel put things in me—in the exoself—about her organization. I need that information."

"I can't believe she could do that. But if she did, it would work the same way I taught you to play tricks with the COP. You'd simply have to know which processor, which factor, to activate. There would be a code. But there is nothing that I didn't put there, or at least authorize."

"Let's get some sleep," Chase said. "Tomorrow, you're *not* doing what you've been told to do. Again. And I'm going rogue."

39

Chase knew when the doctor told him it was all a matter of finding the code that he already had what he needed. Patty told him he could access Mel's information trail if he could figure out how. This had to be it—Mel's gateway to the secrets she'd hidden in the exoself. He slept little that night. How did the code end up in his dreams, or whatever they were? He remembered the voice's last words.

"You are still mine."

He concentrated on the code, sparking the thirty-second processor and pulling the seventh factor. But he was void of the exoself. Nothing happened.

The doctor came in the morning with a gurney and a solution bag. "What's the drip for, Robert? Do you really need to knock me out to reprogram me?"

"We discussed this. Someone might notice if you're conscious. I have to put you under."

"Who's going to know? If the team is not assisting or observing, just put the bag on the gurney pole. Don't put the needle in me. I want to review the programs as they feed into the exoself." Chase stretched out on the gurney. "And I don't want to be slowed down by sedatives. I'm getting out of here."

The doctor shook his head. "I don't see how. How are you going to leave this place? Someone is bound to notice."

"Figure it out. Can't you make me run fast? Or

fly?"

The doctor laughed and slapped his wrinkled forehead. "You've been watching too many movies."

Chase sat straight and grabbed Robert's arm. "This is important. I've *got* to go."

"I know, son. We'll figure out something. But it would take time to install processors in your legs to make you run fast, and I'd *have* to knock you out. And flying is not an option." The doctor hooked the bag to the IV pole. "Unless you want to use a flight pack. There are some stored in lockers in the research lab. Of course, your phobia might be a problem."

"I think I can do it—the flight pack, I mean. Flying doesn't seem so scary anymore. But wouldn't there be a tracking device? They all have one."

"Have you ever used a flight pack, son?"

"No."

"You're right about the tracking device, but I could disable it. You'd have to learn how to use the thing. You can't just snap it on and start flying. And you're afraid to fly."

"Then program me."

"I told you before that I can't program away a phobia," Robert said.

"I said I can handle it. And you can give the exoself a flying lesson. Augmentation means people can gain years of education in only a few hours— remember? So give me some education. It can't take more than a few minutes to learn to use a flight pack."

"The educational programs haven't even been tested yet."

"So who better to try them out on?"

The doctor mumbled and turned to the door as Chase lay back and pulled the sheet to his neck. The door slid open, and Robert pushed the gurney into the hall.

"Will you do it or not? Will you plug me into a flight pack instructor?"

"Yes, yes. I'll do it. Now close your eyes and be still," Robert said. "I've set the cameras in the compound to show the next ten minutes as the last ten minutes, much like I taught you to do with the COP. No one will see us making this trek to the lab. Unless someone is outside, that is. But no one will be outside. They'll use the tunnels."

"This place has tunnels between the buildings?"

"Yes. If the other doctors leave the rear building to come to their rooms in the guest quarters, or to my laboratory, they will use the tunnels."

"So we'll stay up top. I get it," Chase said. "Robert?"

"Yes, son."

"The last time we were here, when you were about to install the NP, you told me there was code to override the system."

"You remember that? You didn't when you woke up from that procedure. The NP wouldn't let you."

"Will I need the code when you're done today?"

The doctor wheeled the gurney out of the guest house and into the open air. "Hush now. You're asleep."

Chase didn't speak again. He didn't move. But he did open his eyes for just a second. Blue sky filled his vision. He could almost hear Mel's voice. He couldn't wait to see her again. And his mom. How he missed her.

"Close your eyes," Robert said. "We're going to get caught. I know it."

"Only because you're talking to someone who's unconscious."

The door to the main building gave entrance. Chase kept his eyes shut as they moved through the lobby. He could tell by the echo of wheels on tile that they were in a hallway. Then he heard footsteps. Someone said hello.

"Yes, yes, good morning," the doctor said. The wheels turned faster, another door opened, and the gurney came to rest.

Chase opened his eyes. "Who was that?"

"I don't know," Robert said. "New tech, or nurse, I suppose. He didn't seem too interested in what I was doing. I didn't know anyone, much less a new employee, was even in the building."

"Do you think he'll tell the others that you're operating this morning?"

"I have no idea, son. Let's get this done."

"What about the code? Will I need it?"

"No, you won't need to override the system. There'll be no programmers, no central processor. You're in charge now."

"Then it's not really an exoself, is it? It won't depend on outside programming anymore."

The doctor paused, and his brow lifted. "We are reprogramming the exoself to continue within its host, without interference from external forces. This is a monumental day in history. But you're moving ever closer to what you're trying to escape. You know that, don't you?"

Chase had little understanding of this. "You're the one making history. After today, I hope you can stop history from repeating itself."

"Time will tell, son."

"What about the access code?" Chase sat on the gurney, but the doctor pushed him back down.

"That's something else entirely. Consider the exoself a freeway. There are exits you'll need to take to use the drone tracker or any other applications I add today, but you have to take the right exit, or you'll get nowhere."

"How will I find the exits?"

"The exoself, if we may still call it that, contains self-modifying programs. To execute programs, you'll have to access the code directly from the exoself."

"I have to access the access code?"

Robert walked around the laboratory flipping switches and touching light panels. "I know it sounds complicated, son. Well, it is. But you can do it."

Chase tried to relax while the doctor brought a massive control panel to life. This was no VPad. Numbers and bars and colored graphs lit up in the middle of the room. Robert walked around the phantom display, poking at it, pulling down lines of code and pushing numbers upward. "I'm adding some other programs," Robert said. "Once you've accessed the systems you'll be able to shut down certain electronics, among other things.

Chase watched as numbers appeared to float up and down in the room. "Can you tell me what thirty-two does?"

"What factor?"

"Seven."

Robert put his finger on the number thirty-two and pulled seven lines of code to cross it. "Nothing. Like I said, the system is self-modifying. Later it may mean something."

"I don't understand how I'll learn to use this thing

if the code changes all the time."

"Once a code is successfully accessed, it won't change. Unless you change it."

"This computer, this thing—does it know what we're doing?" Chase asked.

"Yes, in much the same way you are aware of the exoself, *it* is aware of you."

"Are you saying this is my exoself?"

"That's right, son."

"It's WR property. Will it turn us in?"

"I'm telling it that its primary goal from this day forward is to protect you."

"Before today what was its goal?"

"To use you. To bring you into compliance with WR computer models."

"But it's disconnected from the main brain, right?"

Robert came near and looked at Chase. "Main brain? Well, yes, it's disconnected. For that reason, the data won't update. You'll be going out of here with information that in only a few days will be outdated."

"Doesn't matter. I don't care about housing upgrades and job assignments. What about the COP?"

"No one will be able to activate the COP when you're disconnected from the system. Try to access the data bank, the way you did before," Robert said.

Chase closed his eyes and searched for the exoself. He found the WR information trails just like before, and the processors in his body sparked to life.

"It's coming, Robert." He opened his eyes and looked at his doctor. "Thank you."

"Don't thank me yet. I'm sure you're free of the main brain, as you put it. I like that, main brain. But—"

"But what?"

"The system may send a message that it's been

revived. Each of the team members installed code to protect the exoself from the tampering of the other members."

"So somebody might notice stuff is going in and not out as planned."

"It's possible."

The data from the exoself streamed into Chase's consciousness. It was too late to back out. "You didn't mention that earlier."

"There's an override code. But I don't know what it is."

"Who does?"

"The exoself knows. I programmed it to choose a code and not to share it with anyone." The doctor walked back to the lights and poked a number. "The exoself, hopefully, will use the code that only it knows and make itself invisible, so to speak."

"And if it doesn't?"

"One of the other team members may get a message."

Chase remembered the doctors who came into his suite with Kerstin. "There were four of your protégés at the estate. Team members?"

"Yes."

"Any others?"

"Thirteen in all. Any one of them could know by now what we're doing."

"I need to go," Chase said.

Robert moved to the wall and touched his fingers to a VPad monitor. As he typed, more numbers appeared on the big display glowing in the center of the room. Chase processed what the exoself brought. He didn't want to leave until the programming was complete, not knowing if Mel's input was there yet.

He'd find her information trails using the access code—the one in his head. He hoped. Like Robert said, right now the numbers meant nothing.

"Are all the team members here in the compound?"

"No, only the ones who came back with me from the estate. The rest are doing research from their homes. Or they're traveling—whatever. I don't keep tabs."

"So any one of them, wherever they might be, may know that I just got my exoself back."

"Perhaps we didn't think this through."

"*We*?"

The door slid open and a young man in scrubs walked in. Chase pushed up on his elbows. "Jimmy?"

Robert moved in front of the man. "Chase, this is the man we passed on the way in. You know him?"

"He worked at the estate," Chase said. "You must have seen him there."

"All scrubs look alike to me." Robert got right in Jimmy's face. "When did you get here? You weren't on the jet with us."

"I requested reassignment after you left," Jimmy said. "Got here yesterday."

Chase felt a rush as more of the exoself came in. "Jimmy, why?"

"I came to help you, Mr. Sterling. Patty asked me to find a way to get here."

"You can't just request a new assignment and have it handed to you," Chase said.

"What is he talking about?" Robert asked. "Who's Patty?"

Jimmy stepped around the six foot hologram of a computer screen. He stared at it briefly and shook his head. "What is this thing?"

No time for questions," Robert said.

"You're right about that," Jimmy said. "A message has gone out to someone in Flagstaff. I intercepted it on the institute's main system. It was a communication from the exoself."

The doctor seemed to go into some kind of fit. "Dr. Gaha lives in Flagstaff." He shook his fists and muttered about his life's work and going to prison and spending his final years with an NP in his brain. "And the worst part is," he said. "I've come so close to ending this nightmare for you, Chase. And now they'll come in here and stop us. They'll delete everything and pull out your sensors and processors. And you and I will both lose everything."

"Calm down," Chase said. "Jimmy, are the doctors in the other lab coming this way?

"Not yet."

"Robert," Chase said. "I've got to go."

"But the flight packs are in the other building. And you don't know how to use one anyway—I haven't programmed you yet."

"I can teach him," Jimmy said.

"You can't just walk into the research lab and take a flight pack from a locker," Robert said. "They'll want to know what you're doing. They'll want to know who you are. They'll remember you from the estate. This won't work." He walked a circle around the exoself, his hands on his head.

"You're not helping," Chase said.

"I have a flight pack," Jimmy said. "It's with my stuff in the staff locker room in the basement."

Information continued coming slowly and orderly from the reloading programs. "Can you continue the process if I fly away?" He looked to Robert for an answer.

"By the time he gets the pack and I deactivate the tracker, you'll be done." Robert looked at Jimmy. "Go, young man, and hurry."

40

Chase stretched out on the gurney, his mind filling with WR facts and figures. He caught on Kerstin's reassignment and studied it for a moment, and then let it file itself away. He found Jimmy's information as well. The move, executed by SynVue, was the first of many to reassign SynVue Estate personnel to the Helgen Institute. The network was taking over and Jimmy took advantage, apparently with Patty's prodding. The clock was back—Jimmy had been gone for 8.3 minutes. What was taking so long?

He heard a sound, distant, but coming nearer. Miles away, too far for Robert to notice with the hearing of a normal man, Chase heard the hum of a personal hovercraft. If the institute was its destination...

"Where is that kid?" Robert worked frantically, poking the exoself with both index fingers. "That kid. What's he doing here? We can't trust him. He's probably gone over to the research lab. They're probably coming with guards and weapons to take us away."

"Are you through?"

The doctor waved his arms before the massive display and then walked to the monitor and pushed one number. The exoself faded away. "Yes, son, the exoself is all yours."

"I meant are you through ranting." Chase stood

and pulled a shirt from under the gurney. "Someone is coming."

"How do you know that?" Robert asked.

"Air traffic headed this way. I can hear it."

"Gaha," Robert said.

Jimmy rushed in with the flight pack.

"I can't fly out of here," Chase said. "Not with a hovercraft coming."

"Take the pack with you," Jimmy said. "When you get away from the compound, put it on and go. It'll take you a good hundred miles."

"So I'm just going to walk out the gate?"

"Cyber-guards," Robert said.

"Exactly, they'll catch me."

"No, son, you'll be one."

"Just what I was thinking," Jimmy said. "There are some in the basement. Wake one up and bring it in here," he said to Robert.

"Yes, yes. Then you put on the guard's gear, Chase, and walk outside the gate." Robert went to a keypad on a desk. "I've got one coming. No one will pay it any mind. In fact, we've flown guards out of here before. Even sent one to town for tacos one time."

Jimmy slapped his knee. "This is great. Mr. Sterling, get ready to fly."

While Chase listened to Jimmy's express instructions for using a flight pack, Robert undressed the cyber-guard that had arrived from the basement. When the face shield came off, Chase was stunned to see that the robot had no face to speak of—only a tan, egg-shaped head with a light bar where eyes should be. It wasn't so intimidating with its gear stripped away. The thing was sent to a closet and shut down.

Robert opened up a keypad on the back of the

fight pack, pushed a few buttons, and put the pack under the gurney. "There, its tracker is deactivated."

Chase stepped into the snug-fitting uniform. He'd barely pulled on the helmet with the darkened face shield when the door slid open.

Dr. Bentley walked in. Chase gave a subtle point to the flight pack, and Jimmy quickly pulled down the sheet to cover the shelf beneath the gurney.

"Where is he?" Bentley yelled.

"Jack, I do not appreciate you coming into my laboratory this way," Robert said. "What's the problem?"

"I got a call from Dr. Gaha, who got a message from the exoself. The one we shut down," Jack yelled. "Where is Sterling?"

Chase stood perfectly still beside the gurney. Bentley looked at Jimmy. "What are you doing here? You're a nurse from SynVue Estate, aren't you?"

"Got reassigned," Jimmy said.

Robert stepped forward. "I sent for him. He and I worked closely on Sterling's programs. He will be an invaluable asset to our team."

"What have you done, Fiender? Why is this empty gurney here? Where is your patient?"

"*My* patient is in his room. This guard was just about to retrieve him. If you don't mind, I have much to do to prepare for the extractions."

"Since when do we use cyber-guards for med-techs? And why did Gaha get a message from the exoself? It says it's been reactivated."

"Nonsense," Robert said. "An anomaly, that's all."

"I'll just take a look if you don't mind."

Chase barely breathed when Bentley looked him right in the face. If Bentley powered the exoself, he'd find a system active and reloaded into its host. There had to be a way to hide it. The exoself had the power to become invisible—that's what Robert said. But only the exoself knew the code.

Bentley went to the monitor on the wall and touched it. Chase knew, somehow, he could stop this. The code from his dreams pounded in his head. He sparked to the thirty-second processor and pulled the seventh factor.

"Jack, please," Robert said. "Let it go."

But Jack's fingers stayed on the monitor. He punched the last number, turned to the center of the room, and waited. The light came up in the room and spread open. Nothing was there. Just light.

"See." Robert shook his finger in Bentley's face. "The exoself is dormant."

"I don't understand," Bentley said.

"An anomaly, like I said. Now please, let me get back to my work, and you get back to yours. I'm still in charge of this institute."

"Fine." Bentley headed for the door. "Gaha is flying in from Flagstaff because of this. You need to work on that thing, Robert. Make sure it doesn't bother us anymore."

"Yes, yes. I'll do that."

The door slid open, but Bentley turned before he stepped through. "One more thing," he said.

Chase didn't move.

"Could you send the guard to town for some tacos?"

"Of course. When he's done moving Mr. Sterling, I'll send him for some lunch. But you tell Gaha to go home. Tell her there's no reason to come. I'll never get my work done with her in my lab."

"I'll call her," Bentley said. "I'll tell her it was all a mistake." He went through the door and it slid shut.

Chase breathed a sigh and pulled off the face shield.

"I don't understand," Robert said. "The exoself didn't show itself. It hid from Bentley. It must have used the code. But why didn't it do that sooner, before it sent out a message?"

"*I* used the code. I did it myself." Chase slammed the face shield onto the gurney.

"Son, why do you look so disappointed?" Robert asked. "And how did you know the code?"

"I had the numbers in my head. But I thought they were for something else."

"The exoself told you the numbers. It's miraculous, really. It made the decision on its own to work through its host. It preserved its own life."

"If you say so." But Chase had lost a miracle. Now he didn't have a clue how to find Mel's programs. He'd thought the numbers were the key.

"Mr. Sterling, you need to go now," Jimmy said.

"You're right about that. What about you, Jimmy? Are you going back to Chicago?"

The young man smiled. "This is my new assignment—I guess I'll stay here. For now. Could be I'll need to move again."

Chase pushed the gurney to the door. Robert came beside him. "I'm so sorry, son, for my part in ruining your life." He pushed money into Chase's hand.

Chase put his arm around the old man's neck. "Everything happens for a reason."

"I doubt that, son."

"It's true. My father told me so."

The doctor nodded and sighed. "Whatever you

say. I'll keep them from finding out you're gone as long as I can."

"They'll know you had a hand in this."

"They already think you can shut down the guards. After you're gone, we'll take the stripped down guard to your room and leave it on the gurney. They won't know I helped you escape. But they'll come after you, son."

"They won't catch me. I'm not sure you'd approve of what I'm going to do with your creation. But I'm going and no one can stop me."

"I trust you fully with my creation, as you call it. You're a good man. Much the better man than that imposter, Chase Sterling."

Chase took Robert by the arm. "There's something else you can do for me."

"Anything, son."

"The woman I brought out of the audience that night on the new show — she's really sick. Cancer, and it's bad."

"The vaccine doesn't prevent all types of cancer. Toxic poisoning is just a term given to the ones that were not eliminated. Even worse, the vaccine causes organ failure in about a tenth of the people who receive it — a government cover-up we scientists helped propagate."

"I'll have to process that revelation later. Will you see if you can find her?"

"I'll do what I can," he said. "I replaced the NP with a device that will allow you to send me a message. I won't respond, but later on, when you're away from here, let me know you're all right."

"How do I use it?"

"You'll figure it out. You just used a code no

human could know."

"You put too much faith in me. I haven't got a clue how to do this without you." Chase hugged the doctor one last time, and then shook Jimmy's hand. He pulled down the face shield as the doctor moved in front of him to activate the door. The gurney rolled onto the tile floor as Chase pushed it forward, down the hall, and out of the building. He rolled it to the guest quarters and left it in his empty room, underneath the Picasso. Then he walked outside, used the keypad built into the vest of the cyber-guard's uniform to open the gate, and walked away with the flight pack draped over his shoulder.

"I have no idea what I'm doing," he said. "Or where I'm going. Or how to fly." He could still hear the hover craft in the distance, but the sound was moving away. Gaha wouldn't land her craft here today. Chase wondered if the old woman flew the thing herself.

He pulled the pack on, fastened it around his waist, and touched the panel that covered his chest. A low hum emitted from the flight pack. "I wish I wasn't scared out of my mind." Then, as Jimmy had instructed, he yanked on the silver cord hanging below the panel. And he lifted off the ground.

He swallowed a scream as his eyes were forced open. His legs flailed. He grabbed the hand controls, and solid ground got farther and farther away. He kept his eyes on the desert floor.

But he had to look forward. He turned his face to the white hot sky, he opened his eyes. Nothing but strings of clouds surrounded him. Nothing held him. He was free. "Thank God," he said. And he meant it.

A sound filled him beyond the *whoosh* of the air and the hum of the flight pack. Something was coming.

He looked to his left and there was the hovercraft, not moving away, but toward him. It came so close that Chase could see inside. And there sat Dr. Gaha at the controls, looking back at him.

He gave a proper cyber-guard nod to his superior. She made no gesture in return. After a few seconds, she lifted the brow on her wrinkled old face and shook her head. And then she turned the craft and flew away.

Chase sighed in relief. He faced forward, not knowing what lie ahead or how to find his way to where he knew he should be. Nothing was certain except this freedom. And for the moment, even though he was a hundred feet in the air, he was not afraid.

41

Chase brought himself to the ground in a remote area in the Southwest Territory. The exoself told him he was seventeen miles from Phoenix. The money Robert had given him wouldn't last long. A few people sat around a table outside a food and power stop. They'd be frightened by the cyber-guard getup—those things didn't typically patrol small desert towns. But he didn't dare remove the face shield. He was still, after all, a celebrity. The last thing he needed was a crowd, even a small one, ogling Chase Sterling.

"What am I worried about? The world has probably forgotten me by now."

A woman came near, a VPad to her face. Chase removed the mask and stood in front of her.

"Get out of my way," she said. Then she looked at his clothes and fear lit her eyes.

"I'm not really a guard," he told her.

She looked at his face. "Oh, my goodness, a cyber-guard that looks like Chase Sterling. Is this some kind of new show? Am I on camera right now?" She smiled.

Chase played along. He stared ahead and tried not to show any expression. "I am a SynVue project model recreation of Chase Sterling."

"I didn't know guards could talk like that. You're really cutting edge," she said. "The real Chase Sterling was better looking, but what a jerk. I hope you're not a letdown like he was. What do they plan to do with you?"

"They will gather public opinion. Thank you for your input."

She giggled and stroked her VPad as she hurried away. Chase could hear her talking.

"You won't believe what just happened to me," she said into the VPad. "They've got some robot Chase Sterling going around asking people their opinions. I thought he was a cyber-guard, but he's just a PR machine."

"Mistake number one, you idiot. Don't talk to people with your face uncovered." He got out of sight before the girl had a chance to point him out to the people sitting at the table.

"The real Chase Sterling was better looking?" He shook his head.

The exoself provided information about the town. A block away, he'd find a laundry station. This might be the first day of his augmented life he'd found practical application for the stuff loaded into his head. The only man inside the rundown place sat slumped in a plastic chair, his eyes closed, his breathing heavy.

Chase went through the open glass doors and pulled the handle on the front of the only machine in operation. The wash and dry tumbler was at the end of the cycle, and the clothes inside were warm. He pulled them out and picked a pair of slacks and a shirt, then threw the rest back into the machine. He started to walk away, but then he turned back, pulled out a couple of his few WR bills, and threw them in the machine.

He found the restroom and peeled away the cyber-guard suit. The clothes were a good fit. The guard boots would have to suffice. And the face shield, with a little work, could look like something else.

Using his augmented muscles, he broke the shield away from the helmet. He went back out to the laundry station and pulled a black cord from the edge of a mesh basket. It'd been a few years, but college kids used to cover their faces in protest to WR policies. He ran the black cord through fastener holes on the sides of the shield and then put it up to face and tied it off at the back of his neck.

He caught his reflection in the glass door. Guard boots, jeans, a black T-shirt, a dark mask, and a flight pack. That said it all—dead-beat rebel making a statement while he traveled the country. He hoisted the pack over his shoulder and went out on the street.

A few more blocks brought him to a food truck— Mexican delicacies on wheels. He pulled out the rest of the WR bills and got himself some lunch. "What's with the mask?" The guy handed Chase three tacos and a cola.

"Protesting."

"Protesting what? Nobody does that anymore. You been in a cave for ten years?" The man laughed. "You gotta take that thing off to eat."

"I will not remove the mask until the government admits that toxin poisoning is just another name for cancer."

"Yeah, man, I always thought that. You think it's true?"

"I know it for a fact. Spread the word."

"OK, yeah, I can do that. Thanks, man."

Chase nodded and walked away. He found a dark corner behind an old hotel and pulled the mask up enough to get his teeth into a taco.

He had to get out of the Southwest Territory.

Robert and Jimmy couldn't hide the fact for long that Chase Sterling was not where he should be. Gaha would tell the others she saw a guard with a flight pack well beyond the point of a lunch run.

With his feet back on solid ground, Chase dreaded the thought of flying to Atlanta, but that's where Patty said Mel went. That's all he had now that the code he'd been counting on was not what it seemed. He'd get to Atlanta. But he'd just as soon walk.

He heard a train in the distance. The old-fashioned way of getting products from one place to another was still in operation, especially from points headed south. No passengers on board, only merchandise. He prompted the exoself. Nearest station was in Phoenix. He could fly that far after charging the pack at the food and power stop. But he didn't want to pay the price of a plug in.

He finished his lunch, pulled down the shield, and walked through the small town. He passed a shop with an open door and a storekeeper within earshot. "Mind if I plug my pack in for ten minutes?" he asked.

"No power on the street," the woman said. "Come inside."

Chase walked in, his face still covered. The Asian woman, probably not five feet tall, grabbed the pack off his shoulder and hooked it to the power stand by the pay scanner.

"Thanks. I don't need much. I'm just flying as far as Phoenix."

"You want a ride to Phoenix? My husband is going there to pick up some merchandise." She laughed a bit and slapped her hand on the counter. "What am I saying? You've got a flight pack—you'd rather fly than ride."

"You'd offer your husband to a stranger in a face shield?"

"He won't care what you look like, friend. Why are you hiding? Something bad happen to your face?"

"No, I'm protesting."

"Seems like a waste of time, but OK. You protest." She smiled.

"If you're sure it's not a problem, I'll take that ride."

"I'll go tell my husband. He won't mind. He'd appreciate the company." The woman left Chase standing in the doorway of what seemed to be a gift shop. Or maybe antiques. Chase didn't know the difference, and the exoself offered no information about such things. He stepped to a shelf and ran his finger over a row of delicate vases and figurines. He thought of the cabinet full of knickknacks in the living room of his parents' house.

A man came from the back of the store and gave Chase a firm handshake. "Perry Chang," he said. "Wife says you need a ride. I'm only going as far as the train station. Leaving in ten—is that OK?"

"You're going to the station?"

"Yep, but that's it. Is it close enough to town for you?"

"I'll be out front."

"You need a duffle," Mrs. Chang said. She walked out of sight for a minute or two, and returned with a black zip pack with a shoulder strap. "It matches your mask." She draped it over his arm. "Even a super hero needs something to carry his socks in."

"What makes you think I'm a super hero?"

"Don't worry, I won't tell." She smiled big, and if she could have seen his face, she'd have seen Chase smiling back. "Thanks. What's your name?"

"Zoe. What's yours?"

"The Masked Rebel."

The woman laughed as Chase unplugged his flight pack and headed for the street.

"Thanks for the charge, Zoe, and the duffle." A truck—it must have been thirty years old—pulled up to the sidewalk.

"My pleasure, Masked Rebel." She waved good-bye to Chase and blew a kiss to her husband.

Chase unzipped the black bag and found a sandwich, an apple, and two bottles of water. "This is all I've got to my name," he said. "Thank you for your generosity."

"If that's all you've got, what do you plan to do at the train station?"

"I guess I'll cross that track when I get to it."

"You know that no one really travels by train anymore, don't you? The only people who get on trains are stowaways. You look the part, but you don't seem like you know what you're doing." Mr. Chang turned onto the highway. "Tell me your real name."

He thought about it for a moment. "Um. Charles. Or Charlie, if you prefer."

"Somebody looking for you?"

"Could be." Chase rubbed his hand across the dash of the old truck. "I've heard about antiques vehicles reworked to run on electricity, but I've never seen one."

"You're changing the subject. Why are you running? And where are you going?"

Chase didn't answer.

"Listen, I've got a friend at the station. He helps me with transport. Sometimes it's merchandise;

sometimes it's people. I can get you on a train, but I need to know where you're going."

"Atlanta."

"You got family there?"

"I hope so."

Perry got in the speed lane and passed a couple of cars. "Old trucks beat new Selfdrives every time," he said. "You're a man of mystery, Charles. Why do you wear that face shield?"

"Protesting WR propaganda."

"Well, I don't like too much about the WR. So go ahead and take that thing off—I'm on your side."

Chase didn't move.

"You can trust me. I'm good at keeping secrets."

"It wouldn't be the first dumb thing I've done today." Chase reached behind his neck and untied the cord. The face shield fell to his lap.

Perry looked him in the eye. "Chase Sterling. I wondered what happened to you. I thought they shut you down."

"Is that what people are saying?"

"That and more. SynVue said the things they tried on you needed more work, and they put you in some kind of coma until they could fix you. Your fans are divided. Some say the network will bring you back better than ever. Some say they hope you're gone for good. They say you ruined everyone's chance at getting some augmentation."

"Because of what happened on the air with Larin Andrews?"

"You were a little scary that night, my friend. But the whole show was ridiculous."

"Were you a fan of *Change Your Life*?"

"Not so much. We watched the special a couple of

weeks ago because everybody was saying it would change the world, but normally Zoe and I don't watch much GV. We don't even get the signals for SynVue back there in our little store without catching a link from a rogue source. We live in the basement, pick up some signals put out by the Constitution Rebels."

"You and Zoe are out of the system?" Chase wiped the sweat from his forehead and ran his fingers through his uncombed hair.

"For ten years now."

"But you live like normal people. You're a business owner."

"The WR doesn't concern itself with small-town junk stores."

Chase looked out the window as the desert became dotted with office buildings and housing. The traffic grew heavy. "I didn't know people outside the system couldn't get GV signals." He turned to face Perry. "I'm surprised you even knew who I was."

"Everybody knows who you are, Chase. Better put that mask back on."

He pulled the face shield tight and tied the cord.

42

Chase got a little money from Perry Chang. Not that he asked for it. The man just handed it to him. Perry left him in the care of a Western Republic Rails worker named Frank. And Frank put him on a train bound for Atlanta.

Nothing in the old forty-foot boxcar indicated Chase would travel in style and comfort. The air was hot and dry. Frank had offered him a choice — ride in a hot car or a refrigerated car. Chase opted for heat. His augmentation did nothing for temp control. At least he wasn't shivering.

"Atlanta, here I come" He settled between two crates and pulled off the face shield. "Somebody tell me what to do when I get there."

He tied Zoe's black zip bag to the flight pack after he gulped from a water bottle. He'd eat again when the sun went down. Right now he had to rest. The exoself told him how many stops the train would make before it reached Atlanta. He had plenty of time and nothing to do. He drifted off.

❧

"See, Charlie, I told you your mother could get it out of the bottle."

"What does it say, Dad?"

"It's the code, son. The numbers you need."

"What are they?"

"Thirty-two, seven."

"I don't think so, Dad. I already used that code."

"Do it again, Charlie. Or you'll—"

Chase pushed himself up between the crates that hid him among the cargo. He panted and wiped the sweat from his face. The numbers played in his mind. They danced. They sang to the tune of some old childhood song. "I don't know what to do. Help me."

The train was still. Chase pulled up the schedule in his head and noted they'd stopped in Roswell. "Aliens. Great, that's all I need."

He thought about Robert. Chase could track drones now, but the doctor didn't tell him how. Was he just supposed to figure it out?

"What am I doing out here on my own?" Sunlight barely filtered in through a few holes in the old boxcar. The darkness made him lonely. And hungry. He powered his night vision, pulled the sandwich from the zip bag, and removed the poly wrapper.

"Smells like turkey." He bit into it. "Tastes like turkey." Before he could swallow the first bite, the door of the boxcar slid open and a man rolled onto the dirty floor. He came to a stop not ten feet from Chase.

Chase grabbed the shield and covered his face before the man sat up and looked his way.

"I don't want no trouble," the man said. "That mask you got looks like something off a cyber-guard." He came closer and poked Chase in the chest. "You a robot?"

"No. Just a traveler like you." Chase tied the cord behind his neck. He wrapped the sandwich and stuffed it back in the bag.

"What's with the mask?"

"Protesting."

"Oh, yeah, I did that back at Berkley."

"You went to Berkley?"

The man rolled backward and laughed. "No, man. I didn't go nowhere."

Chase faked a laugh and turned so that he didn't face the stranger directly. But he kept an eye on him. The man scooted a few yards away and settled in between two crates. "Getting off in Shreveport," he said. "Looks like we'll be together all the way through what used to be the great state of Texas."

"Let me guess," Chase said. "You're with the Dissenters of the Republic."

"That's right. You?"

Chase didn't know what to tell him. He wasn't a part of the man's group of rogues. He wasn't a Constitution Rebel. He was looking for the Underground Church, but he didn't belong to that group either.

"Just set out on my own," he said after a moment. "Heard something I thought I should share with the world, but I don't want to go to prison for it."

"What'd you find? Got some dirt on the WR?"

"Cancer vaccines cause organ failure. Big government cover-up. Tell your people."

"I didn't get no vaccine. I knew they'd screw it up. I guess I was right."

Chase had gotten it—all normal working citizens of the WR got one. He thought about his replicated parts. At least organ failure was one thing he didn't have to worry about. The train lurched forward and quickly worked up to full speed. The boxcars were old, but the engine was nuclear, and the tracks were revamped for speed. That's what the exoself reported.

With the train on the move and the sunlight dimming, Chase decided to drop the mask. The old guy wouldn't come close enough to see him in the dark. He put the face shield at his side and got out the sandwich.

"Can't see it too good from here," the man said. "But it smells like turkey."

Chase scarfed another bite, but then he wrapped the poly around what was left and slid the sandwich across the boxcar floor.

"Thanks. I ain't eaten in two days."

"You're welcome."

"Wonder how long it takes to get to Shreveport," the man said with his mouth full.

"Six hours, seventeen minutes, allowing for stops in Abilene and Fort Worth," Chase said it too quickly.

"How'd you know that? I thought you said you just set out on your own."

"Well, I studied the schedule before I left."

"Oh. Sure. What's your name, stranger?"

"It's Charles, or Charlie. Yours?"

"Gabe," he said. "In Abilene, I'll get off and get us some more food."

"That sounds good, Gabe."

Hours passed, and Gabe said little else. He slept for two hours. In Abilene, he slithered off the boxcar. Chase thought he'd been snagged or else had a change of plans. But right before the train started moving, the rogue food grabber returned with a bag of burritos, two colas, and a cherry pie.

"How'd you end up with a whole pie?" Chase asked.

"Little old lady was taking it to her grandkids."

"And you just took it?"

Gabe laughed, the way he did before. "Man, you are so green. Ain't no old ladies getting on this train. Let's just say I bought it with tokens I had coming to me. How else would I survive?"

"Oh." The exoself made Chase smart. But he wasn't too bright.

They ate in companionable silence. They still had a long way to go. Gabe kept his distance, and Chase stayed in the shadows, the face shield still at his side. Conversations came and went. Gabe had been an oil rig worker in his younger days. When the world stopped drilling, he dropped off the grid. He had a wife and two kids when he joined the DR, but his wife couldn't deal with it. She left him and integrated back into the work force. He hadn't seen his kids in years.

"They must have kids of their own by now," he said.

Chase wondered, if he tried, maybe he could tell Gabe where his kids were. Maybe the exoself could reunite long lost family members. It would make a great show. He shook his head and smirked. "Idiot, those days are gone."

"Well, don't insult me, man. I can't help thinking about what I lost."

Chase lifted his eyes and looked at Gabe's dark form. "No, not you. I'm sorry, my mind wandered. I was calling myself an idiot, not you."

"What's your story, Charles?"

"I told you, I'm protesting."

"You said you just took up the cause. What'd you do a month ago? A year ago?"

"I had a good job. Better than most. I worked for SynVue."

"SynVue—don't get me started. You left because

of all that mess with those two game shows, didn't you? Everybody's gonna get smart and live forever. Bunch of liars. I hope they shut the whole network down. The whole blasted thing. The world don't need more lies. The world just needs to know the truth."

"What's the truth, Gabe?"

The man moved back between the crates until all Chase could see was his legs.

"The truth is this world is messed up, friend. You did the right thing—getting out of that circus. You'd be welcomed by the DR if you want to join us."

"Thanks," Chase said. "I'll think on that. Right now, there's someplace I've got to go."

43

Chase said good-bye to Gabe in Shreveport. Hours to go before he got to Atlanta. He settled back and thought about the night he'd carried Larin off the stage. Gabe said there were promises that everyone would be smart and live forever. Is that what Larin told the audience when Kerstin sent him back to the stage?

What a world it would be if everybody had what Chase had. Not that he expected to live forever. But he'd live longer than he should, and he knew more than he needed to know. If everybody became like him, could they end war and poverty and social injustice?

Or would smarter people who live longer only add to the world's problems? "I've got to concentrate on what I *can* do."

He sparked his processors—all of them. "Somewhere in there is a drone tracker and a trail of information about the Underground Church." He stretched his arms. "Maybe if I just start combining processors and factors, I'll get lucky." He pulled the apple from his bag. "Or maybe I'll accidentally call the WR security force and tell them where to find me." He took a bite. "Or maybe I'll blow up the world."

He knew better than to start some random coding process. In the dream he'd had earlier, his father told him to use the code again: 32-7. But it was just a dream—not like the ones from before. Not that they meant anything either.

"I need an instruction manual. Come on exoself, old friend. Give me something."

At once the visual of the phantom screen that had hovered in the lab filled his mind. Numbers were there, and lines of code. They moved up and down until numbers and lines crossed. The exoself had given him his request.

He did not find the number thirty-two on the mental screen at all. What did pop out brighter than the others was the number fifteen. Three lines of code pushed the number to the top.

He sparked the fifteenth processor and gave a mental tug to the number three. And a complete grid of drone deployment was there. No S-drones active— not within the borders of the WR. But thirty were in ready position in and around Atlanta.

"Drones around Atlanta means I'm headed in the right direction. Thank you, Robert. You should have told me all I had to do was ask the exoself for instructions."

He watched the screen in his mind again, and the number twelve intersected with two lines. He sparked the twelfth processor and pulled twice. And he knew the device in his ear—the one Robert used to replace the NP—was installing a link to an information route that would end at an old laptop. The antiquated system was registered to Robert Fiender. That's where Chase could send a message.

"I'm on a train, Robert. Headed for…" He decided against giving too much information. Somebody might intercept. "I'm going to the place I belong. I don't know how I know that, but I do. I'm working with the exoself to gain access to the programs I need. Thanks for all you did for me."

He let the lines drop the number and the transmission ended. The drone tracker, he sealed in place. He wasn't sure how he accomplished this, but the tracker was connected permanently. This new manipulation of the exoself was a mental and physical chore. Chase closed his eyes and let the screen fade away. "I've got to find somebody in the underground. Give me a few minutes." Sleep nearly took him, but the train slowed enough to get his attention.

"Must be coming in to Birmingham." It wouldn't be long now before he arrived in Atlanta.

The next time he opened his eyes, the train was at full speed. He checked the exoself's familiar program of mapping and mileage, and knew he was only forty miles from his destination. He'd better get the phantom grid back up and see if he could find Mel's information trails, or else he'd be wandering around Atlanta at sunrise with no idea where to go.

But the exercise produced nothing that he didn't already know. The number of secret churches in particular cities of each territory was there. No way to find the exact locations of the underground operations. Three base churches were in or around Atlanta, but that limited information didn't do him any good. Some church houses in certain cities showed directions, but not one in Atlanta listed a location. Maybe he was just tired. The process did seem to wear him out. Or maybe some things were so hidden that they didn't come up easily. The train slowed, and he tied on his mask and grabbed the flight pack. Once the old boxcar gave its last grind on the tracks, Chase eased his way to the big door and slowly pulled it open. He peered through the crack.

Workers came and went from the train, removing crates from the boxcars and swiping their VPads or taking crates off pallets and stacking them on electric loaders. Before he could jump out of the door, it slid all the way open and a man began yelling instructions.

"Get this car emptied. We've got twenty minutes."

Chase backed against the wall. He held his breath. But the man came onboard and it didn't take long for him to spot the stowaway on his train.

"Get out of here. You got your ride," he yelled as he pulled a metal rod from behind his back. "Now get."

Chase jumped to the track and took off. He slowed when he realized no one was after him.

The Atlanta station was one of the largest in the country, so said the exoself. All supplies for the Southeast Territory came through here. Dozens of people filled every walkway. Chase found an old terminal that was probably used when the trains carried passengers. A few loners were huddled in corners or stretched on the floor of the dilapidated building. "Larin's village would be a step up for these people."

The bathroom was filthy, but it didn't matter. After he washed his hands and face, he walked back into the budding daylight. He noticed two cyber-guards and turned and went the other way. But he listened for anything coming from their direction.

"I am the resurrection and the life. He who believes in Me, though he die, yet shall he live." The voice was feminine. Chase could hear the shuffle of guard boots and the resistance of the woman as she continued speaking. "He who believes in Me will live, even though he dies."

Nearby, he could see a guard transport. A blunt sound like the smack of a cyborg's arm against flesh filled his ears, and then the two guards came by him with the woman in a laser band. She was young—probably no more than twenty—and her arms were bound at her side by the beam of light. Long blonde hair fell against her ripped green shirt. She was forced onto the open-sided Selfdrive and hauled away. Chase powered down the hearing enhancer. He didn't want to hear this anymore.

"Though he die, yet shall he live," Chase said. He considered this in light of his own recent revival from death.

"Lots of guards around here 'cause of all the stuff that goes on in Atlanta." The voice came from just behind Chase, and he turned around. "What's with the mask?" A small boy stood before him.

Chase studied the child. Grime covered his sandy blond hair and tan face. "What are you doing here by yourself?" he asked the boy. "How old are you?"

"Goin' on ten. I'm here 'cause I get fed. Boss man gives me chores. And dinner."

"Where are your parents?"

"Jail, I guess. Haven't seen them in a while. But when they get out, I'll be here. They'll find me."

"Did they get arrested like the young lady? Were they proselytizing?"

"Huh?"

"Talking about religious stuff when they should have been quiet."

"No, they're not Christians, just DR people. All of them go to jail, though. Everybody with a message goes to jail."

"And there are a lot of guards around Atlanta, because there are a lot of messages. Is that right?" The exoself streamed information about the number of cyber-guards in Atlanta, but Chase made the correlation on his own. Even this kid knew why the guards were plentiful here.

"Yep. All kinds here. Dissenters of the Republic, Constitution Rebels, all kinds of religions. But Christians get the most trouble. I don't know why they take grief from the guards. They don't talk too much, and they're good people. Fed me lots of times."

"Do you know where they hide out?"

"Underground."

"Yea, I know it's called the Underground Church. But do you know where I could find some of them?"

"Mister, you ever been to Atlanta?"

"Not since I was a kid."

"You go downtown. Get on MLK, go past the old parking garages—they're all boarded up. So are the tunnels to the underground, but a smart man can get inside."

"You mean the Underground Church is really underground? Underground Atlanta?"

"Hey, you didn't hear it from me," the boy said. "But yeah, that's it. Under the roads, down where the stores used to be. That's where they go before the sun comes up. If you got a VPad on you, it'll give you better directions to get downtown."

"I can get directions," Chase said. "Thanks, kid."

The boy stood there, staring. "Mister?"

"What is it?"

"I hope I didn't just turn in all those people. You standing there with that face shield on makes me wonder if you're a guard."

"You ever heard a guard carry on a conversation like this?"

"No, they don't say nothing but 'move along,' or 'stop,' or 'come with me.' That's about it."

"That's because they can't talk like you and me. Their programming is basic enforcement stuff, and I'm not one of them." Chase pulled the boy closer to the wall. "I'm protesting. That's all. That's why I'm wearing the shield."

"I heard guards can talk more than they used to. They got a guard in the Southwest Territory that looks like Chase Sterling."

"You heard about that? What else did you hear?"

"He's showing up all over the place, asking people what they think, giving them cars and flight packs."

Chase smiled. Not that the boy could see his face. "Really? Cars and flight packs?"

"Yeah, some new game show. I guess it'll be on GV soon."

"Well, it might just be a rumor. People have a way of blowing things out of proportion." Chase hefted his pack over his shoulder and held out his hand to the boy. "Thanks. What's your name?"

"Thomas." The boy shook his hand. "What's yours?"

"Charlie. Maybe I'll see you around, Thomas."

"Be careful out there, Charlie."

Walking away, Chase waved to the boy. Then he pulled a map from the exoself and headed for downtown Atlanta.

44

The exoself gave Chase more information than he needed about the old shopping venue and the night clubs that used to draw people to the underbelly of Atlanta. The WR didn't maintain the place, and it shut down.

He figured the best way to get to downtown was to fly. It wasn't far. He hooked up the pack and powered it. Takeoff was easier this time. But the sky over Atlanta was filled with flyers. Even with the sky grid marked clear by the exoself, maneuvering brought a new level of fear. He wouldn't make a habit of this mode of transportation. At least not in metro areas. The heart of this city was not where he'd expected to go. This was not the place to find an open field like the one in his dreams. He looked as far as he could see to the outskirts of the city. Just business parks and housing. A couple of sporting areas spread out to the south.

Chase put his feet on the ground in a parking lot between two skyscrapers. A man in a booth yelled at him for landing in a parking space instead of on the personal landing pad at the north end of the lot. The exoself hadn't explained anything about parking lot protocol.

As he came to the boarded-up tunnels that hid Atlanta's past, he searched the exoself for anything Mel might have programmed. A cyber-guard walked the distance from the nearest parking garage to the boarded-up entrance. When Chase passed within ten feet of the guard, it stopped and seemed to study him. "Move along," was all the simpleton said.

But Chase knew better than to defy orders. Even with his augmentation, the thing was stronger than him. So he walked away. A few blocks brought him to a lady with a cart selling hot dogs. He ate one as he walked back to the tunnels, and he hid behind an old dumpster and watched the guard.

He also watched for people sneaking into, or out of, the place. For six hours no one even walked by. Except the cyber-guard.

But before the sun was completely gone, a real live policeman came by in a Selfdrive with a light band on top. He stopped a hundred feet from the dumpster and got out of his vehicle. Then he whistled like a man would do to call his dog. The cyber-guard walked right to the cop, and the human stuck his hand in the robot's shirt. And he shut him down. He looked around before he grabbed the guard by the arm and hauled him in the direction of the dumpster.

Chase squatted close to the backside of the green receptacle, but the officer came to the rear, the guard in tow. Chase could run, but he knew he couldn't get away.

The cop didn't seem surprised to see him hunched there. "Guard's off duty 'til dawn, buddy. Go on in if you want." He bent the guard so that its face shield came an inch from its knees, and he walked away.

Chase stood up and followed him. "How...Why did you do that?"

The cop turned around. "You must be new around here. He's a cylon—an old model. Easy to mess with. I put a program disk under his shirt almost two years ago. When I call him, he comes. And I turn him off. He regenerates in ten hours. Gives the people inside time to come out and make their rounds, newbies like you time to go in and get acquainted." He headed for his car. "So, go on in. The old entrance is covered over with refuse blocks, all except for two tunnels. Boards over the second tunnel come off easily."

"Are you one of them?" Chase asked.

"Me? No, I got too much blood on my hands to join their group. I just look out for them."

"Nobody ever comes to check on the guard? What about cameras in the area?"

"They come the second Thursday of the month. The night before, I take my disk. The night after, I put it back. And the guard lets me. He seems to like me." He pointed to the top of metal pole. "As for the camera, I shot it out before I started messing with the guard. Nobody ever came to fix it."

"That's amazing."

"Yeah, yeah, it's a miracle. That's what you people say. By the way, I don't care what guard you took that face shield from, but you can't walk around the city like that and expect to go unnoticed.

"I'm protesting."

"The people underground—at least the ones I know—don't protest. They're real quiet. You might want to think about that before you go in."

"Thanks."

The officer drove away, and Chase went to the closest tunnel entrance and pulled the boards loose. He stepped inside and put the boards back. And then he turned around.

"Hello?"

No one answered. Chase hid the flight pack

behind an old metal trash can. He started walking.

The night vision allowed him to see the boarded-up store fronts covered with graffiti. Some of the writing was old and faded. And vulgar. But some seemed newer and orderly. And purposeful. This was a school of some sort. Simple sentences and math problems filled a fifty foot section of plywood. After that, the work got harder, and farther down the walk, harder still.

"People teach their children here." Chase rubbed his hand over a poem written on the wall where kids must study their lessons.

The wicked draw their sword and bend the bow
To bring down the poor and needy,
To slay those whose way is upright;
But their swords will pierce their own hearts,
And their bows shall be broken.
Better the little that the righteous have
Than the wealth of many wicked.
Ps. 37:14-16

More writings covered the wall. He stopped before one that was only a line, really, and not a poem.

You are my hiding place; you will protect me from *trouble and surround me with songs of deliverance.* Ps. 32:7

Chase studied this one. He repeated it aloud. He uttered the numbers. The code. "Thirty-two, seven. A hiding place." The exoself had hidden itself when Chase used the code. And here was a message of some kind about hiding, about being kept from trouble. And it had the code written beneath it.

"P-s—what is that? Post script?" He walked back and forth in front of the verse. "No. It's from the Psalms."

He went farther into the dark chamber. If anyone

were hiding there, they didn't show themselves. The walls and boarded-up storefronts here contained more writings, but the farther he got, the less the place seemed like a classroom. It became more like a conference room. Maps of Atlanta were taped to the walls, locations marked in red. Chase studied the routes and roads the people he was looking for might travel. But where were the people? He walked a little farther. And then he saw words written on a board that made him stop.

Day after day they pour forth speech; night after night they display knowledge.

Ps. 19:2

Underneath this was an instruction.

Listen and learn.

And a name.

Mel

Chase touched her name. No one called her that but him. She'd left him a message. A key. A code. But why leave this for him when she was here somewhere?

He sparked the nineteenth processor and pulled the number two. Another message flooded his mind.

Four *S's*—sympathizers, supplies, safe travel, secret houses. Search the Psalms.

That was all the code got him. It wasn't much. But he smiled under his darkened mask. He turned to go farther down the walk, but his hearing enhancers picked up a sound. A whisper.

Somewhere nearby, someone prayed.

45

Chase followed the low resonance of the man's voice back toward the tunnel's beginning. He'd passed them. A store boarded up and covered with writing—potential code, he guessed—was where he stopped. He pulled a board loose and dropped it, and the praying stopped. He tore another board free and stepped through to the other side. A few lit candles lined the walls where a dozen people were on their knees, their heads bowed. Some were shaking. Some of them peered at him. One of them screamed.

"It's OK. I'm not here to cause you any trouble. I'm just looking for someone."

A huge man, deep black skin and all muscles, stood from the group. "Drop the mask. Show yourself."

Chase hesitated, and the big man lunged and tackled him to the floor. More by instinct than anything, Chase turned the man over and pinned him.

More than one scream went up at that. Chase quickly got off the man and stood with his hands in the air. "I don't want to hurt anybody."

"You're stronger than you look," the man said. "Now drop the mask. I won't go so easy on you next time."

He untied the cord and pulled off the face shield. And waited.

The big black man was the first to laugh, and soon

they were all laughing. Some fell to their bottoms. Some stood. One of the women who'd screamed came to put her arms around Chase.

"Chase Sterling." The woman seemed to weep now more than laugh. "Thank God. We've been praying for you."

Chase returned her hug with a pat on the back, and then he pulled away. "Were you expecting me?"

"We only hoped you'd end up somewhere in the underground," she said. "A message went out that you escaped. We're just so glad to see you."

"Melody Reese," he said. "That's who I'm looking for. Is she here?"

"No, Chase. She was here, but she's gone back up north."

The news sank deep, even into his manmade heart. "She's gone?" He turned to the wall and then turned back. "My mother?"

The big man came near. "Melody said she met your mother in New York, but I don't know if they're together now. Last we heard, Melody was gathering supplies to take to the Far North Territory."

"I can't believe she didn't wait for me." Chase rubbed his eyes and then crossed his arms.

"She didn't know you'd come here. She thought that you thought she was in New York. She said you called her there."

"I did, but I didn't get a chance to talk to her. Then someone told me she was here."

"Communication is difficult. But it'll be easier now." The man smiled.

"How so?"

"Because you tapped into Melody's database. Right? How else would you have ended up here?"

"I'm only just getting into Mel's programs. A kid at the train station told me where to find you." Chase looked over the crowd. "He said this was the place in Atlanta to find the Underground Church."

The woman who'd hugged him handed him a glass of water. "How'd you end up coming to Atlanta? Who told you Melody was here?"

"A nurse named Patty. Do you know her?"

"Melody never mentioned a nurse," the woman said. Chase drank the water in one long series of swallows. He slid down the wall until he sat on the cold floor with his elbows on his knees and his head in his hands.

"I'm sorry you're disappointed," the woman said.

He looked up. "Isn't there any way to reach Mel? Don't you have VPads or, I don't know, two-way radios or something?"

"No—too much chance of getting caught." The big man sat across from Chase, and the rest of the group moved close and settled around him.

"If it's any consolation," the man said. "She left you a message just in case you ended up here. It's written on a board down the walkway. It may seem kind of cryptic, but she said you'd know what to do with it."

"I found it. She left me a code, and I used it to get to another message. But I don't know what to do now."

"What was the message, Chase?" Someone in the crowd spoke up. The voice was young and feminine. Chase looked up to find the girl he'd seen get hauled off by the guards at the station.

"I saw you earlier today," he said. "They let you go?"

"We've got a friend at APD. We don't usually stay

in too long."

The young man next to her poked her arm. "We don't usually get caught."

The girl poked back and made a face.

"I met your friend a little while ago," Chase said. "He found me hiding behind the dumpster."

"It's been an hour since he shut down the guard," the big man said. "Now's the time we go out of here."

"Where do you go?" Chase asked.

"To church." The man stood and gathered a few books and some empty sacks. "Listen up, people," he said. "You go without me tonight. I'm staying here with Mr. Sterling."

"Chase Sterling was just a stage name. Those days are over. It's Redding. Charles Redding. But my mom nicknamed me Chase, so that'll do."

"All right." The man held out his hand. "They call me Bear. I guess that's my stage name. This is my stage." He looked around. "Only name I go by since I got saved."

Chase knew what he meant by that, sort of, but it struck him as funny that the man would consider hiding in the underground anything close to salvation. "You don't have to hang back on my account," he said to Bear. "I just need time to figure out what to do next."

"I might be able to help you. I'll stay."

Bear gave instructions to the group that seemed to be under his leadership. Some of the followers introduced themselves on their way out. The blonde girl was Emmy. The lady who'd hugged Chase was Beth. A sad-looking young man with tattooed arms called himself Van Gogh. Not all of these people used their real names, it seemed.

When the last of the group had left the tunnel, Chase walked with Bear back to the message from Mel.

"Emmy asked you what the other message was," Bear said. "You didn't answer her."

"I'm not sure I understand it."

"Well, let me hear it. Maybe I know something you don't."

Chase sat on the floor and leaned against the wall. "Four *S's*—"

"Sympathizers, supplies, secret houses, safe travel." Bear recited it without hesitation. "Underground lingo. Melody was telling you what we need. People on the outside to help us. Food, water, clothing. Shelter, hiding spots. And last, transportation to get from place to place unnoticed."

"Basic stuff. But it's not easy to come by, is it?"

"Not at all, Chase. And the lack of communication makes it more difficult. Somebody still in the system has access to data banks. But we don't. No electronics allowed in the underground. Too risky."

"But you have people you can count on, believers in the system. Mel was one until she went under. They help you, right?"

"That's where my people went tonight. Church houses are up top. Good working WR citizens stay there as long as they can, and they help those of us who've gone under. Others are out of the system but managing to stay up top for various reasons."

"Why do they go under?"

"In the past it's been to stay free, to stay out of prison. Or the crazy house. But now…things are changing."

"Augmentation?"

"Yes. More people will be joining us if it happens."

"Strange," Chase said. "Some people want it, and some people don't."

"I can't speak for anybody but myself and, I think, for those with me. We don't want some lab-grown enhancements giving us life. We got life. Nobody's turning me into a wired-up, death-defying freak."

Chase looked to the ground.

"Man, I'm sorry. I got a mouth on me that doesn't quit. I didn't mean that you're a freak, Chase. Forgive me."

"It's nothing—forget it. I know what I am." Chase looked the man in the eye. "I'm here to learn how to use what's in me to help your people. That's why this happened to me. Not to make money for SynVue, or to lead the world into the future, or to take an evolutionary leap. I'm just here to help people. That's all."

"Melody said as much. She said there was a reason God allowed this to happen to you."

"God and I haven't really talked that out. If it were up to me, I'd have found another way, Bear."

"It's not always easy for us when God makes up His mind to do something."

"There was something else after the four S's," Chase said.

"Study the Psalms." Bear stood and rubbed his hand across Mel's message. "This verse—'Day to day pours out speech. And night to night reveals knowledge.' I think Mel was telling you to take some time. Listen and learn. You see? Speech and knowledge."

"So, she wants me to get some help to study the Psalms to find the rest of the code. Why? Why didn't she just write it down? Why didn't she just tell *you* the code so you could tell me?"

"Suppose the WR raided this place. They'd have the code if she'd written it down. They might give me something to make me talk. Surely they can access the systems they put in you. Then all that information would be theirs."

"Not anymore. The exoself is all mine. I'm disconnected."

"The what?" Concern showed on Bear's face. "Chase, they've got to be tracking you. How long before they come in here? Will you know when they're near?"

"They're not coming. At least not because of me. Like I said, the stuff in me is no longer connected to the system. But I have to say, your security is lacking. You've got a cop who knows where you are, and at least one kid. A boy named Thomas pointed me right to you."

"I know the cop. We call him Cruiser. And I know Thomas. Others know we're here. Wouldn't be surprised if the mayor knew where to find us."

"You don't seem worried about it. Why are you so concerned about *me* being here?"

Bear went a distance down the walkway, then turned and looked at Chase. "Good people still exist in the world. But the WR—the people who run it and the puppets at SynVue—are far from good. They want us gone. For the most part the cops don't care. Local government—what's left of it—they don't care. Poor folks sure don't care. We feed them and they look out for us. But the WR is another story, Chase. My concern is that you'll lead them right to us. Surely they want you back."

"I wouldn't have come here if I thought that

would happen. I'd know if they were tracking me. My doctor unhooked me. He set me free."

"Why would he do that?"

"Guilt, I think."

"A change of heart can be a good thing," Bear said. "Let's hope nobody forces this doctor of yours to go back on his plans to free you."

Chase thought about Robert hiding the truth while WR higher-ups tried to make contact with the exoself. "The woman, Beth, said you all heard I went missing. Is the world looking for me?"

"We heard it from our sources within the church houses. But it's not public knowledge, as far as I can tell. It's not news. You got any idea why they'd keep it quiet?"

"So they can find me first," Chase said.

"So you don't fall into the wrong hands."

"Too late. You would be, in their opinion, the wrong hands."

Bear smiled. "Let's find what we're looking for." He pulled a small book from his pocket.

46

"Earlier I saw that you had real books. Bibles? I haven't seen a paper Bible in years."

"WR stopped the sale of electronic Bibles nine years ago. Of course, you can still get it that way. You can get just about anything if you try. But since we don't allow electronics in the underground, we keep these old paper copies coming in."

"Your people went up to the church houses," Chase asked. "What do they do there that they can't do here?"

"They collect supplies. They trade. What we've got, we give. What people in the system have got, they give. Somebody up there needs a Bible, we give them one. It'll get us enough food for a week. All of us."

"You trade Bibles for food?" Chase asked.

"They need the Good Book up there, we need food down here."

"There are no children here. I saw lesson plans written on the boards. Where are the kids?"

"We've got work to do, Chase. I'll answer your question once we spend some time listening and learning." He opened the little book. "This is a New Testament and Psalms." He held it out for Chase to see. "Here's the verse from the wall. See? 'Day to day, night to night.' Now, what's the first S?" Bear asked.

"Sympathizers."

"OK, we find a verse that might tell us something

related to getting the help we need." Then he started reading. Out loud. From the beginning. Chapter one, verse one.

Chase settled back against the wall. He expected to find the words confusing, and some of them were. He also thought this process would put him to sleep. And while he did find the ancient text and the smooth tone of the big man's voice relaxing, he didn't once close his eyes. While listening for a verse that might lead him to the first code, he learned some things about these people.

Maybe they'd always been in trouble. Maybe they always needed rescue.

Maybe they always got it.

An hour passed before Bear slowed down. He set the book aside and rubbed his eyes.

"Tell you what. Let's take a walk. I could use some coffee," Bear said.

Chase stood and stretched. "You lead the way."

The big man headed farther into the tunnel. Chase followed. It seemed the path went into the depths. Bear kept the candle in front of him. After nearly a quarter mile, they came to a concrete barrier in front of an opening. Bear handed the candle to Chase. He put his full weight on the heavy blockade. It hardly moved. "I usually get two other men to help me. You up to it, Chase?"

"Let me give it a try," Chase said. He handed Bear the candle, put his hands on the thing, and scooted it to the side.

Bear's eyebrows went up. "They do that to you, Chase?"

"Yep."

"What the devil intends for evil, the Lord uses for

good." Bear led the way, and soon they were in a room filled with old electric lamps. Dozens of people moved about, laughing and talking. Children played. Several men and women stood behind a table where they stuffed sacks with sandwiches and fruit.

A few primitive hot plates were plugged in to outlets on the far wall. The smell of fresh coffee filled the place.

One person prodded the next, and soon they were all looking at Chase. A few gasps were followed by cheers. The adults came to surround him. The younger children went on with their games.

Chase took a cup of steaming coffee and settled on a padded chair. Soon most of the crowd went back to their tasks. But some came and sat with Bear and Chase. Whispers filled the place. Chase could hear that while these people were glad to see him, they were afraid he'd bring their secret world to an end.

"The kids don't seem too interested in me," Chase said. "But the adults are worried."

"Most of these kids don't know who you are. Some of them have never even seen a GV. As for their parents, I'll make sure they know you're not a risk." He turned to those sitting around him. "We need some help," he said. "We're looking for a verse in the Psalms that has something to do with receiving help."

The few gathered there didn't ask why Bear needed to know this. They pulled out little Bibles and began reading. Some combinations of chapter and verse numbers that the people noted, Chase had already tried. Then a woman read aloud, "'May he send you help from the sanctuary and give you support from Zion.'"

"Chapter and verse?" Bear asked.

"Chapter twenty, verse two," the woman said.

Chase sparked the processor and pulled the number. And a flood of information came from the exoself. Lists of names and places from across the WR were followed by data in various languages. Chase understood every one. When the Mexican girl at the institute had led him to his room, Chase was grateful for the VPad translator. Sometime between now and then the exoself had gotten some language lessons. Robert must have added the program. Or maybe Mel built it in to this information trail.

"I've got it," he said. "I know where you can find crates of Bibles in the EU. There's a tent in Egypt filled with fresh fruit, but it's just a cover. Trucks are transporting people into safer territories." Chase knew this information was current, not outdated like the WR data banks. "I don't understand."

"What's the problem?" Bear asked.

"Mel put this stuff in me soon after I was injured. And then she left. Who's updating the information? How can anybody send updates to the exoself when the WR can't?"

"All I know is Melody said you were hooked to computers around the world. Must be believers still in the system exchanging information with each other, and somehow you're getting it."

"I had her making coffee and picking up my dry cleaning." Chase laughed. "I knew she was smart. She's outdone the best of them. Robert, my doctor, would be impressed."

Bear raised his brow and shook his head. "I'm glad you know what's going on in Egypt. What about Atlanta?"

Chase closed his eyes and searched the trail.

"Cargo plane leaving here tomorrow night. Headed for New York City. They can take four people. No travel documents. No questions." He leaned forward and clasped his hands. "Anyone here like to come with me?"

The people turned to each other. No one volunteered.

"You can't leave tomorrow," Bear said. "We've got to find the rest of the code."

"Now that I know what I'm looking for, I can keep searching on my own. I've got to get to New York."

"I hate to bring this up. By the time you get there, Melody may already be in the Far North Territory."

Chase sipped his coffee. A young girl came near and handed him a sandwich. "Thank you," he said. She smiled and returned to an older woman's side. The gray-headed lady nodded and put her arm around the girl.

"Do you know exactly where Mel's headed?" Chase unwrapped the sandwich and took a bite.

"Somewhere in Quebec. It's a big place," Bear said. "But if you can get into her programs, maybe you can find her. I just don't see how jetting off to New York City will do you any good if you don't know where to go when you get there. It's not as believer-friendly as Atlanta."

"Then we'd better get back to work. Read me some more of the Psalms."

A man stood and put his little Bible back into his pocket. "Lights go out in ten," he said.

"How do you know that?" Chase asked. "How do you even get power down here? Who pays for it?"

"We've got a friend," Bear said. "Newer buildings up top produce more energy than they use. Some techno-rebel hacker borrows from the grid and sends the power our way. God bless him. Lights come on for five hours every night. And nobody gets a bill for it."

A woman approached. "If you want to read more you'll have to wait for daylight, Mr. Sterling. Right now, we'll be getting our children to bed."

"Call me Chase. Thank you all for your hospitality. But I'll keep reading. I can see in the dark."

"They do that to you, Chase?" Bear asked.

"Just like the upper body strength." He looked around. "And fair warning, when you talk about me, I'm probably listening. My hearing is enhanced." He smiled. "You don't have to worry about anybody following me here. And I'm not going to turn you in."

A couple of women standing nearby blushed. They turned away and went on with the chore of preparing for darkness.

"Let's you and me go back in the tunnel," Bear said. "You read, I'll listen. If I'd known earlier you had cat eyes, you would have been reading all along."

"Right behind you, Bear."

The big man threw the stub of a candle on the floor. "You lead the way. You're the superman."

"I'm not sure he had night vision," Chase said as he came to the room's narrow doorway.

47

The second S showed itself quickly—twenty-two, twenty-six. "'The poor will eat and be satisfied; they who seek the Lord will praise Him—may your hearts live forever!'" Chase laughed when he read the last part.

"What's so funny?"

"My heart—it *could* live forever. It's not real."

"That's nothing" Bear said, and he pounded on his chest. "This heart in my body will stop beating one day. But I've got something in me that will never die. And I didn't need no augmentation to get it."

Chase pondered this. But he had to keep searching Mel's trails. "Some of the information jumps categories. This trail leads to the same Bibles in the EU."

"Makes sense. People are listed as sympathizers. The goods or services they offer are listed elsewhere. Did you find names of individuals or groups when you used the first code?"

"Yes. Some of them were fake names, I'm sure."

"People have to protect themselves. Those names will likely show up again when you find the code for safe houses. And the plane to New York will show up in safe travel. It's good to cross reference. Gives you confidence that the information is legit." Chase thought of the man who'd given him supplies and a ride to Phoenix. He let the twenty-second processor go and sparked the twentieth again. There he searched for the name Chang. He didn't find it, but he found Junk Store Perry. He smiled. "I was getting assistance even before I knew it, Bear. I just found a trail to some people I met two days ago."

"I'm not surprised. God's got his hand on you, my friend." Bear let out a yawn. "I think I'll take a break, Chase. You need to rest?"

On the train, working the exoself had drained his energy. But now he felt no desire for sleep. He must have adjusted to the process. "You rest," he said. "I'll keep reading."

The next chapter brought the third code—twenty-three, six. Mel had laid them out in order. Chase read it silently. *Surely goodness and mercy shall follow me all the days of my life, and I shall dwell in the house of the Lord forever.* This was familiar. He'd heard Psalm twenty-three before, but he didn't know when. Someplace, sometime in his childhood, he guessed.

He sparked the twenty-third processor and pulled on the sixth factor. Locations of church houses and hiding places filled his mind. He looked for Perry's store and found it with cryptic directions from the center of town. He scanned all of Quebec and found only three main underground locations. That was good news, considering his search would likely take him there. He tried to pull names of individuals working or living at the locations but got nothing. The three churches in Quebec, like most of the secret places around the world, had strange names. The first was called Mist Covered Hill, the second, Storm on the River. And the third was called Blue Sky Field.

"Blue Sky Field." Chase dropped the Bible and reached to shake Bear awake. "I've got it. I know where to find Mel and my mother."

The big man sat straight and rubbed his eyes. "You found them? You got a data trail that tells you where they are?"

"No, but I know where they're headed if they aren't there already."

"How?" Bear stretched and pulled a candle and match from his pocket. "I know you can see me. I'd like to see you, too." He struck the match, and the light burned softly in the tunnel.

"I just know it, Bear." He had to give the man an explanation, even if it sounded crazy. "When I was getting worked on, you know, by the doctors, I had some dreams. I think I talked to God. And I think He told me to go this place. I think it's like what you people call the Promised Land."

"Israel?"

"No. Canada."

Bear laughed.

"What's so funny?"

"You might have a computer for a brain, but you've got a lot to learn."

"I'm going to Quebec. I'll take that plane to New York, and then I'll make my way north."

"You've got all the S's?"

"Only three. I don't have the last one."

"I can't believe you got three in one night." Bear stood as the group that had gone out of the tunnel came back from their venture in the night. The eleven men and women carried sacks spilling over with bread and fruit and glass jars filled with what looked like peanut butter. The weary-looking crowd greeted Chase and Bear and then continued down the tunnel.

"Daylight's coming," Bear said. "The guard will be

waking soon. That plane of yours is leaving after dark tonight, I hope. You got a fight schedule?"

"The plane leaves at noon."

"What? What kind of fool made plans to take believers out of here in broad daylight?"

"Somebody called Windsong," Chase said. "You know anyone by that name?"

"Doesn't ring a bell. Where is takeoff for this foolhardy flight? Strip outside of town?"

"Hartsfield-Jackson."

Bear put his big hands on his hips. "Atlanta International? I don't think so."

"That's what the exoself tells me."

"Who is this exoself?" Bear asked. "I'm not sure you should believe everything he says."

"Can I get there on time?"

"In this case, time is the least of your problems, Chase." Bear looked toward the boarded mouth of the tunnel. Daylight barely shimmered through. "Sun's up. Must be after six o' clock."

"It's six fourteen."

Bear looked at him. "They do that to you?"

"Yeah."

"You're just full of gadgets, aren't you?"

"Can we do this, Bear?"

"I don't see how. You've got no pass for the solar rail. You could walk if you left right now."

Chase walked as far as the metal trash can. He pulled out the flight pack and held it up. I don't need to walk. I'm flying."

"Where did you get that?" Bear asked.

"From the place of my creation. Don't worry, my doctor unhooked the tracker."

"I'd like to meet this doctor of yours someday."

While Bear went to get them some breakfast, Chase continued through the Psalms. Chapters twenty-four through thirty. The number combinations produced no trail into the secret world of the Underground Church. He'd find it before he reached the end of chapter thirty-three—he only had so many processors.

Bear came back with hard-boiled eggs and peanut butter sandwiches and a thermos of hot coffee. "You have chickens down here?" Chase asked.

"Somebody from a church house sends them. Always boiled—they travel better. What I wouldn't give for some scrambled eggs and bacon." Bear stuffed half a sandwich in his mouth and made a face.

"Real bacon? That stuff will kill you."

"Maybe so. Something on this planet will get me. But I'm laying up treasures in Heaven where moth and rust and bacon can't destroy."

"Is that in your Bible?"

Bear laughed. "I might have gotten it wrong. Don't quote me."

"How do you know you're going to Heaven?" Chase bit into mushy white bread and peanut butter. "How do you even know it's real?"

"I know because I know. Because I took the gift."

"What gift?"

"Grace, my friend. Undeserved. Unearned. Unattainable."

"You people speak in riddles—you know that, don't you?"

"Nobody ever told you about grace? Not Melody or your mother?"

"Mel wasn't too open about what she believed. She worked in the entertainment industry. She lived, on the surface, by the rules of the WR. No proselytizing. And my mother, the last I knew, was OK with shipping Christians off to a desert island."

"Melody was afraid. Christians learned to be quiet years ago. The WR made threats, and we shut our mouths. But we struggle with it. We're called to spread the Gospel, not hide in a hole in the ground." Bear took a breath and looked toward the tunnel exit. "As for your mother, I think she might have changed her mind, Chase. And God might have changed her heart."

Chase counted the beats of his own heart—the only one he had. "Is that how it works, Bear? God changes your heart?"

"It's no riddle. Sure, it comes off that way to some people. It's foolishness, 'til you believe it."

"Too bad."

"What do you mean?"

"It's too bad I can't get what you've got. I haven't got a heart—not a real one. Not anymore."

"Man, that doesn't matter to God. You are still—"

The sound of boards dropping to pavement filled the place and daylight overtook the darkness. Guards appeared, and Chase felt Bear's strong grip on his arm as the two rushed into the room where he'd first discovered the group.

The face shield was still there on the floor. Bear picked it up and tossed it to Chase. Then he crouched in a corner and motioned Chase to take the opposite corner. The sound of guard boots filled the tunnel.

"Dear God, Father in Heaven, do not allow this. Protect my people," Bear whispered the prayer.

Chase shut his eyes tight. This was his fault. They'd tracked him.

48

"You got some gadget in you to turn off robots?" Bear whispered.

"Even if I shut them down, somebody sent them here. I'm sorry, Bear." Chase threw down the mask and ran back into the tunnel. Bear was close behind him.

"Go back—it's me they want," Chase said. But it was too late. They were both surrounded by speechless, mindless guards. Six of them.

"You think we can stop them from going any further?" Bear asked.

"Run, Bear. I'll do what I can."

"I can't let them take you, Chase. We need you. Turn them off or something."

The guards circled. Chase pictured the exoself and demanded a code that he wasn't sure existed. The number thirteen immediately crossed three lines of code, and Chase sparked the processor and pulled the factor. The guards froze. Chase put his hand against one and pushed. The thing fell over.

"Glory," Bear shouted.

"There's probably an army outside. I've got to turn myself in."

"No. We're going back into the tunnels together." Bear pulled on Chase.

"You'll lead them right to your people. I'm going out alone. They want *me*, Bear." Chase pulled away and walked into the daylight. Only one armed cop waited there. The one who'd turned off the guard—Cruiser. "I'm coming out," Chase said. "There's no reason for you to go any farther. I surrender."

"I'm here for the Christians. They're under arrest," the cop said. His voice carried no urgency or emotion. His tone didn't waiver. Something was wrong.

Chase stepped close. "You didn't come here for me?"

"I'm sending data now. If they want me to take you in, I will."

"They?"

"WR specialty forces."

"Cruiser—that's what they call you, isn't it?"

"I am outfitted to weed them out." His eyes were blank. His expression didn't vary. He pulled out a weapon and aimed it at Chase. "Step aside."

"Cruiser, only yesterday you were shutting down a guard. You were helping these people. Do you remember that?"

The cop straightened his arms and readied his laser. Chase stood in the aim of the weapon.

Bear came out of the tunnel. One long scream rose from the big man as he ran. With his arms opened wide, he lunged at the cop. Cruiser turned and the weapon buzzed as the laser met its target.

Death seemed to claim Bear even before he fell backward and thudded on the pavement.

The code, thirty-two, seven, sparked from exoself, not by Chase's instruction. It just happened.

The cop grabbed the sides of his head before he hit the ground. Blood trickled from his left ear.

Chase dropped to his knees beside the dead body of the man called Bear. Guilt flooded his mind until he wept. He looked at Cruiser. Someone had put an NP in him—Chase was sure of that. He reached over and clutched the man's arm. The Wilberton told him the cop was dead.

"This is my fault."

"Not true." The voice was soft. "It's not your fault Cruiser turned on us."

Chase looked up to find Emmy standing with two young men from the secret world of the Underground Church. "I'm sorry. You will all have to get away from here. I'll find you a place to go." He turned his eyes to the ground. "I should never have come here."

One of the men knelt next to Chase. "First, we get these men out of sight. Can you carry Bear's body? You're super strong, right? Sam and I will get Cruiser." He motioned for the other man to come alongside the cop's body. "Emmy, you get the weapon and anything else on the ground."

"Got it." Emmy grabbed the laser gun and stuck it in the waistband of her pants.

The two young men each took a leg and pulled the cop to the tunnel. Chase wiped his eyes and hoisted Bear over his shoulder. He carried him into the underground and laid him gently in the hidden room. People stood along the walls, some crying, and some singing.

"I'm so sorry." Chase knelt to the floor. "I said they couldn't track me, but they did. I'll find you all a place to go, and then I'll get out of here. You and your church will never see me again."

The woman named Beth approached him. "Chase, what exactly happened? There are six guards out there in the tunnel doing nothing, and the cop who helped us is dead." Her voice wavered and tears fell. "And our Bear is gone." She sucked a breath and wiped her face. "Tell us what happened."

Chase told the people how their leader came to die by the weapon of their friendly cop. "But this is because of me," he said. "Why else would they put an NP in Cruiser and come down on this place now?"

"From the way it sounds," Beth said, "you being here didn't have anything to do with it. We've heard of other underground groups getting flushed out just in the last few days. Things are changing rapidly. Finding you here may just have been a bonus to whoever is behind all this."

Chase couldn't believe that. Not with Bear lying dead before him. But these people didn't seem to blame him. "I destroyed the device they put in Cruiser, but my image may have gotten through." He lowered his head and closed his eyes. "If they didn't know where to find me before, they probably do now."

Beth knelt beside him and cupped his face in her hands. "This is not your fault. I'm sorry you had to kill Cruiser. But you saved us from whatever he was going to do to us."

"I delayed whatever he was going to do. Others will come, and soon."

"Then turn on that stuff inside you and tell us where to go." She stood and held out her hand. Chase let her pull him up. Candles were lit as more people came in. Whispers filled the place. And tears. But no one blamed Chase. Not one of them said a word against him.

The leader of these people and the cop who'd turned on them were covered with blankets and prayed over. The believers thanked God for the men, for their lives. They treated one as the other. No animosity showed for the man who wasn't one of them. But when the prayer for Bear neared its close, the man praying laughed through his tears. And all those gathered with him smiled. Chase remembered his dream and those who died in the field under the blue sky. They'd flown away and Chase had laughed. Bear had gone home, and his friends were glad for him.

But the urgency of getting to that place in the dream and protecting Mel and his mother overwhelmed him. He had to get these people to safety, and he had to get to Atlanta International. He checked the time. Eight fifty four. Three hours.

Chase noticed a young girl carrying her little Bible in one hand and a candle in the other. He went to her and asked her to read the next Psalm. Thirty-one. The girl asked no questions, but opened the book and began to read.

It didn't take long.

"'You have not handed me over to the enemy but have set my feet in a spacious place,'" the girl read. "'You have set my feet in a broad place.'"

"Stop right there," Chase said. "Verse?"

"Eight."

Chase wasted no time sparking the processor and pulling the number. "I've got it." He didn't wait for the exoself to give up the secrets of safe travel the world over in its normal orderly fashion. He and the exoself were coming to understand each other. Chase wanted only to know how to get these people out of Underground Atlanta, and he wanted to know now.

"How many people are here?" he asked.

"I think sixty-eight total," the girl said. Her face fell. "Well, sixty-seven."

He lifted her face and brushed the tear from her

cheek. "Run and find Beth and Emmy, and tell them to gather everyone at the mouth of the other tunnel—the one that's still boarded up." He stood and looked at the young girl. "Hurry." She got up and ran with her Bible still in her hand.

Things were happening in the exoself that Chase could not explain. He didn't take the time to figure it out before he contacted the computer system of a corporation housed in one of the buildings somewhere overhead. This was the hacker who supplied power to the tunnel every night. This person, or people, had a bus. A big, old fashioned, gas powered bus. And the bus was fueled and ready to go.

"Where are these people getting gasoline?" Chase left that information trail and moved to the twenty-third processor. A grid of safe houses in the foothills of the Appalachians came up, and Chase linked to a system offering a closed private resort with thirty cabins deep in the wooded hills. The people gathered their meager belongings, their children, and as much food as they could carry, and assembled in the second tunnel to wait for the bus.

But Chase sensed something in the exoself. S-drones were coming. Three of them. He knocked the boards loose at the tunnel's exit and stepped into the daylight.

The little planes hovered over the paved area outside the tunnels. They were no more than a foot wide. Their silvery shells gave them the look of old bullets. Big ones. Chase sparked the thirty-second processor. It had concealed the exoself when he'd first used it. But it was a weapon—he was sure of that now. He wasn't sure, however, that he could control it. He focused on one drone. It dove straight into the tunnel and crashed, sending the people inside running back into the underground.

"Be careful," Chase told himself. He set his eyes on another. It fired a beam at him, but he rolled to the ground unharmed. Then he brought the thing straight down. It blew to pieces when it hit the pavement. The third lifted and seemed to retreat. Chase blew it up anyway. "God help me. I don't know what I'm doing or how I'm doing it. But thanks."

He turned to the tunnel to find the people slipping back into view. "Is everyone all right?"

Beth came forward and motioned the others to follow her into the open. "We're fine. That was quite a show, Chase. You rescued us again." She smiled.

"There are more coming. The bus will be here in two minutes."

"How do you know?"

"I just know. Get everybody onboard as fast as you can. You've got to get out of here."

"You too, Chase. Come with us."

"No. I'm going to the airport. I'm flying to New York, and then I'm going to Quebec."

"I wish you'd change your mind," Beth said.

He looked her in the eye. "I've got to go. I've got a flight pack in the other tunnel. I'm ready to fly as soon as you are all out of here safely."

She nodded, and he touched her hand. She turned to gather her people as the bus approached. Chase walked to the driver's side of the old bus and the darkened window cracked open. A middle-age man smiled. "Here to pick up some folks moving north." The man's brow crossed, and he tilted his head. "Hey, aren't you—"

"Name's Chase. You get them out of here in a

hurry. Understand?"

The man looked at the ruined S-drones. "What happened here?"

"Never mind. How fast does this thing go?"

"It's an old bus. It moves like one."

The last of the displaced believers loaded the bus. Beth stood at the door before she got on. Chase came to her, and she put her arms around him. "Go," he said as a tear fell down his cheek. "Tell the driver to take 75 north. In a few minutes I'll fly after you and make sure you get out of town without any more S-drones tagging along."

"Chase, you're a good man. You will be a help to many people."

"I hope so, Beth. I hope I don't cause so much death and destruction everywhere I go."

She looked him in the eye. "You did not cause this, young man. You are our hero." She smiled, and he kissed her forehead. "God be with you," she said.

He nodded as she boarded. He waved to them all as they pulled away.

50

Chase ran into the first tunnel and grabbed his pack. He needed the face shield so he went back into the room where the bodies were left. A few candles still burned there.

Bear had become a fast friend. Chase would never forget him. He deserved a proper funeral, but there was no time. But maybe Chase could keep his friend—both these men—from rotting in this tunnel.

"The prayers have been said. I can finish this." He tipped the first candle and it fell to the ground and smoldered there. He'd have to do better than that. He took the next candle and touched the flame to the edge of the blanket. "Good-bye, Bear. I don't even know your real name." Another candle lit the cover over Cruiser. "It wasn't your fault, man. I'm sorry I killed you. I wish there could have been another way."

With the room ablaze, Chase strapped on his mask, grabbed his gear, and carried one more candle into the tunnel. "Best to burn these too." He tried to light the clothes on the cyber-guards, but the material didn't burn. So he tossed the candle into the metal trash can. Refuse there caught fire easily, and Chase rolled the blazing thing down the tunnel. "This will keep city cops and rescue busy for a while."

He went into the daylight and powered his flight pack. "Good-bye to Underground Atlanta. May you rest in peace."

Flying north, he heard the sounds of emergency vehicles headed for the fire. No smoke rose yet from the underground, at least not enough to see from the air. Chase used the exoself to warn the source that had sent the bus. Their office had to be in one of the buildings he'd just flown over. He sent a message to the unknown computer system: *Underground is on fire. Evacuate.*

Inter-territory 75, at least headed out of the city, was open and the traffic moved at a good pace. Chase spotted the bus easily and dropped in altitude as he approached. He sensed no drones in the area, but three more were headed for the fiery underground. Seemed no one knew the believers were high-tailing it out of town. Maybe the forces investigating the fire would think they'd all died.

With the bus leaving the city limits, Chase turned and headed south, thinking about how he was going to get into Atlanta International and sneak on a cargo plane. Bear was right—it was a foolish plan.

But this Windsong person had to know what he was doing.

When he got there, Chase put his feet to the ground where other flyers landed. The entrance to the airport's security arena was only a hundred feet in front of him. He'd never get in with his face covered. Even if he did, he wouldn't make it past the scanners— his DNA would give him away. He stayed back as the other flyers put their pack in lockers and headed for the building.

"What do I do now? Give me some good news, exoself." He sparked the processor and pulled the number for information on the last S—safe travel. Running through the program, he found the plane, and the pilot, Windsong. And he found the way in. A truck would load the plane in fifteen minutes. It was parked in a cargo building two miles behind the farthest runway. Chase would have to fly with his pack to the backside of the airport. He quickly strapped up, and he was in the air in record time. "I'm getting better at this."

He couldn't fly directly over the runways. He wasn't sure he could fly anywhere near the airport, other than around the pad he'd just lifted from.

Fourteen minutes.

He flew five miles out and circled, then came down a mile from the buildings clustered at the back of the airport. He stayed ten feet off the ground and maneuvered through security pillars, sure he would be shot to pieces at any moment.

He made it to the twenty-foot laser fence surrounding the place. How would he get through this?

Six minutes.

He could see an open bay on the closest building. The truck inside hummed. A man came from around the truck and stepped outside. He looked around and shook his head before he turned and went back to the truck. This must be it—no other trucks were ready to roll. No bays were open but this one.

Chase summoned his exoself and viewed the phantom screen in his mind. "Can I breach this fence?" The number twenty-four fell into six strands of code. He walked to the fence as he put to use this latest discovery. Did Robert think of everything?

Five minutes.

The fence didn't change, and Chase knew of nothing to do but walk right through. He was not stopped. There was no pain of electric shock, and no alarms sounded in the vicinity. The truck pulled out of the bay just as Chase ran to it.

The driver stopped. "Looking for Windsong?"

"Yes." Chase stood at the side of the truck and looked up to the driver.

"I've got four minutes to get this truck to the plane. You couldn't have gotten here sooner?" The driver reached and slung the passenger door open. "Get in."

Chase followed the man's order and climbed into the truck. He sat straight in the seat and faced the windshield. "I'm sorry."

"Nice to meet you, Sorry. You're not riding there. Pull down the seat back and crawl through."

Chase didn't say anything else to the man—he just did as he was told. He found the open space behind the seat led from the cab to the cargo section. Pulling his flight pack behind him and appreciating the night vision, he settled into a tight spot between tall crates.

"You got two minutes to find an empty crate and get yourself inside." The voice from the cab of the truck was not any friendlier. The seatback slammed into place. Chase stood and reached for the top of the crate to his left. He forced the lid off and peered inside. No room for a man. He did the same to the crate on his right and got the same result. Moving quickly, he banged on crates until he found one that made a hollow sound. He threw the lid open, dove inside, and pulled the lid down. The truck came to a stop before he managed to catch his breath.

Soon voices surrounded him. He kept perfectly still and silent. The crate was lifted by a machine of some kind and practically tossed through the air. At least that was how it felt. And then all was quiet. But that didn't last long. The engine of the fuel-cell jet started up, and Chase had a sudden rush of panic at the thought of being lifted into the clouds by the giant plane.

"Calm down," he said under his breath. "You're not afraid of this anymore." He closed his eyes tight as he felt the plane leave the ground and climb with its nose pointed at the heavens.

As soon as the plane leveled, a strong but feminine voice called out. "OK, you secret servants of the Lord, you can come out. How many have we got this time? I'm guessing not too many, considering the location of our departure."

Chase stood and pushed the lid off his crate. He looked around. No one else had popped up but him.

"Well, I guess you're it, masked man," the woman said. "Welcome aboard. Keep your seatbelt fastened and your tray in the upright and locked position."

Chase stared at her. She tossed her long blonde hair over her shoulder and laughed. "Just kidding. Do what you want. But can you lose the mask? It makes me nervous, and I don't like flying when I'm nervous."

"Who's flying the plane right now?" Chase asked.

"It's on auto."

"Are you Windsong?"

"That's me. Who are you? And seriously, take off the face shield."

"Are you a believer?"

"Who's asking?" She crossed her arms.

Chase pulled off the mask. "Are you?"

Her mouth came open, and her eyebrows rose. "Are *you*?"

❧

An hour passed as the plane travelled north. Windsong promised to keep secret that she'd seen Chase Sterling. She was a believer, still in the system, and she moved as many people as she could with her cargo shipping business. Chase knew how he'd gotten on board—tricks he managed with the exoself. But he didn't understand how the average person without credentials could get into a major airport and stow away on a plane subject to frequent inspections.

"Never tried it at a major airport until today," Windsong explained. "I really didn't expect anybody to show up, but my driver—the guy in the truck—said we should do it. He said he had a feeling. I told him he was nuts. Turns out he was right."

"Where do you usually make your pick-ups and drops?"

"Small strips. I won't try this again. I'm surprised I got away with it considering I've got a rogue, augmented superstar in my plane."

"You can't tell anyone."

"Are you kidding? If there's one thing I avoid, it's attention." She sat in the pilot's seat. Chase sat beside her. "But you've got to tell me about it, Mr. *Change Your Life.*"

"How do you communicate with other believers? Have you heard anything about the Underground Church in Atlanta?"

"So much for *me* asking the questions. We've got old cell towers in use. Hackers make it work on our VPads. Any call that comes in from an unapproved base, the call disconnects before the receiver can be tracked. Of course, some of us have to keep tapped into commerce bases. Even then, if a call came from what we consider a hostile source, like a direct WR base, it'd get cut off."

"So that's what happened," Chase said as he thought of the last time he'd heard his mother's voice.

"What happened?"

"Nothing. What about the church? Any rumors flying around?"

"Heard the underground caught fire. They found two bodies. People are saying the rest of the group probably died from the smoke." She sighed and wiped her face with her sleeve. "I don't know if they'll even go in there to look for them."

"Good."

She turned her eyes on him, and her anger showed. "I kind of got the feeling you weren't totally against us? Was I wrong?"

"No. What I meant was it will give them more time if the authorities think they're dead. They're on a bus headed for the mountains." Chase looked out the plane's windshield. "All but one of them—their leader. The other dead man's a cop."

"So you were there."

"Bear, their leader, died saving my life. And I killed the cop."

"I've heard of Bear. Heard he was a good man. If he died to save you, he did the right thing. He followed Christ. As for the cop, you did what you had to do, I'm sure."

Chase watched the graying sky for the rest of the flight. He spoke little. Windsong hummed a soothing tune. She occasionally stopped her song and prodded him with questions about how he'd managed to hide from the government and how long he'd been involved with the Underground Church. She even asked him when he'd become a believer.

"You're making assumptions," he told her.

The plane came down on a private strip outside of the city. Chase thanked his pilot, strapped on his flight pack, and headed for Brooklyn. He'd used the exoself to locate a church house a mile from the WR office where Mel worked after her reassignment. The same office Kerstin now occupied.

S-drones were numerous in and around New York City. If the ones in Atlanta had scanned him and reported his identity, the ones here would soon be after him. He came down a block from the church house. According to Mel's information trail, the place was behind a clinic. The digital hologram in front of the building read Clarkson Avenue Family Clinic. The place closed at six o'clock. He'd find something to keep himself busy until dark. Eating seemed like a good thing to do.

He walked the streets, stepping inside a small deli and ordering a turkey sub. No one seemed to mind the mask. The people here didn't even look at him. No wonder—others passed by in stranger getups than his. A man in a dog collar, and little else, barked to hail a cab. A pretty girl walked toward Chase with a live snake curled around her neck. Even the cyber guards on most every corner had no interest in Chase. He found a public bathroom in a park and huddled in a stall. The face shield rested on the back of the toilet while he ate his sandwich.

Night fell on the city, and Chase headed back for the clinic. He watched from across the street for a while. The people who took the alley to the back of the building, unlike everyone else in the city, seemed aware that a masked man watched them. The way news traveled among these people, he thought they might know who he was. Maybe they were expecting him.

But one by one, two by two, they looked his way, and then disappeared into the alley. He crossed the street and fell in line with a group of five. They all turned to look at him. Five laser weapons came out.

Chase didn't waste time pulling off the mask.

51

When the people of the Brooklyn church house stopped their murmuring, Chase heard the news he'd been expecting. Mel and his mother—they called her Birdy since she sang all the time—were in Quebec. They'd been gone a week.

"I'm not surprised," he said. "Disappointed, yes, but I had a feeling they wouldn't be here."

"Then why'd you come?" a man asked.

"I hitched a ride on a cargo plane, and this is as far as it went. I thought I'd better at least check to see if they were still here." Chase looked over the forty people in the room. "I'm headed for Quebec—place called Blue Sky Field. A truck leaves from Manhattan in three hours."

A young woman with a skeptical look in her eye approached. "Did you find that out from the stuff Melody put in you?"

"Yes, I did." Chase walked to the center of the room. "Is there anything I can tell you; anything I can do for you before I go?"

"You can try not to set us on fire." The request came from a young man with big silver lightning bolts dangling from his ears and a tattoo of a cross on his arm.

Chase turned and walked to the wall and then faced the crowd with his arms folded.

The man who'd spoken first was quick to chide

this candid believer. "Shut up, Fryer. We don't even know what happened." The older man walked to Chase. "We heard the believers in Underground Atlanta got burned up by the WR forces looking for you. Is it true, Mr. Sterling?"

"They're all safe. All except for their leader, Bear. He was killed. I got a bus to move the rest of the people." Chase looked at the young man called Fryer. "I sent them to an old resort in the mountains. And I set fire to their hiding place. Seemed like the right thing to do at the time."

"How do you know they're safe?" Fryer asked.

"I got a message from the computer system run by the hackers who provided the bus."

The Christians of Brooklyn stood there looking at him. "I'll go now," Chase said. He headed for the door.

The older man stopped him. "We could use some supplies. We've got a huge body of believers out of the system here. They need food and clothes, and we're the ones to get stuff to them. You got anything in you to indicate where we could restock?"

"Mel and my mother took a great deal of supplies with them, is that right? I'm showing supplies were delivered to Blue Sky Field."

"Yes. We were expecting a shipment on a train two days ago. It got confiscated."

Chase searched the trails and found the confiscated material, courtesy of a hacker in the Bronx. "Your supplies are in a WR warehouse. Five guards surround the place, but I can shut them down."

Three of the men accompanied Chase to the warehouse. One drove the ugly old truck in need of brakes. The other two sat in the back and questioned Chase about his involvement in the underground.

When they reached the place where the goods were hidden, the guards were disabled, the cameras, too, and the food and other essentials were loaded onto the truck.

"I'll fly to Manhattan from here," Chase told the men. "You should be fine getting the supplies back to your base."

The men kept loading, scarcely looking at Chase. But the truck driver muttered his thanks. Chase knew he'd have to work at gaining the trust and respect of some of these groups. But surely they realized how much they needed him. He lifted into the night and headed for the tallest buildings. He dodged other flyers—a skill he'd rather not have the occasion to master.

He came to an area clearly marked for night landings, and brought his feet to the top of a skyscraper on the east side of the island. Other flyers came down as some lifted away, their packs emitting a glow in the darkness. Street landing after dark was illegal—Chase knew that much. He'd have to take the elevator to the ground level and walk six blocks to the pick-up spot.

The exoself seemed to quiver, if that was possible. A processor sparked. Something wasn't right. Chase looked around the lighted landing pad. Lockers were to his left for storing flight packs. A bathroom on his right flashed a display to indicate availability. And a massive recognition scanner encircled the whole rooftop. Chase stood motionless, surrounded by machines that could run his fingerprints, iris pattern, and DNA in a matter of seconds. And he didn't have to consent or even be near the device.

He—the exoself—shut the thing down. But it was

probably too late.

He walked to the nearest exit and swiped the lighted panel. None of the multiple elevator doors opened. He turned to the door leading to a hundred and fifty staircases. The sound of the door bolting shut let him know he needn't bother. The flight pack needed a charge but he slipped it on and powered it anyway. He lifted three feet off the roof, and then the pack shut down. He fell to the rooftop and his knees buckled as he hit.

He was trapped.

No other flyers were there on the roof. The ones who'd landed shortly before or after Chase had made it into the elevators before the doors quit opening on command. The blue beams that moments ago lit the pad had retracted so flyers would know they needed to land elsewhere. He listened to the sounds at street level. No rush of police cars seemed headed his way. But they wouldn't come with great force. They'd send a liaison to bring him in quietly. Now that the WR had his location pinpointed, it wouldn't be that long before somebody joined him on this rooftop.

Chase climbed to the observation platform where a translucent barrier came to his waist. He broke the lock on a power outlet and plugged in his pack. Maybe a ten minute charge would get him to the truck and out of this awful city. But after only seven minutes, an elevator door opened behind him. He turned around.

Kerstin.

52

She swiped her VPad and then jabbed it with her fingernail. Her hair lifted from her shoulders in rhythmic waves as the night air came over her. She walked toward him.

"It won't work, Kerstin. You can't shut me down."

Darkness fell across her sallow cheeks. Her steps were slow, her breathing labored.

"Then I'll call the guards from below to come and carry you away," she said.

Chase sparked the exoself. "I just shut down every guard within a block of here."

"So I'll call the NYPD. You cannot keep running, Chase. Just come with me."

"How did you get here so fast?"

"I was in a cab a block from here when I got the call that you'd been detained, and I asked if I could be the one to bring you in. It was providence, Chase. Come with me."

"I can't, Kerstin. I have to do this. Nobody can stop me."

She came onto the platform. "What is it that you're doing?"

"I'm helping people."

"What sort of people, Chase?"

"The ousted. Those surviving underground. Those still in the system who are barely hanging on for the sake of the ones gone rogue. Believers."

"That was not the plan, Chase. Not at all. You we're not created to become a hero for the poor and misguided. Certainly not for a bunch of rogue Bible thumpers. That's not why we made you."

"Then I'm an accidental hero. I don't care why you made me, Kerstin. I only care about what I can do now."

"Do you care about Robert?"

Chase stepped so close he could feel her breath on his face. "What have you done?"

"I haven't done anything. They've got him confined to his lab. They're searching for evidence that he reprogrammed you and let you go. No one believes you could have gained access to the exoself on your own."

"It came back to me, its host, and we don't need anybody telling us what to do. Not Robert, not the WR or the network. Not you. I'm fully independent of systems outside myself." Chase reached for the flight pack and strapped it on. He climbed onto the rim of the skyscraper. "It's what you wanted, isn't it? An evolutionary leap? Well, I made it. Consider your experiment a success."

Kerstin came after him. She grabbed his arms and a desperate cry came from deep in her throat. "I will not let you do this!"

In her rage she stumbled, and her heel turned under. Chase dropped to his knees and grabbed her arm as she slipped over the edge.

She dangled there, her spiked heels scraping against the glassy wall. "Chase, please, don't let go," she cried. "Don't let me go."

He pulled her up, wrapped his arm around her waist, and set her on her feet.

She brought both hands over her mouth and sobbed.

"You're the one who has to let go, Kerstin."

"I can't, Chase. I'll lose everything."

"And what if I go with you? They'll pull me apart. Study me. Try to fix me. For what? I know they're already putting NPs in cops. Things are moving ahead so fast that before long, I'll be obsolete." He looked for a glimmer of empathy. "Tell them I got away. Tell them I'm just a man who wants his life back. And then leave me alone. For God's sake, Kerstin, just leave me alone."

"Chase, I can't face the WR without you. You said you want your life back. If I bring you in, they'll give me back *my* life."

"No, Kerstin. People need me, and I'm going to help them."

She wiped the tears from her face and crossed her arms. "Funny, I thought those people already had a hero," she said. "Didn't he already save them?"

He grabbed her and pulled her close and then reached into the pocket of her black silk blazer and pulled out her VPad. He tossed it over the edge. "You need a kidney." He pushed away and looked her in the eye. "I'm serious. Go to Robert. Tell him I said to give you one."

Her face turned down, and she wrapped her arms tight around her trembling body. She said nothing else. Nor did she stand in his way. He tied on the face shield and prayed he had enough power to fly off this building.

"Good-bye, Kerstin." With the pack powered, he went over the side. Dropping to thirty feet above street level, he flew between buildings until he spotted the waiting truck. He came down in the middle of a crowd. No one cared. The city was a noisy tangle of night prowlers and drunken revelers. Chase climbed into the back of the truck with a few others. Like the group in Brooklyn, these people were quiet and seemed on the defense against a man in a cyber-guard face shield. Chase said nothing. He didn't show his face. Before he drifted into restless sleep, he only thought of Kerstin, the look in her eyes, the sickness in her body. The fact that she'd let him go.

And her disconcerting insinuation that the people he was trying to protect already had a hero.

53

When Chase came fully awake, two of his six fellow travelers were gone. Four Hispanic men huddled in a corner at the far end of the big rig. They no longer seem concerned about the lone masked man. Good thing—Chase had grown weary of explanations.

The truck arrived in Montreal and pulled to a stop. Chase pushed up the rear door and lowered his feet to the ground. Daylight smacked him and the cold air added another punch. The rest of the men remained in their corner. Chase pulled the door shut, and the truck drove off. He'd been deposited in an alley, out of sight of pedestrians and drivers. He hadn't noticed these past few days as he traveled from west to east to north that the climate was changing. Now the autumn chill gave an undeniable first impression of the Far North Territory. Chase hoped the people of the north were just as blasé about the mask as the New Yorkers. But he didn't plan to stay in Montreal long enough to find out.

He found a pay-for-power outlet and deposited the last of his WR bills. A half hour later, he powered his pack and left the city beneath him. The exoself pointed him to a town called Herouxville. That's where he'd find the open field under the blue sky. Well, today the sky may not be so blue. Low clouds hung in the northeast. Chase followed them.

He arrived in the little farming town by

midafternoon. The site of the underground hiding place called Blue Sky Field was not in the information trail. The locations of the main branches of the Underground Church were kept secret, even from the exoself. But the location of an untitled church house appeared with sketchy directions. This land seemed right to reveal the beautiful place in his dreams. Even though white cirrus clouds now covered the sky with angel wings, the fields were as wide and welcoming. The hills surrounding the open land were familiar, even though Chase had never been here.

He set down on a narrow street and wondered if he should wait until dark to approach the small house at the end of the row. But he'd waited long enough. He walked to the door and knocked. A small woman, old and bent, peered through a window. She shook her head. She would not open her door, it seemed.

Chase removed the face shield and stood before her.

The woman lifted her hands and bounced on the other side of the glass. The door opened, and she pulled Chase inside and slammed the door closed in one motion.

"Birdy told me to watch for you," she said with the slightest French accent. "She told me you'd come, but I didn't believe her."

Relief was instant and undeniable, and Chase couldn't hide it. A tear fell to his cheek as he dropped his pack to the floor.

The woman patted his shoulder. "You want some tea? I've got cookies in the oven."

"Where's my mother?" He let the old woman drag him to the parlor, and he collapsed into a soft chair.

"In good time, Mr. Redding."

"No one's called me that in a long time. Did Mom tell you my real name?"

"Yes, of course it was your mother who told me. Melody just refers to you as her boss."

Chase laughed and cried altogether. "Is she all right?"

The little gray-headed lady seemed flustered by this. "Which one? Birdy or Melody?"

He wiped his tears and laughed again. "Both."

"Oh, they're as fine as can be," she said. "Living the way they do."

"How are things here? In the underground, I mean. I've been worried I wouldn't get here before it got bad."

"Things are changing. But you know that, don't you? You're part of the change."

"Yes, ma'am."

"Come to the meeting room in my basement. I'll bring you some tea and cookies. There are towels in the bathroom, clean clothes in the closet. I'm set to fit all sizes—you'll find something there. Clean yourself up and get some sleep."

"I really just want to go to Blue Sky Field. I'm sure I must have passed it on the way here, but I didn't know where to go. Is there an old house or a barn?"

The woman shook her head. "Do you think that's where you're going? To a literal field?"

"I saw it in my…"

"Your what, son?"

"What's your name?" he asked.

"Molly. May I call you Chase?"

He nodded. "What is Blue Sky Field?"

"You'll see. But for now, come with me." She led him to a paneled wall and pushed a button hidden behind a painting. Stairs that one minute weren't there, the next were descending into a dark cavern.

"I'll get the light for you," she said.

"No need. I can see."

"I'll be back in twenty minutes with cookies and tea, Chase. Bathroom is to your left."

"Thank you, ma'am."

Just as Molly had said, Chase found clean clothes to fit him. He stood under a spray of hot water and relived every moment since he left Robert. What could he do to help his doctor, his friend? Nothing, he decided. Not now. He prayed Jimmy or Patty could do something.

He dried off and picked up a razor from the counter by the sink. But looking in the mirror, he decided to let the few days of growth go, and he simply trimmed the edges of his beard. He pulled on worn jeans and a blue sweatshirt. Tennis shoes replaced the guard boots. A sofa against the far wall of the basement welcomed him, and he stretched out and closed his eyes.

Before he could find sleep, Molly came to the stairs with her cookies and tea. She turned on the light. Chase put his feet to the floor and sat on the sofa.

"Sorry," she said. "Maybe you can see in the dark, but I can't."

"Thank you for the snack." Chase sipped the warm tea and ate a butterscotch shortbread. The little woman stared. "Is something wrong?" he asked.

"I like the beard. Let your hair grow out and wear some dark shades, and pretty soon people will forget what Chase Sterling looked like. Then you won't need that silly old mask."

Chase laughed. "I feel ridiculous walking around

in that thing." He picked up another cookie. "Will people come here after dark? My mother and Mel?"

"They come on Tuesday nights. This is Friday."

"I'm not waiting that long."

"I know. After it gets dark, I'll tell you how to get to Blue Sky Field. It's easy—right in the middle of town. But I won't go with you, Chase. I'm too old for such adventure."

"An augmented game show host in your basement is enough for you, is it?"

She giggled. "More than enough."

"You must see plenty of adventure if you're willing to keep a church house going here."

"The Lord protects me. He knows I'm old. You go be the hero, and I'll stay here and pray for you."

"A good lady in Atlanta told me I was a hero. But I think she was mistaken."

"I heard you saved some people down there. Rumor was they all perished, but then we found out they'd just relocated. Thanks to you."

"You can thank Mel for that—she's the one who programmed me."

"You're the one facing danger to rescue our people. That makes you a hero. But heroes are not infallible. You can't save everybody. Fact is you can't save anybody—not really. Don't get it into your head that you can, Chase. Only one can do that. Only Jesus."

"I won't let it go to my head. Thanks for the advice, Molly."

"Rest now. After dark I'll tell you where to go to find your mother and Melody." She clasped her hands and smiled wide. "They will be so happy."

Chase lay back on the sofa. "Don't let me sleep too long."

"I'll be back in three hours." She left the tray with the cookies and tea on a table, and walked up the stairs. The light went out, and Chase closed his eyes.

54

"Blow it up, boss. You can do it."

"No, I can't, Mel. I can't stop this from happening."

"If I tell you a secret, then will you blow it up?"

"Mel, this thing is coming, and I can't save your people. Telling me a secret is not going to change anything."

"Yes, it will. It changes everything."

"Then tell me, Mel. Tell me now."

Chase opened his eyes wide and sat straight on the sofa. His breath came in gasps, and his body was drenched. He pulled off the sweatshirt, went into the bathroom and splashed cold water on his face. Dabbing himself with a wet towel, he quickly felt the chill of the basement. The closet gave up another sweatshirt—a black one. He grabbed a black windbreaker as well, and put on both and headed up the stairs.

Molly sat in her parlor, staring out the window. She turned when Chase approached. "It's not time yet, son. You mustn't hurry."

"I need to go. Something's wrong."

"How do you know?"

"I can sense S-drones. They're close." Chase walked to the window and looked at the dark sky. "And I had a dream."

"S-drones are manufactured nearby. Did you

know that?"

The exoself had not revealed this. "Do they test them at night?"

Molly shook her head. "I really can't say, Chase. Could be. Maybe that's why you picked up on them."

"I think there's something else coming. Something bigger, more powerful."

Concern showed in Molly's eyes. "All right, Chase. Go to *Rue de Saint Paul*. Can you find the street with your programs?"

"Yes, I've got it."

"There's a building that was a painter's studio. It's called *Musee de Nouvel Art*. It was never a museum but the young proprietor fancied himself a great artist. The sign still hangs there—not a digital thing. It's just an old printed sign by the door."

"OK."

"Go behind the building, and you'll find a door with no handle, no knob. You must knock on the door, and your knock must be in code."

"What's the code?"

Molly made a fist and pounded on the little table at her side in a series of bursts. The exoself told Chase what it meant.

"Christ our Lord," he said.

"That's right. You know Morse code."

"Apparently."

Molly stood and walked to a closet by the front door. She pulled out a black knit cap and dark glasses. "Leave the mask behind, Chase. It'll only attract attention in this small town."

The cap covered his hair, and he pulled it down almost to his eyebrows and then slipped on the glasses. The flight pack waited by the front door—Molly had plugged it in to charge. Chase strapped it on. "I wouldn't know it was Chase Sterling under there," she said. She pulled on the cap and patted his cheeks. "Now be careful."

"Yes, ma'am. Thank you for taking me in." He went out the door and walked a hundred yards before he took flight. His drone sensor registered activity, but nothing came into view. The menacing dream faded as the brief flight came to an end.

Nightlife in the little town was practically nonexistent. A café took up a corner with patrons eating and drinking. Lights came from apartments above closed stores and businesses. A few people walked the streets. No cyber-guards, not even a local policeman patrolled the place.

Chase found the abandoned art studio and walked behind the old brick building. The door with no knob was there, just like Molly said. Chase pounded the code.

A tall man, black and muscular, cracked open the door. The resemblance to Bear brought Chase a sense of relief. And guilt. Without a word, he pulled off the knit cap and the dark glasses. The man nodded, opened the door, and stepped aside. Chase followed him into a hallway. Doors lined each side.

"It's about time you showed up." The man led him through a door and into a room where paintings filled every wall. They were all landscapes.

Chase stopped in front of the largest of the paintings—it practically covered a wall. The cloudless blue sky and open field welcomed him, masterfully replicating the dream. Or was it the other way around? A small placard, fastened to the bottom of the frame, told the painting's title.

Ciel Bleu Domaine. "Blue Sky Field," Chase said.

"You speak French."

"Among other languages."

The man swung the painting wide and stepped through the portal behind it and then looked back at Chase. "This is the new brain of the Underground Church, computers and everything. Melody's got us hooked up with systems the WR can't touch. Soon we'll be able to keep the whole thing running from here. World-wide communication. But Melody says you've got programs in your head that we need, Chase Sterling." The man rolled his eyes. "That's what the girl says."

"What's your name?"

"They call me Switchblade."

Chase smiled. "You don't think too highly of me, do you, Switchblade?"

"I got nothing against you. I just hope you don't disappoint."

Chase followed him into another hall and then down spiraling stairs. The man opened a last door, and Chase stepped into a spacious room filled with light and activity.

He quickly spotted Mel and his mother among a crowd of a hundred or more. Both women studied monitors positioned on a table in the center of the room. His mom looked up, and the cry she let out caused everyone to stop what they were doing.

She ran to Chase, and he scooped her off the floor and swung her around. "I'm here, Mom," he said. "I'm here." He held her tight, and she wrapped her arms around his neck.

"Welcome, son."

He stepped back enough to see her face, and she

smiled. He wiped her tears and kissed her cheek. A hand, small and brown, came to rest on his shoulder, and he found Mel beside him. He turned to her and pulled her close. Her arms came around him as he closed his eyes. A feeling overwhelmed him of being gone a long time and finally coming home. Whispers and giggles echoed through the place. Chase opened his eyes and smiled. Perhaps a crowded room wasn't the best place for this reunion. Mel lifted her head off his shoulder and backed away.

"Good to see you, boss." She brought her hand to her mouth in an attempt to cover the grin.

"It's real good to see you, Mel. I've missed you." He turned to his mom and pulled her close. "Both of you."

"Chase," his mother said. "I never dreamed the two of us would end up in a place like this."

"Neither did I, Mom." He wouldn't try to explain his dreams. After ending up in this deepest of the deep in the Underground Church, and not in a beautiful field, he wasn't at all sure he'd ever understand the dreams.

He turned to Mel. "But you've got a lot of explaining to do. Why didn't you ever tell me you were some kind of techno-genius? And why did you put all this stuff in me?"

She lost the smile then. "I'm sorry, boss." She crossed her arms, and her eyes turned down. Then she looked him in the face. "Well, not really," she said. "I'm glad I did it."

He touched her soft cheek. "Me, too, Melody. But please explain how somebody like me ended up bent on being of service to the good people of the Underground Church. Was that in one of your programs? I've got questions. Lots of them."

"I'm not the one who made you want this. That's the truth. God brought you here. I hope you know that, boss." Her smile returned. She slipped her hand in his, and he laced his fingers with hers.

"Call me Chase."

Thank you for purchasing this Harbourlight title. For other inspirational stories, please visit our on-line bookstore at www.pelicanbookgroup.com.

For questions or more information, contact us at customer@pelicanbookgroup.com.

Harbourlight Books
The Beacon in Christian Fiction™
an imprint of Pelican Ventures Book Group
www.pelicanbookgroup.com

Connect with Us
www.facebook.com/Pelicanbookgroup
www.twitter.com/pelicanbookgrp

To receive news and specials, subscribe to our bulletin
http://pelink.us/bulletin

May God's glory shine through
this inspirational work of fiction.

AMDG